Hannah Emery studied English at the University of Chester and has written stories for as long as she can remember.

Her favourite things are her family, friends, books, baking on a Saturday afternoon, going out for champagne and dinner, and having cosy weekends away.

Hannah lives in Blackpool with her husband and two daughters.

hannahcemery.wordpress.com

 twitter.com/hannahcemery

Also by Hannah Emery

THE NEW YEAR'S EVE PARTY

HANNAH EMERY

One More Chapter
a division of HarperCollins*Publishers*
1 London Bridge Street
London SE1 9GF
www.harpercollins.co.uk
HarperCollins*Publishers*
1st Floor, Watermarque Building, Ringsend Road
Dublin 4, Ireland

This paperback edition 2022
1
First published in Great Britain in ebook format
by HarperCollins*Publishers* 2021

A catalogue record of this book is available from the British Library

ISBN: 978-0-00-851973-5

This novel is entirely a work of fiction. The names, characters and incidents portrayed in it are the work of the author's imagination. Any resemblance to actual persons, living or dead, events or localities is entirely coincidental.

Printed and bound in the UK using 100% Renewable Electricity
by CPI Group (UK) Ltd

For Dean

Prologue

FRANKIE

New Year's Day

Apparently, they'd pulled Red from the water first. Frankie hadn't even seen him. She'd run straight past where he lay, towards the others: their faces strange hues of ghostly greys and blues.

She must have left Red behind when she came to the hospital, but she didn't remember.

Frankie reached out and touched the silent head beside her. The blonde hair was crisp with dried lake water. *Come on. Wake up.*

The resolution was still in her pocket, rustling each time she moved. She took it out and tore it up, her fingers trembling like they had been since just before midnight. Perhaps she'd never stop shaking. The shards of card stuck to the crumpled blue fabric of her dress and she brushed them onto the floor. Somebody – Frankie couldn't even remember who it was – had offered to bring her a change of clothes to the hospital. Nice clean clothes. But she didn't want them. She didn't want to smell of laundry powder and shampoo and a new day in a new world where nothing made sense. Instead, she hugged the folds of her dress and closed her eyes to the scents of the night that clung to it: sour water; the woody pop of fireworks and spilled drinks; Chanel and lipstick; marshmallows and melted chocolate.

Frankie knew how fast things could spiral out of control if you didn't have one eye on them all the time. She knew that if you took your eye off a pot for just a moment, it bubbled over. So how had she got things so wrong?

She closed her eyes.

If she went right back to the beginning, it started when her real parents (or was it just her mother, sixteen and round as a ball, frightened and desperate?) decided to give her away.

It started when Frankie's new parents plucked her from one life and carried her into another one.

It started when she was sixteen and stuck a cool glass bottle of beer into her woven rucksack, when hope and desire fluttered around inside her like pretty little birds.

It started when Verity decided to chop down those trees so that the ground suddenly became the freezing lake, up to your neck without warning. It started with the party: with the invitations and resolutions and the champagne that Frankie could still feel the acid fizz of in her blood.

Chapter One

FRANKIE

7 December

'They'll kill you, Verity,' Frankie said. 'You can't do it.'

They were silly words, because *of course* Verity would do it.

'Aren't you worried about how everyone will react?'

Verity looked genuinely puzzled. 'Not really, no. Why would they all care so much about me chopping down a few trees?'

'The trees aren't under a preservation order,' said Frankie's husband, Red.

'He's right,' Verity agreed. 'Max looked into it. Those trees belong to us, so we can get rid of them whenever we want.'

'But we live in *White Fir* Lake. If you cut them down, it'll—'

'Oh, it'll still be White Fir Lake without those trees. There are plenty of others. People will get over it,' interrupted Verity with a wave of her hand. Her enormous cut diamond flashed beneath the spotlights, and Frankie looked down at her own plain solitaire, then stole a guilty glance at Red to see if he'd noticed. He hadn't.

'If you're sure,' Frankie said. She never had been able to change Verity's mind, and now she sometimes wondered why she still tried. How odd it was that you did things without really knowing why, that sometimes your thoughts and behaviours were as independent to you as a jerking knee that had been hit with one of those little reflex hammers.

'They'll probably all thank me in the end,' Verity said, opening Frankie and Red's giant fridge and retrieving the bottle of Chablis she'd started on twenty minutes ago. 'Everyone will be able to see a bit more of the lake with the trees gone. You'll probably even be able to see my house from here, won't you?' She wandered over to the French doors, bottle still in hand. Then she turned, flashing her brilliant smile at Frankie. 'Look, don't worry. Even if they're all mad about the boring old trees to start with, they'll all come crawling back on New Year's Eve so that they can come to my party. I've invited *Hills Daily*, and they'll all want to be in that. Hey, which reminds me, you didn't open your invitation.' Verity swiped the gold envelope she'd left on the worktop when she'd arrived and jabbed it into Frankie's hand. 'I've sent it out in DMs too, obviously.'

Frankie opened it carefully, sliding out the gilded card.

A NEW YEAR'S EVE TO REMEMBER AT NO 1, WHITE FIR LAKE.
EIGHT TILL LATE.
RSVP TO VERITY AND MAX.

'Gorgeous, aren't they? Come on, Frankie, aren't you going to have a drink with me?' Verity waved the wine bottle in the air.

Frankie placed the invitation down and looked at her watch. Maisie and Bella were at their Christmas party, twenty minutes away, due to be picked up in one hour. Harry would wake from his nap in forty minutes, all warm-cheeked and dependent. Frankie loved being a mother: honestly, she did. But sometimes she felt like she based her whole life around nap time and snack time and picking people up from school and parties. One of her favourite things about Verity was that she always wanted to have fun, regardless of who needed waking or feeding or picking up. If Frankie didn't go along with it at least *sometimes*, there would be a bridge so long between Frankie and Verity that it might one day be impossible to cross, and that couldn't happen. 'A small one,' she said, taking a crystal glass from the cupboard next to her.

Verity grinned like a child and sloshed the glass full. 'We're celebrating the new look of White Fir Lake. Plus it's Christmas! Our first as neighbours.' She took her phone out and snapped a photo of herself with the glass. It'd be on Instagram within seconds. 'Tagged you,' she said, showing Frankie: #*celebrations*. She'd put a little tree emoji followed by a winking face. The whole of White Fir Lake would see that and be speculating what it was all about within minutes.

Frankie sipped the wine: sharp and cool and crisp. 'We seem to have a different reason to celebrate every day.'

'Oh, you love it,' Verity said, pawing Frankie like a playful kitten. 'It's taken you so long to move here, we might as well make the most of it now you're just around the corner.'

Frankie looked across at Red and caught his eye. *It didn't take that long.* She tried to reassure him with a smile. They'd managed to move from their sensible detached house at the nice end of Lower Hill to the more affluent and more attractive White Fir Lake in the Cotswolds six months ago. Lower Hill was fine, but it had never been enough for Frankie and Red. It had been their dream to buy this house across the lake from Max and Verity for about twelve years. It had finally gone up for sale just as they were reaching the amount they needed to save for the gargantuan deposit. *Meant to be.*

Red smiled back at Frankie, seemingly oblivious to Verity's comment about how long it had taken them to save. Perhaps it was just Frankie being oversensitive.

'Fun, fun, fun,' Verity was saying now, taking out some olives from the fridge. Sometimes it seemed like she was more at home here than Frankie. Even if Frankie couldn't quite believe this house was their life now, Verity could. Her easy conviction was comforting. 'That's what we need.'

'You know what we should do? Send the kids to Red's parents one weekend,' Frankie said, taking another delicious sip of wine and tasting red apples and the slightest hint of vanilla. 'Then we can have a weekend like we used to.'

'We can do it on New Year's. Mum and Dad always stay in on New Year's Eve, so they're bound to say yes,' Red said, cracking open another beer. 'Your party will be like the old times, V. I can take them over first thing, leave them there a couple of days.' He grinned and rubbed his hands together. 'A decent bit of kid-free time.'

Frankie looked at Verity, who was studying her glass, her lashes elegant and black against her pale doll's cheeks. She hoped Verity didn't think she and Red were ungrateful for their children. They weren't, not at all. 'We need to be able to give the party every second of our attention,' she said to Verity brightly, in way of explanation. 'I can't wait to see what you have planned.'

Verity looked up again with a wide smile and Frankie tried to work out if her eyes were filled with tears or if they were just shining under the billion spotlights Red had insisted on fitting in their ceiling. 'Oh, it's going to be full-on Gatsby! Without the deaths, obviously,' Verity said. She leaned forwards and brushed an airy kiss against Frankie's cheek, and Frankie smelt the sharpness of apples on her friend's warm breath.

'Why are we here?' Maisie whined as Frankie carefully drove through the open gates and stopped on Verity and

Max's enormous driveway an hour and twenty minutes later.

'Because Verity left her bag at our house by mistake. I'm returning it to her,' Frankie said, pulling up the handbrake button. She turned to the backseat, where Christmas party-bag contents were strewn across the girls' laps. The December weekend party was an annual tradition for all the children at Middle Hill Primary School and was known for its extravagance and excellent party bags. The girls were currently mid-glitter lipstick application, mid-candy cane crunching, mid-everything that was in the bags. Harry clutched a snowman cupcake in his podgy hands, and his delicious little mouth was shimmering with jam. Although the state of them would be good for a Facebook photo – one of those wry before-and-after posts – taking Harry into Verity's immaculate palace without giving him a full bath first was impossible. But then, leaving them in the car, even in broad daylight—

'Mum-my, Harry stinks,' said Bella, dropping a gluey white candy cane onto her dress and putting her hand over her nose and mouth.

Decision made. Thanks, Harry. 'Right. Wait in the car. I'll wind your windows right down. I'll be one minute. I won't go in,' Frankie said, and the girls let out a joint squeal of delight at the prospect of being left alone with their party haul. She glanced up at the darkening sky. She never usually left the children alone in the car, let alone with the windows open, because she always imagined the worst: returning to empty car seats, or to no car at all or to some kind of garrotted... *Stop it.* 'I'll be one minute,' she repeated as she clambered out, and shut her door with a thud.

The Bentley mansion was completely covered in fairy lights, and a giant wreath hung in the centre of the house with a lavish red bow sweeping down towards the front door. Frankie and Red had ordered the same decoration, albeit smaller, and Frankie felt a glimmer of bright satisfaction as she stood beneath Verity's. She'd always adored the way Verity dressed her house at Christmas, and now she had finally been able to do the same.

Max answered the door after a few minutes. A tiny paintbrush was balanced behind his ear – a nod to his status as one of the most successful artists in the country. Frankie stared at it for a moment too long, then felt herself blushing. Even after all these years.

'Hey, Frankie! Good to see you.' Max's words puffed into the icy air in a plume. He leaned forward and kissed Frankie softly on the cheek like he always did. Verity liked to refer to Max as having a 'cocktail of cultures': his accent American; his home English and his habits European. His scent lingered after he'd moved away again: cash, oil paint, a slight hint of Verity. 'Verity didn't say you were coming. Is everything alright?'

Frankie and Verity used to turn up at each other's houses unannounced all the time. When had that changed into this?

'Is she in?' Peering past him, she saw the enormous

hallway, yawning empty and silent. There were no shoes, no coats, no sign of life. How did they *do* it?

'She's taking a nap at the moment.'

'Oh,' Frankie said uncertainly. Verity had only left Frankie's house about forty minutes ago. And she was already in bed, asleep? 'She left her handbag at ours. I thought I'd return it.'

'She was out like a light,' Max said with a grin. 'It's these daytime soirées you keep having.'

Frankie smiled weakly. 'Oh, it was only a glass or so. It's the weekend, after all.' It had to be Red's comment. *Kid-free time*. It hadn't been the best thing to say to a woman who had never been given the chance to ever have any other kind of time, had it? 'Well, I'll see her soon then, instead, I suppose.'

Max glanced behind him. 'I won't wake her, if that's okay?'

'No, course not. Tell her I dropped it off,' Frankie said, trying to keep her voice casual, her smile bright. Was it wrong that a part of Frankie wanted Max to invite her in, even though she'd only just seen Verity, even though she had her own life waiting a few steps away, with its sticky hands and adorable little faces and brand-new furniture they'd waited twelve years for?

She turned and crunched her way back over the thousand-pound gravel.

Chapter Two

FRANKIE

7 December

'Max said Verity was asleep when I went round,' Frankie told Red as they sat around their glass dining table. She dipped a fat golden chip into the pool of sauce on her plate. Her mushroom sauce was one of their favourites and she'd done a particularly good job of it today: creamy and velvety with the pleasant bite of pepper to save it from being too sickly.

Red speared a piece of steak with his fork. 'A nice afternoon nap. Lucky for some.'

'I had the kids in the car, so I couldn't have gone in for long anyway.' Frankie cut up a chicken nugget and gave a piece to Harry. She frowned. 'I was a bit worried that Verity might not want to see me, for some reason. Do you think she was offended about us talking about child-free time?'

Red chewed his steak as he thought about this, and Frankie saw a flash of red flesh in his mouth. Perhaps she should try cooking some more veggie food. She'd seen an article online that said red meat was bad for the heart. 'Nah,' Red said calmly. 'Won't be that. Verity doesn't offend easily. And anyway, she probably barely took any notice. She'll be obsessing over the party.'

Frankie felt herself loosen a little at his words. Red knew Verity as well as she did, and of course, he was right. Verity wasn't the type to get upset about a throwaway comment. And anyway, if there was a problem, Verity would tell Frankie because they were best friends. That's what Verity always said, and even though it was a bit of a ridiculous label for women in their thirties, when Frankie heard Verity use it she felt a sweet, nostalgic satisfaction, like she got when she ate one of the children's strawberry laces or chocolate mice.

'It was probably just Max, wanting her for himself,' Red continued. 'Did he have a paintbrush behind his ear?' he asked with an amused grin.

Frankie shrugged. 'Not sure. I didn't look.'

Red shovelled some more salad onto his plate. 'He will have done. You know it.'

'You sometimes have a pencil behind your ear, Daddy,' Bella piped up, her little mouth gaping open to show a half-chewed chicken nugget.

Red pointed his fork at Bella. 'That's right, Bel. I do. But it's just for safekeeping so I have one right there if I need to take measurements. It's not an accessory.'

'Maybe Max wants to keep his paintbrush safe too,' offered Maisie, an eight-year-old voice of reason. 'Maybe he measures his pictures?'

'Eat your dinner, girls,' Frankie said.

'I'm sure he does,' Red said, a laugh teetering beneath his smile.

'What's a naccessory?' Bella asked.

'Jewellery,' Maisie answered with the exaggerated patience of a sage. She was only three years older than Bella but she acted like she had at least fifteen years on her.

'Max wears jewellery? But he's an old man. You have to be a girl to wear jewellery,' Bella said, baffled.

'Actually,' Frankie began, 'that's not strictly true—'

'I would love to see Max in earrings and necklaces,' Maisie interrupted, as Bella snorted with laughter.

'That's enough,' Frankie objected, tapping Red on the arm to stop him from laughing too. 'Don't ever be mean about Max like this in front of Verity. We don't want to make her sad, do we?'

'Okay, girls, your mummy's right. We shouldn't laugh at people. It's not nice.' Red tore into another piece of his steak with his fork so that bloody juice oozed from it. Frankie would try that little vegan deli over the Christmas holidays. Georgia Booth, who had twin girls in Maisie's year at school, said she'd bought her husband some sausages from there and he didn't even notice the difference.

'No, it isn't nice. Let's talk about something else,' said Frankie, feeling a little sorry for Max. What was the big deal about the paintbrush anyway? Was he meant to hide the fact that he was a famous artist?

'Okay, well, I got the apartments in Glasgow,' Red said. 'We'll start work on them in a couple of weeks. People want to be in as soon as possible. We've signed them all out already, within an hour of releasing them. Can you believe that?'

'Glasgow? The old church renovation?' Frankie felt a lurch of fear. 'When did you... You weren't sure you were going for them, were you? Didn't you say it was a bit of a headache, with all the extra planning and building regs?'

'Well, yeah. It might be a bit of stress. But this life don't come for free,' Red said in a terrible American accent, making Frankie think of Max's voice.

'But it's not just stress, is it? I thought you said you might start slowing down now, Red. After...' She looked at Maisie and Bella, who stared at her, waiting to pounce on her words. They were like sponges, filling themselves with everything she said, whether it was appropriate or not: usually not. Harry wailed something incomprehensible, bored by the silence, and flung his little fork on the floor.

Red bent to pick up the fork and resurfaced, pink-faced. 'I'm fine. I'm not letting it stop me. Jesus, I *can't* let it stop me. Okay? You need to stop worrying about it.'

Frankie leaned over to kiss Red's cheek. He smelled of nothing; perhaps a faint whiff of meat if she really strained to get something. She shouldn't push him about this. He probably felt just like she did, as though none of this was going to last; as though their new house could be snatched from them at any moment. Was it really any wonder he wanted to do well at work, earn more money so that their dream felt less like a dream and more like reality?

'Okay.' She stood up and took her phone from the worktop. 'I think I'll phone Verity.'

'Yeah, Max told me you'd brought it,' Verity said on the phone a few minutes later. 'Thanks. I really need to stop leaving my things everywhere I go. I'm like a bloody toddler.'

'Or maybe we need to stop drinking before four p.m.,' said Frankie.

'Oh no, I'd rather leave stuff places than go teetotal.' Verity laughed and Frankie laughed too.

'Did you look inside it?' Verity asked suddenly.

Frankie felt her stomach turn with the change in Verity's tone, like she'd gone over an unexpected hill on a fast road.

'As if I'd look!' Frankie said, feeling a defensive blush creep over her cheeks. She'd thought of looking in it. But she'd come to her senses within seconds. And there wouldn't be anything in there anyway.

'Ha! You're right. As if you would. I'd have looked in yours, obviously.'

'Course you would,' Frankie said. 'But you wouldn't need to. You know everything about me,' she said, the words rolling off her tongue quite nicely. 'So you had a good sleep then?'

Verity's answer came quickly. 'Oh, it was wonderful. Well, anyway, thanks again for dropping it off.' Verity's words were stretched out of shape by a yawn. 'I'm tired again.'

'Again?' Frankie asked. 'It's not like you, is it? Ooh, you don't think that you might be—'

'Nope. My period came a few days ago. I think I'm more exhausted with not being pregnant than I would be if I were pregnant.'

Frankie felt the familiar guilt stir in her. 'I'm sorry,' she said quietly, because there was never anything else she could think of to say.

Chapter Three

FRANKIE

16 December

They almost didn't hear the doorbell amongst the detritus of noise in Frankie's kitchen-diner: CBeebies, Harry's incessant clanking of a poor toy mouse against the tray of his highchair, the rhythmic thrum of the washing machine from the utility room. Verity had just been telling Frankie that she might start painting again, and Frankie had been deep in thought about this. Did it mean Verity was giving up on having children, or that she wasn't letting it bother her so much? Either way, Frankie decided as she made her way down the hall, it was good news. Verity was so good at painting: it was her thing. She was lucky to have a thing.

When Frankie opened the door, a frightened-looking woman was standing on the step. She wasn't local, Frankie's initial assessment told her. She was wearing jeans that were faded at the knee and scuffed flat boots. The same age as Frankie. No makeup or jewellery. She definitely wasn't a Middle Hill mum.

'I'm so, so sorry,' the woman said. 'It happened really quickly.'

Frankie mentally checked where all of her kids were: Harry inside with Verity, Bella and Maisie at school for another few hours. This woman was nothing to do with the school or Red's business.

'What happened quickly?' Frankie asked, craning her head out of the front door.

'I drove into your wall,' the woman said, fumbling with her handbag and taking out a battered notebook and a biro.

'Oh God! Are you okay?' Frankie asked. Red had said that this would happen one day. And now, one day was here.

'I'm fine, honestly, just a bit shaken. It's such a sharp bend!'

'It's so sharp,' Frankie agreed apologetically, as though she'd planned the road and built the damn wall herself. 'Are you sure you're okay? Whiplash can take a while to come out.'

'Yeah, I'm sure. Here, I'll write down my number and my address, and you can let me know what I owe you. God, I'm shaking. I really am so sorry. Let me show you the damage. I think I must have hit a patch of ice.'

Frankie stepped outside and, shielding her eyes from the

low sunlight, let the woman lead her to where the white wall at the front of their house had crumpled with the force of the car. Her heart sank. 'Oh,' she said with a wave of her hand. 'It's nothing much. Easily sorted. And it's honest of you to tell me. Most people would just speed off. Is that your car there? Is there much damage?'

'Only a little,' the woman said, her voice fracturing slightly. 'How embarrassing. I was going to have a look in the village to see if there might be any work for my daughter. I don't really think I'm in the right frame of mind for that now,' she said, putting a shaking hand up to her face.

'Honestly, it's really no big deal. I'm Frankie,' she said.

'I'm Alice, and I'm sorry again.'

'No need for any apologies. I'm just glad you're okay. My husband said this would happen one day. If it hadn't been you, it would have been someone else.'

'Oh no, will he be mad?'

Frankie thought fleetingly of Red and smiled at the thought of him losing it over a wall. She'd never seen Red angry, really. 'Don't worry about him. He won't even see it, he'll come straight onto the driveway at the back. Look, why don't you come in and have a coffee? You probably don't feel like getting straight back in the car.'

Alice hesitated. 'I wouldn't want to impose. I've completely interrupted your day.'

'Not at all. Come on. My friend Verity is here too, and she works in the village, so she might have some advice for your daughter.'

'Well, okay then. That would be lovely,' said Alice as

they crunched over the icy ground back to the warmth of the hallway.

––––––––––––

'Sorry about the mess,' Frankie said as she kicked a Lelli Kelly shoe to the side of the wide hall. She did try to keep things tidy, and they obviously had a cleaner too, but she just couldn't ever seem to keep on top of that deluge of *stuff* that came with three kids. Christmas was even messier than any other time of the year too: Sellotape and Amazon orders and cards all over the place as well as everything else.

'To be honest, it's just nice to be somewhere that isn't covered in boxes,' Alice said as she followed Frankie down the hall. 'I've only just moved here,' she added.

'Welcome to White Fir Lake.' Even though she and Red really lived on the outskirts, pride bloomed in Frankie as she said the words.

'Verity, meet Alice,' Frankie said as they reached the kitchen, where Verity sat at the breakfast bar. 'She ran into some black ice on the bend at the front of the house and had a bit of a bump. She's in need of strong coffee.'

Verity flashed Alice one of her million-pound smiles and Frankie felt a wave of gratitude for Verity's friendliness. Frankie couldn't bear for people to feel left out: one of her hangovers from childhood, probably. A counsellor would have a field day with that, if Frankie had the time to see one.

'Alice, gorgeous name,' Verity said. 'That bend is an

absolute bugger. I nearly crash into that wall every time I come round here.' It was as Verity stretched out her hand, for Alice to shake, that Frankie saw it: a purple bruise snaking up the side of Verity's wrist.

'Oh, V! What did you do to your wrist?' Frankie asked.

Verity pulled her cashmere sleeve back over the bruise. 'Fell the other day. On the ice, actually. So you're not the only one slipping all over the place,' she said to Alice.

'Thanks, that makes me feel a bit better. I'm normally a pretty good driver. Fifteen years no claims,' Alice said.

'Do you want an icepack to put on your wrist?' Frankie asked Verity. 'It looks sore.'

'No thanks. It looks worse than it is. Fifteen years no claims, really? You've got about fourteen years on me,' Verity said with a laugh.

'Driving isn't Verity's favourite thing to do,' Frankie explained to Alice.

'Well, it's so bloody boring. Look at this, check that. Who's interested in all those rules, really?' Verity said. 'I just want to get where I'm going. If people are in my way sometimes, that's their problem.'

Alice laughed. 'I'll be sure to stay out of your way if I ever see you behind the wheel! And who's this?' she asked as she stood before Harry in his highchair. He held out his mouse to Alice and shouted 'hiya' repeatedly and rather manically at her.

'Oh, that's Harry,' said Frankie. 'He's two in the spring. Growing fast!'

'He's gorgeous.' Alice took the mouse from Harry and

dangled it in front of him by its tail, which, Frankie noted with quiet embarrassment, was quite filthy. 'What lovely green eyes.'

'Alice has just moved round here, Verity,' Frankie said to change the subject. It always felt so wrong to indulge in chatter about her lovely children and their lovely eyes when Verity was around.

Verity had got pregnant for the first time on their honeymoon in St Tropez about ten years ago. When they came back, she had a permanent sort of wide-eyed, surprised expression on her tanned face.

'I'm pregnant,' she'd whispered to Frankie. Then she'd said it again and again, her voice giddy and getting louder every time she said it – 'Pregnant. Pregnant. PREGNANT!' – until it lost all meaning. 'It's very early. Max didn't want to tell anyone yet, but I had to tell you.' She'd taken Frankie's hand and squeezed it so tightly that there still was a red mark later that night where Verity's ring had pressed into Frankie's skin.

Frankie had always thought she'd be the one to have children first. It wasn't that she'd been jealous of the pregnancy. It wasn't as simple as that. She'd been happy for Verity and fascinated by her heartburn and faint nausea and random cravings for Weetabix ('*Weetabix! Me!*' Verity had gasped, as though the baby should have been making her want caviar instead). But something inside Frankie had deflated somehow, making her feel a bit less like who she was meant to be. So when it came – the pain and the blood and Verity's pale, glassy stare in her private hospital room –

Frankie had felt guilty, as though someone, somewhere might have known that Frankie hadn't been one hundred per cent okay with Verity's baby and had snapped their fingers to make it go away.

It was a stupid way to have felt, Frankie thought now. She unclipped Harry from his highchair. He'd finished his lunch a while ago and she should have taken him out of it then, but she was guilty of keeping him strapped into it just so she knew where he was and that he wasn't about to cause himself some kind of gruesome injury.

'New blood is always good round here!' Verity was gushing to Alice excitedly. She never seemed to notice Frankie carefully changing the topic, steering it gently away from children. Frankie didn't mind. It was quite nice actually, as though Frankie was working behind the scenes of some successful show, not particularly acknowledged but valuable all the same. 'Where from? Have you come far?'

'We've come from London,' said Alice. 'That's probably why I'm not used to country roads. My first mission here is to find my daughter Luna something to focus on for the next few months. Just a little part-time thing. She's really into art, and we're looking at colleges for her, but for now, I think it'd be good for her to have a bit of world experience. She's not very confident.'

'How old is she?' asked Verity. 'You don't look old enough to have a working-age daughter! You must use bloody good cream!'

'She's seventeen,' Alice laughed self-consciously. 'I had her young. I was a lot more outgoing than she is,' she said with a conspiratorial grin. 'I'm hoping this move will do her good, though. I did it for her.' She looked down to where Harry played obediently with his toy animals on the rug. 'She was nothing like him when she was that age,' she said. 'He's so quiet and good.'

'He's given up trying to make noise,' Frankie said. 'He has two older sisters.'

'I run a gallery in the village. If your daughter is into art, she might like it,' Verity said. 'It's actually my husband Max's gallery. He's an artist, so he exhibits some of his pieces there, and other people's too.'

Alice gasped. 'Your husband isn't Max Bentley?'

Verity laughed as the kettle screamed on the hob. 'Yeah, that's him.'

It was still hard to get used to, Frankie thought as she made the coffees, that strangers knew who Max was. He'd always been a success in the art world, but it was only recently that his name had become mainstream. He was like a celebrity, minus the plastic face. His bright, bold artwork was on overpriced mugs and tote bags and biscuit barrels. He had his very own stands in all the department stores, his huge, scrawled signature hovering above the merchandise like a spider. He was quiet about his success: modest, charming, intimidating only because of his perfection.

'Well,' Alice said as she took her steaming mug and accepted a shortbread petticoat tail from the plate Frankie held out. 'Not much gets a reaction from Luna, but this definitely will. I knew he was from round here but I didn't expect this! Can I bring her to the gallery sometime? Would that be okay?'

'I'd love that!' Verity said. 'In fact, if she's wanting work, I could probably set her up with a few hours. She can see if she likes it. Max won't mind. He's done schemes for students in the past. He's a very good citizen,' she said with a grin.

'He really is,' agreed Frankie. *Oh, it was just Max, her best friend's husband, nothing more.*

'So you've all known each other for a while, then?'

'Yes,' said Frankie. 'Verity and I were friends at school.' Verity, with her blonde bouncing ponytail and a laugh that sounded like music, had changed Frankie's life. Her effervescence and charm were like nothing Frankie had ever experienced before; addictively different, like lemonade after a lifetime of tap water.

'Best friends,' Verity said.

Frankie bit into her biscuit. Nice: perfectly buttery, perhaps a little too crumbly. Her eyes went to Verity's wrist, but it was still covered. 'Sometimes it's hard to believe so much time has passed.'

'It has!' Verity said. 'Do you ever feel like you're still twelve?'

'All the time,' Alice said. 'It's a relief to hear someone else say it.'

'And people expect you to have it all worked out! Well, I don't!' Verity was on a roll. She loved nothing more than confiding like this. She could get a nun to reveal her dirty secrets over a glass of Chablis if she wanted to.

Alice gazed around the kitchen, at the vast ceiling with its endless rows of spotlights, the enormous Christmas tree in the corner of the room (red and gold: the unfortunately garish homemade offerings that the girls brought home from school each year were safely stowed away on their own mini trees in their bedrooms). 'You two look like you're pretty close to having it all worked out, to be honest.'

Verity gulped down her coffee and jumped up. She flung open the fridge door. 'Who wants a little glass of fizz?'

'Sure,' Frankie said. She'd have to add more bottles of champagne to her next online shopping order. They were going through it faster than milk and bread. Verity and Max had a wine cellar at their house: a cavern of never-ending Moët. Frankie and Red needed to at least install some kind of wine fridge to keep up. She'd mention it to Red later. 'What's the celebration today?' she asked Verity with a grin.

'Our new friend Alice, of course!' Verity said.

'Oh, don't open anything on account of me,' Alice said, but the cork had already popped and landed on the floor (Harry racing towards it with Olympian determination) and the champagne was fizzing out of the top of the bottle onto Frankie's worktop.

'Too late! You need it anyway, to calm your nerves. You can leave the car here if you want more than one, can't she, Frankie? We'll pop you in a cab home if you like. Unless your partner can come and…'

Alice laughed. 'No partner. Just me.'

'You're here on your own? Well, then that's even more of a reason to celebrate you. All this fresh start stuff with no backup. Wonderful,' Verity said, a bright smile of admiration on her face.

'I shouldn't really. I'll be getting the girls from school

soon, Verity,' Frankie said as she bent down and took the cork from Harry, who emitted an unpleasant 'Mine!' in protest. Some things could slide when Verity was around, but she could hardly fail to pick up her children because she was drinking in an effort to be more carefree. Her parents were coming round tonight too, and she couldn't be too drunk in front of them. Life was full of so many lines, so much working out if you could cross them: a giant cat's cradle.

But nobody even heard her say it anyway, because as she spoke, Verity gasped and rushed over to the French doors.

'Look! They're doing it! It's finally happening! They said they'd get started today!'

The first tree had fallen, and as the three women watched, another one lumbered to the ground. They looked bigger coming down than they did standing, somehow. The lake quivered with each movement, the ripples fluttering all the way across the water to the side they could see here, from Frankie's kitchen.

'It looks so different,' Frankie said. Before today, only the glimmer of lights and the very peaks of Verity and Max's house had been visible. Now the bright white mansion was revealed in patches where the first trees had fallen.

'Oh, Frankie!' Verity said, her cheeks a new shade of pink and her voice slightly higher than usual. 'Look at my house! Now there'll only be the lake between us. We'll be able to signal to each other like people in a film! No secrets,' she added with a smirk.

'It doesn't sound like you two have many secrets from each other,' Alice said as she gazed across at the spectacle of the falling firs.

Frankie smiled, pleased with how things had come across. 'Oh, we don't,' she said, taking another petticoat tail.

Chapter Four

FRANKIE

16 December

'So they've just walloped them down, have they? Did they not ask anyone what they thought first?'

Frankie placed a bowl of homemade pitta crisps and some tzatziki on the coffee table. 'They didn't need to ask, Mum. The trees on are their own property.'

Frankie's mother screwed up her nose. 'It's common courtesy though, don't you think?'

'If you ask people, you get nowhere,' Frankie's dad said. Harry was sitting on his knee, fiddling with his tie. 'Isn't that right, Red?'

'It's absolutely right, Robert. Max and I both checked. There's no preservation order.'

'Well, then you can't say fairer than that. Good on them, that's what I say.'

Frankie's parents were forever on opposite ends of every spectrum of ideas. Frankie's mother, Ruth, always cautiously perched on one end as though she were on a particularly rowdy bus; her father reclining at the other, ready to forgive anyone anything. Frankie sometimes wondered about the days when they decided to adopt her. Was her mother as dubious about that as she was about everything else related to Frankie? She'd never dared ask.

'Mummy, what are these?' Bella asked, taking a pitta crisp from the bowl.

'Pitta crisps. Crisps made from pitta bread,' Maisie said. She was turning into a bit of a know-it-all. Another thing to talk to Red about when they had a minute to themselves. Maybe they needed to rein her in a bit.

'I don't like pitta bread,' Bella said. She licked the crisp and pulled a face, then put it back in the bowl.

'Ooh, Bella, we don't do that.' Ruth pulled Bella away from the table. 'If we take something, we eat it up. We remember our manners.'

'Right.' Red sprang up from their gigantic corner couch. 'I'll get us some drinks.'

'Doctor Pearson has already mentioned it,' Ruth said. 'I saw Susan this afternoon. She'd been to see him about her leg, which still isn't better you know, and anyway, Doctor Pearson was livid about it all. His wife had phoned him up and told him, as soon as it happened. Those trees have been there for years.'

Frankie had tried to get Red in at the doctor's the other

day when he'd had one of his turns. 'Nothing till next week,' the receptionist had said bluntly. 'No wonder there's no appointments if all the GPs are busy on the phone to their wives about Verity's trees,' Frankie mumbled.

'But that's just the thing! They're not Verity's trees, not really. They belong to everyone.'

'Did Verity not use her manners when she chopped down the trees?' Bella enquired.

Ruth beamed, delighted at the concept of manners spreading so rapidly. 'No, Bella, she did not!'

'Hey, Frankie?' Red appeared back at the doorway of the living room. 'Where's the last bottle of fizz gone?'

'Oh, I had some friends round today,' Frankie said. Verity and Alice had stayed at the house with Harry whilst Frankie went to get the girls. They'd only left about five minutes before Red got in. 'One of them is new to the village. Actually, she had a bit of an accident, hit our wall at the front. I meant to show you.'

Red groaned. 'Is there much damage?'

'She was fine. The wall is a bit of a mess, but we'll sort it.'

'I'll go and have a look,' Red said, disappearing out to the hallway.

'How much will that cost to fix?' Frankie's mum asked, standing up and looking in her bag for her glasses. 'Who was this woman again?'

'The lady was called Alice,' Maisie said.

'She had short hair,' Bella offered.

'She lives in Lower Hill,' Frankie said. 'She's probably not too far from you.'

31

'Oh, are you sure she's good enough for you?' Ruth teased. 'Friends from Lower Hill, Robert, even after they've moved up in the world! Fancy that! No wonder she crashed into your wall. Riff-raff, I hear, those people from Lower Hill.'

Frankie ignored her. She should have told Red straight away, to save all this with her parents here, but as soon as Verity and Alice had gone home this afternoon, she'd had to listen to the girls do their reading and straighten up the kitchen and wrap the teachers' Christmas presents. Then Harry had fallen and hit his head on the side of the granite fireplace in the front lounge and screamed the house down for at least thirty minutes. Then Bella had dropped her favourite Barbie down the toilet, so they'd had to wash her and dry her and spray her with perfume so that she wasn't stinky. There'd been pitta crisps and dip to make. Then Frankie's parents had arrived. There'd been something else to do too, although what it was had evaded Frankie all day, getting further from her with each sip of her drink. She thought again now. What was it?

The front door slammed and Red appeared again.

Suddenly, it came to Frankie. Swimming lessons! She'd enrolled Harry into a prestigious baby and toddler swimming school that her friend Anna had told her about. It was expensive, but the children were given mini robes and mini slippers to wear and a free milky smoothie after every class. They met at 1.30 p.m. every Monday, even through the holidays... and Frankie had been sipping the last bottle of champagne with Alice and Verity all the way through it instead of being there.

'What's the damage out there, mate?' asked Frankie's dad.

Red looked at Frankie. 'It'll take a bit of sorting out. I'll get one of the builders from work to have a look. Was this woman drunk when she crashed into it?'

Frankie laughed. 'No! Of course not. We just had a bit of fizz after her accident, to welcome her. It was Verity's idea' – Frankie noticed a raised eyebrow from her mother – 'because she's nice like that.'

'Did you get her insurance details?' Red asked.

'Sit down, Daddy. I want you to colour with me,' said Bella.

'No, I said it didn't matter.' Frankie waved her hand as she spoke, the way Verity would wave away something that bored her. She wondered if she should call the swimming people. She did feel bad for forgetting, but in her defence, there was so much admin to do when you had children. Surely it wasn't humanly possible to remember every tiny detail at every given moment. But next Monday was the day before Christmas Eve, and the children were meant to be at another party, this time one at Harry's nursery school. He couldn't miss that.

'So we have to pay for her mistake?' Red was asking.

'Well, if you get someone from work to do it, then...'

'There will still be all the materials to buy,' Red said, his tone a little sharper than usual. Frankie felt herself blush.

'Not to mention the labour,' Ruth chipped in. 'Even if you get a friend to do it, their rates are through the roof these days, aren't they? I don't suppose it matters to you now you're here, in Fancyville, with money growing on trees! I hope they weren't money trees that Verity chopped down!' Ruth hooted at her own little joke.

'They'll sort it out,' Robert said, pulling his tie from Harry to avoid being strangled by his own grandson, although that was perhaps preferable to this conversation. 'Leave them to it, Ruth.'

'Yes, we'll sort it!' Frankie said breezily, looking closely at Red and feeling familiar guilt settling on her shoulders. He had moved on now, and was going to the kitchen for red wine, bringing it back and holding a handful of glasses by their delicate stems, pouring and smiling nicely at her parents. His muscles were visible underneath his charcoal jumper. He'd been going to the gym a lot lately. He looked like a different person to the one Frankie had gone to school with and kissed on a Cape Cod beach when she was sixteen. She grimaced. Even the memory of that night made her taste cheap tequila. And what were the crisps they'd had? Some kind of sour cream ones. She'd never been able to eat that flavour since.

'Daddy, colour!' Bella demanded, pulling Red down next to her and providing him with a pink felt tip. 'The mermaid. Do the mermaid.'

Red did as he was told, and coloured the mermaid's impossibly long hair pink, and Frankie watched him and drank her Merlot, and promised herself she would be a better wife from now on.

Chapter Five

FRANKIE

30 December

Frankie applied another coat of mascara and then sat back and looked at her reflection in the mirror. She'd put on more weight: she could see it in her face. She'd bumped into Nicole Wren today in the village and Nicole, in full gym gear, had done an unmistakeable full body glance up and down at Frankie. Who needed scales when you had Nicole Wren staring at your curves from the safety of her Lycra leggings? That look had told Frankie everything she needed to know about her body and overindulgences of late. Thankfully, Frankie had just come out of Sak's, so her blow-dry had probably saved her a bit. The dark waves covered her rounded shoulders and her long fringe softened her face, which was becoming hardened with age and tiredness and too much wine. Christmas never helped either. How other people managed to get through Christmas – with its glass jars of smooth goose fat and chocolate-covered nuts all over the place; drinks here, restaurants there – and not put stones and stones on, she could never fathom.

It'd been Verity's idea to go out for drinks with Alice tonight. They were having cocktails and canapés at Frankie's first, whilst they waited for Red to get home and watch the children. Then they were going to have drinks at GLASS. All the bars in the village were excellent, but GLASS was the best and almost impossible to get a table at because of its status and size, especially the week before Christmas. All it had taken had been a quick call from Max.

Frankie spritzed some extra hairspray over herself, even though she was never quite sure it achieved much.

'Getting dressed up?' Red's voice came from the doorway of their bedroom.

Frankie glanced at him in the mirror. 'You're home early. I'm going out tonight, remember? Alice and Verity are coming here first.'

'There was no power on the building site. It was too dark to do anything. Where are you going?'

'GLASS. Max got us a table.'

Red said nothing.

'Jealous?' Frankie asked. 'Of GLASS, I mean,' she added hurriedly.

Red shifted from one foot to the other, uncharacteristically hesitant. Frankie frowned, then saw her reflection, the early signs of horrible wrinkles, and immediately straightened her features. 'What?'

'It's just... GLASS? Again? It's not cheap there. I don't know why you don't just have a night in. Or at night at the Three Trees.'

Frankie swung around. 'What? Since when are you Mr Moneysaver? You love it in GLASS.'

'I know I do. But we were only there last week. In fact, you went twice last week. I just... It's fine for Verity and Max to go there all the time...'

'But not us?'

'Keeping up with them, drinking champagne all day, paying for walls that other people have crashed into. It's a lot. I'm just saying that we need to be careful.' Red rubbed his hands over his face and closed his eyes briefly, as though he was trying to explain a difficult phenomenon to a small child.

Frankie felt a wave of faint nausea roll through her. She stood up. 'Red, what are you saying? That we're broke?'

'Not yet.' He sighed and suddenly looked very tired. 'Just go easy on the champagne tonight. That's all. We're not broke. But we also don't have unlimited funds.'

Frankie sank back down at her dressing table, thinking of her mum's bad joke about Verity chopping down money trees. She touched her perfectly styled fringe. Should she have done her own hair and saved forty pounds? Is that what Red was saying? Dejection rolled in her stomach like a stone. They'd spent so long getting here.

'So this is why you're doing the church apartments, even though it's going to be really stressful?' Frankie thought of her latest Google search following Red's diagnosis a month ago. *Some genetic heart conditions may be exacerbated by stress.*

'I don't have much choice.'

He'd wanted to live here too. But how much had Frankie pushed it? Too much, probably. And now here they were, bleeding money. Red was trying to stop the flow and Frankie had been gouging more cuts.

'I could get a job,' Frankie said, remembering that she'd recently promised herself that she'd be a better wife. She hadn't had a job since she was a waitress at university, and she'd been awful at it. She'd once dropped a whole teapot of boiling water onto an old man's knee. He'd had to go to the hospital. Her scraped degree in English hadn't prepared her for much in the way of employment. She'd only gone to university because Verity was going. Frankie had always toyed with the idea of being a chef. But wasn't that long hours? Who would see to the children whilst Frankie was puréeing peas and creaming cabbage? She thought of Gordon Ramsay screaming at chefs in chaotic kitchens, and the sweating and stress of it all. 'I'm not sure where,' she admitted.

'No,' Red said, looking more unsure about everything than he had in a long time. Maybe he was still in there after all, beneath the Armani shirts and muscles: that skinny teenager who burned in the American sun, who carried all of their Walkmans and secret alcohol in his backpack without ever complaining.

'I could ask Verity if she knows anyone who has any work,' Frankie began dubiously. 'She might—'

'No!' Red was the newer version of himself again: sure,

forthright. 'Promise me that you won't mention anything to Verity. She'll tell Max, and I don't want this getting out. We'll handle it. I'll get back on top of things when the church apartments are finished, yeah?'

'Okay,' Frankie said, relieved. She dabbed some perfume on her wrists. Ninety pounds a bottle. She could keep a secret from Verity. Another one.

I love your husband, and I'm not as rich as I pretend to be.

'Just be a bit more careful,' Red said again and Frankie nodded and put the lid back on her perfume.

That was all very well, and she really did want to help Red out. She *had* to help him out. Google had told her so and she'd promised herself. But it would be so hard, like going to Disney World and not going on any rides. You couldn't be careful if you lived in White Fir Lake.

Chapter Six

FRANKIE

30 December

'These are good. Verity's missing out. Is she still coming?' Alice asked later that evening, taking her third fig canapé and making Frankie wonder how she was so tiny. Maybe she was a social eater and starved herself in private. Verity did that sometimes. For Frankie, skipping a meal was about as realistic as skipping breathing.

'She's just held up at the gallery. She's going to meet us at GLASS,' Frankie said.

'How amazing that she runs her own gallery,' Alice said, licking her fingers. 'I'd love to have a decent career. But kids ruin all that, don't they?'

Frankie shrugged. 'I don't know. Some people do

both...' In fact, the thing that had stopped Verity's true career as an artist was *not* having a baby.

After the first miscarriage, Verity still painted: huge, colourful pieces that looked much more happy and feminine than Max's brooding strokes. But then there was more 'exciting news', followed by more pain, more blood, and another private hospital room that looked exactly the same. And then there was Maisie, and Bella. And then Harry. And for Verity, meeting Frankie's newborns one by one, holding them carefully, touching their faces with her perfectly manicured fingers, patting their little backs and watching as Frankie took them back to feed them.

The paintings had stopped somewhere around the time Bella was born. Verity had cleared out her belongings, like a bird calmly picking apart its nest. She'd given all of her paintings away: Frankie had one of a rose hanging in her bedroom, right above their bed. Verity's brushes and jars and paints had been absorbed into Max's studio. And she'd given all of her baby things to Frankie, who was ready to give birth to Bella any minute.

'Have it all,' she'd said. 'Just promise me I can be super close to her or him. I might have to make do with being fun Aunt V.'

'I don't want to take your stuff,' Frankie had said, staring around at the Harrods bags, the huge bundles of soft lemon baby clothes wrapped in cellophane and topped with giant bows.

'It'd make me happy. It needs to be used, not stored up.'

And a few months later, when the lemon clothes and blankets were spotted with stains and lost to chaotic piles of washing, Verity turned up at the door with her positive test and a giddy shriek. It had worked, she said. Moving on, forgetting about what they wanted had given it to them after all. And no, she had laughed, she did not want all the stuff back now.

But then there was more pain, more blood and more waiting. And now there was the gallery, but still no painting. Verity hadn't mentioned painting again since she'd first brought it up a few weeks ago. And who was Frankie to suggest that someone should push their career?

'Not that you lot need to work, do you?' Alice's voice cut across Frankie's thoughts. 'You're all living your best lives. Should have bagged myself a rich man. Rookie mistake,' she said.

Frankie laughed, but thought of Red's pale, unsure face, his teenage self-doubt etched into his features that evening before Alice had arrived. 'It won't be long before Verity turns up for drinks.' She eyed the open bottle of wine on the worktop. 'Shall we finish the wine? Or head out to the bar?'

Alice grabbed another canapé and popped it into her mouth. 'Out.'

———

GLASS was the same as always: the right amount of busy with sleek waitresses gliding around with silver trays and perfect faces.

'How's Luna doing?' Frankie asked as their waitress popped open a bottle of Veuve Clicquot. They wouldn't have champagne all night. She'd try her best to save a bit of money and perhaps order a bottle of house white next time it was her round, but what was she meant to say when the whole point of tonight was going out for fizz?

'She's already a bit different!' Alice said, clinking her glass against Frankie's. 'Before we came here, she was just glued to her Xbox, but since she's spent time at the gallery she's been a bit more lively. I knew if I brought her somewhere arty, she'd come out of herself.'

'That's great. It must be a relief for you.' As Frankie spoke, her phone lit up the glass table with a message. 'It's Verity,' she said, frowning as she read the message. 'She's not coming.'

'Why not?' Alice said, sipping her drink once, then again and again.

Frankie stared at the words, at the lone kiss when Verity always signed off with about ten, the wording that didn't quite seem like hers.

Not feeling too good. Rain check? X

'She isn't well.'

Alice raised an eyebrow. 'Luna was at the gallery with her today, and she didn't say anything about Verity not feeling well. She said they had a good day.'

Frankie took a huge, fizzing swig from her glass. 'It'll have just come over her. It does sometimes, doesn't it?'

Alice raised a pale eyebrow and finished her drink. 'I wasn't going to say anything because it doesn't really seem my place but...' Alice lowered her eyes, then shook her head as if to say, *Forget it*. She topped up her glass. 'Tell me about how long you've lived here. Have you been round the Cotswold way a long time?'

'Yes,' Frankie said, knocking back the rest of her drink like a teenager. 'We didn't live too far away before we moved to White Fir Lake. We love it.'

'I'm not surprised! Even Lower Hill is a million times nicer than where Luna and I came from. Our new place isn't big, by any means. But it's more than enough for just me and Luna. She hasn't been having a good time lately, and I thought a nicer area would be better for her in so many ways. Living the dream.' Alice smiled.

There was a short silence, with the tinkling of glasses and conversation in the background only just preventing it from being awkward. They needed Verity. They'd all be laughing if she were here, ordering another bottle already.

'I'm really grateful for you including me in things,' Alice said eventually. 'I hope Luna makes good friends too. She loves kids, you know, so if you ever need a babysitter, I'm sure she'd oblige. She's awkward as hell with her own age, and adults, but give her a few kids and she's a different girl.'

'Maisie and Bella would love that. Maisie thinks she's a teenager herself. And there are some other couples around with young kids too. Luna will make a fortune if she's up for it.'

'I'm sure she will be. Except for New Year's Eve, that is. Luna is a bit taken with Max and his art. Verity invited us to their party, and Luna would rather die than miss it.'

'I don't blame her. It's always the party of the year,'

Frankie said. The conversation had snaked back to them, because it always, always did.

'They throw it every year then?'

'Oh yes. For as long as I can remember.'

'I heard about the parties, actually. Verity and Max's reputation precedes them round here, doesn't it? I went for a coffee in the village the other day with Luna. The people behind the counter were talking about New Year's Eve, hoping they'd get an invitation to the Bentley party. I kind of wanted to boast that I already had one.' Alice covered a laugh with her hand. 'How terrible is that? Do they do that to you, too?'

'Do what?'

'Make you feel like you want to be their favourite?'

Frankie laughed, feeling herself blush. 'A lot of people look up to them.' That wasn't what Alice had asked but it seemed to satisfy her.

'I wish I had what they had,' Alice said, suddenly wistful. 'Luna's dad isn't on the scene, not properly anyway. How long have you been married to Red?'

'About ten years. But he went to school with me and Verity too, so I've known him forever. We even still call him by his high-school nickname. Our surname is Redmond,' she explained, seeing Alice's confusion. 'Red's real name is Thomas, but I don't think I've ever called him that. He's just always been Red. Sometimes I wonder if I should start calling him his actual name.'

'Oh no, that's so nice that he's still just Red to you. High-school sweethearts!'

Frankie laughed. 'Not quite. We were just friends for

quite a long time. We all used to go to Cape Cod together every summer when we were teenagers. Max knew Verity's dad, so he was there one year with us too. That was the year Max and Verity got together.'

'Wow. Friends with her dad? I knew Max was older, but I didn't know he was that much older! And Verity was only a teenager?' Alice was looking doubtful.

'Well, she was sixteen. And Max was only in his early thirties,' Frankie said quickly. 'It wasn't like it sounds. He didn't seem that old,' she said with a smile. She remembered Max as he was that summer: arms the colour of hazelnuts, his intense salty scent that made her want to lick his skin, a smile so *adult* that it floored her.

'Did you want him for yourself?' Alice said, teasing.

'I did a bit,' Frankie admitted carefully, making sure she used past tense. She downed the last of her drink. She waited for Alice to react to it all: to Frankie's intense friendship with Verity that even a man couldn't come between, and the outrageous idea that Frankie had once been on a level playing field with Verity. It, of course, seemed unlikely now. But Frankie had been different when she was a teenager. Wasn't everyone? She'd been gorgeous, and she'd known it. She had taken pleasure in flipping her long black hair over her bare shoulder when she knew Max was watching, glancing at him from the corner of her eye. Frankie had been a late developer: that year she'd had neat, rounded little breasts that looked amazing in every single bikini she slung on. She'd lost it all now, of course. There was nothing neat about her body these days and today the hairdresser had remarked on a few more strands of silver peeping through at the roots.

She poised herself, ready to tell Alice, ready to show her the throwback photograph of herself as a teenager that she'd posted on her Facebook page a few years ago. But Alice said nothing, just tapped the empty bottle. 'Another?' she said. 'I've got quite a taste for champagne these days.'

After the next bottle and then a few cocktails, Frankie noticed her words stretching out. Her laugh was louder than it should have been and her movements were subtly out of time so that she missed the table with her elbow and bumped her glass against her lips. And then before she knew it, Alice was talking about Max again, saying things that Frankie didn't want to hear.

'So the girls in the coffee place… They were saying that he has some big secret. They seemed to feel a bit sorry for Verity, as though she doesn't know it.'

Frankie shook her head vehemently and somehow knocked over her drink as she lifted her arm to gesture about how wrong the coffee-shop girls were. She registered a small knot of embarrassment inside her, ready to unfurl itself like a peacock in the morning. 'I don't think so,' she said.

'So it's all as good as it seems?'

Frankie nodded.

'And the bruise? You believe her that she *fell on the ice*?' Alice asked as Frankie mopped up the sticky river on the table with a napkin. When Frankie looked up at her, Alice held up her hands in surrender. 'I'm honestly only asking. You know them better than I do.'

'I...' Frankie squeezed her eyes shut and felt as though she was on a particularly rocky boat, so opened them again. Max? Hurting Verity, hurting anyone? Verity keeping something as huge as that from Frankie? No. Impossible. 'I believe her, yes.' She put her fingers up to her hot cheeks. 'I mean, maybe things aren't as perfect as they might seem. But what marriage is perfect, really? They aren't having an easy time of it.' Damn. She shouldn't have said that. She was trying to defend them and doing an awful job.

Alice nodded. 'Let me guess, they want a kid? Once you want a kid, you can't think of anything else. So I've heard, anyway.' She laughed loudly. 'It was never like that for me. Luna came along before I'd had a chance to decide either way. But for Max and Verity, it must be so hard. And I think it's harder for the man sometimes, isn't it? They're the ones who want to feel virile, like the Big I Am. So when they can't do it, they get a bit aggressive. I've read about this kind of thing before: manhood being asserted through control or violence. Perhaps it's something along those lines with Max. Sorry,' Alice said, lowering her eyes and messing with her straw. 'I get a bit obsessed with human behaviour. Luna always says I talk rubbish after drinking.' Alice pushed her glass away with an apologetic smile. 'She's probably right. Come on, let's pay and get some air before I do more psychobabble.'

'Oh God,' Frankie said when the bill came. She took out

her credit card and slapped it down on the tray. 'Red's going to kill me. I wasn't meant to spend this much.'

'*You* weren't? I'll have to tell Luna she can't eat for a week,' Alice said with a short cackle. 'But at least I don't have a husband checking my every move.'

'He doesn't check my every move,' Frankie said, surprised at the defence in her tone. 'He's just worried, that's all,' she said, trying to soften her words. 'We've spent a lot lately, on the house and moving across to White Fir Lake. Money doesn't grow on trees,' she finished lamely.

'Interesting. I got the idea that it does round here. Look,' Alice said as she put down some crumpled notes. 'I don't want you to get the wrong idea about me. I would never have said all that stuff about Max if we hadn't had so many drinks. I'm really grateful to Verity for including me. Please don't tell her I've been talking about her and Max. I wouldn't want to upset her, and I don't want to upset you.'

Frankie shrugged on her coat, finding it harder than she should to get her arms in the sleeves. 'I won't tell her. Although Verity's used to people talking about her. She's pretty tough. She knows the rumours aren't true.'

Even so, after Frankie and Alice had climbed into separate cabs, Frankie found herself slurring Verity's address to the driver, rather than her own. It was only a five-minute drive from the centre, all fairy-lit bars and elite restaurants with the dramatic backdrop of graduating trees.

'Gates are closed,' the taxi driver grunted as they pulled up. 'You want to use the intercom?'

Frankie shook her head and tossed a ten-pound note to the driver. She slammed shut the cab door and crunched over the ground to the gate, punching in the code that she'd seen Verity use many times over the years. The house was in darkness. Frankie took her phone from her bag and pressed her recent contacts, but before she could call Verity, the phone slid from her fingers down to the gravel. She bent to pick it up, and as she did, she heard movement from within the house. There was a shout, or did she imagine it?

The door swung open. Max, obviously.

'Why do you always open the door these days?' Frankie asked, feeling like someone else playing a part. She hadn't believed the things Alice had intimated. But she wanted to see it for herself, to be invited in for late-night coffee and prove the rumours wrong, all wrong.

Max frowned, glanced behind him. No air kisses today. Frankie ached to take a step closer towards him.

'Frankie, it's pretty late. You seem upset. Is there something I can do? Can I call Red for you?'

'I wanted to see Verity,' Frankie said, her voice softening into her own. 'I just feel a bit worried about her lately. And you, too.'

'But it's past midnight. Verity's sleeping.'

Frankie stared at him, tried to see into his pale blue eyes to his thoughts and secrets. She remembered looking into those eyes all those years ago and felt like she was sixteen again. What would have happened if she had fought for him a bit more? But no, that would have changed things beyond repair. That had been the holiday that had fixed her friendship with Verity in concrete. Frankie gave Max to Verity. And Verity loved her for it. Maybe Max loved her for it too, in a way. Perhaps sometimes, just sometimes, he wondered about if things had been different, too.

'But she's okay?'

'Yes. She's okay.'

Eventually, when it was clear that Max was going to say nothing more, Frankie turned around and began walking away. The walk back to her house, all the way around the edge of the lake, through the village, and down her own street, was quite a long one in heels. But that was okay. She'd need it to sober up a bit.

'Frankie?' Max said just as he was still in earshot.

Frankie turned. 'Yes?'

'You know what the matter with Verity is, really. You know what she wants, why she's not quite herself, why you guys aren't as close anymore. She's a little bit sad. It's really that simple. There's no mystery to solve, nothing to go digging about in. She's tired and sleeping more. That's all. So please, don't worry so much, Frankie.'

The door closed softly, and Frankie frowned at it, at Max's words that scorched her insides. He was usually the type of person who said what you wanted to hear, but tonight he'd managed to say the exact opposite. *Why you guys aren't as close anymore.* She was still mulling over the words as she turned again towards the private road that glittered with midnight frost; as she saw the silhouette of Verity watching her from the upstairs window, still and pale as a ghost.

Once Frankie had swiped a makeup-remover wipe over her face, brushed her teeth and pulled on some fleecy pyjamas, she crawled into bed next to Red.

'Good night?' he mumbled.

'Yeah,' she said.

'Did you stick to house wine?'

'Course.'

'The swimming woman rang,' Red said, his voice still drowsy.

Frankie's stomach churned. 'What? Why?'

He turned over. 'Dunno. She just asked for you and said she'd call back.'

Frankie said nothing. She'd phoned the company the other day and asked if she could transfer the lessons to another time, after Easter perhaps. But the woman on the phone had been almost gleeful in telling Frankie that the full down-payment on a block of lessons was non-transferrable and non-refundable. Great. She'd lied when Red had asked her about Harry's first lesson. She'd even washed his swimming shorts and put them on the radiator ostentatiously to dry. Harry couldn't turn her in; someone who couldn't talk in full sentences yet was really the only choice of person to do this kind of terrible thing to. Frankie would never have got away with it with Maisie or Bella. She would tell Red the truth, but the lessons were so expensive (free milky smoothies! Cute robes!) that after his panic about money she'd have to wait for the right time. *Stress can be a key factor in the worsening of such conditions.*

'That Alice woman who came for drinks before,' Red said, yawning and turning towards her again. 'I feel like I've seen her somewhere before. Do you?'

Frankie closed her eyes and tried to ignore the violent swaying that took place beneath her eyelids. Thank God he'd moved on from swimming. She pictured Alice: cropped blonde elfin hair that Frankie wouldn't be able to pull off in a million years. Big, bright blue eyes with hooded lids. Pale skin. Petite limbs and a neat little waist. Naturally pretty but not stunning. Had she seen Alice before that day when she turned up at Frankie's, all upset about crashing into the wall? 'I don't know,' she said eventually. 'I don't think so.'

Red grunted, his interest already lost to the sleep that was clawing him back. But for Frankie, sleep felt impossible. Her thoughts were like little pins, jabbing her so that she would take notice of them. First of all was what Alice said about Max. What was the phrase she'd used? 'A bit violent', or something like that. No. It couldn't be true, and there was no basis for it. One bruise, which Verity had explained.

Frankie flipped over her pillow to the cool side, stifled by central heating and too much alcohol in her blood. There was something different lately. That was something she couldn't deny. Verity seemed more distant than usual. But Max had just explained that, hadn't he? Verity was exhausted and sad because of all the fertility problems. The last thing she probably wanted to do sometimes was hang out with Frankie, a walking emblem of motherhood. That's probably how they both saw her, with her bulging handbags of baby wipes and crayons, her widened hips. It's probably how Max saw her.

How things had changed.

She glanced over at Red now. Funny how a whole marriage, children and the lot, should be based on the rather questionable start of too much tequila on their last night on holiday in America. But Red had seemed really into Frankie and she wasn't having Max, so it seemed a bit of a no-brainer. She'd needed to kiss *someone*.

Seeing her phone light up, Frankie rolled over to read the text that had just come through.

Loved hearing more about you tonight! Can't want for NYE partying tomorrow! Alice xxx

Frankie lay back down on the pillows with a thud. She'd felt like at some points tonight she might have told Alice too much. But she hadn't really. She had probably held quite a lot back without really even realising it. Because you never tell anyone everything there is to tell, did you?

Chapter Seven

VERITY

7 December

There had probably been others.

Verity had just got in from Frankie and Red's and was taking off her new Chanel boots when she spotted the envelope lying on the stone floor.

It was a pink envelope with a bear clutching a plump red heart on the bottom right corner. Looping, feminine handwriting spelled out their address, with Max's name at the top. Obviously, Verity wasn't going to open it. She put her boots back on, slipped the envelope into her pocket, swung open the front door again and went out to Max's studio at the side of the house.

He went pale when he saw it, as though he knew what it was.

'It's nothing,' he said, mixing some Indian Sun with Buttercup in his palette. 'Put it on the fire.'

'You don't want to open it? See what's inside?'

'I know what's inside. It'll be something stupid, a threat. It's children wanting money. Daring each other.'

'It doesn't look like a child's writing.'

An image shot into Verity's mind: Betsy's handwriting, on pink and turquoise paper. *To Verity. Will you play with me?*

Max shrugged.

'Can I open it?'

Verity watched Max's jar of water bloom with a yellow explosion as he dipped in his brush. 'If you must,' he said. 'Although it won't say much. I've had them before.'

'Why didn't you tell me?' Verity said, slipping her fingers underneath the seal of the envelope. She'd barely bothered opening Betsy's letters. She'd been much more interested in magazines and nail varnish, the Backstreet Boys and her mother's jewellery. She couldn't be bothered working out the scrawled pages of Betsy's writing, if she was honest with herself. What she wouldn't do for one of those letters right now.

'I didn't think it was big news.' Max spoke casually, but he was avoiding eye contact. It was that – the lack of his silver-sapphire eyes locking with hers, the absence of him coming over to her and putting his arms around her – that made Verity do it. She yanked the note from the envelope.

The handwriting, the same as on the envelope, stared up at her brazenly.

Have you ever told anyone?

Verity looked back up at Max.

'Have you ever told anyone what?' she asked, wondering if this was it, if this was the moment everyone had been waiting for since they got together. *That age gap! Her father's friend! He'll break her heart,* people sang. Verity and Max mocked those people who had no idea about reality. *We'll show them,* they said. *We'll prove them wrong. We'll have a perfect family and a beautiful house on a hill.* How was it this hard to get what you wanted? Things you wanted so much that the ache became part of your soul? She put her hand to her head. The Chablis she'd had with Frankie was wearing off too quickly.

Max put his paintbrush down. 'Verity, I don't know what to say. It's bullshit. People hate that we have it all.'

'All? Really?' Verity thought back to when she'd left so that Frankie could go and get the girls from their Christmas party. Harry was just up from his nap, deliciously floppy and warm. She'd kissed his cheek, a little pink marshmallow beneath her lips.

'Wealth. Glamour. People can't stand success. They can't stand happiness. It could be anyone in this place writing those damn notes.'

'I thought you said it was children who had sent it?'

'Well, I don't know, do I?'

Verity felt her heart vibrating, its strings rippling. 'I need a drink.'

Max moved out from behind his easel, putting his hand on her arm. 'Tea? I'll make us a pot.'

'Yeah, right!' Verity laughed sharply. 'This conversation has really made me want *tea*.' The rippling in her heart became deeper, so that she could hear it in her mind. *Thrum, thrum, thrum.* She squeezed her eyes shut and felt hot tears rushing from her eyelids. 'Are you lying to me?'

When she opened her eyes, Max was staring at her. 'I don't want to lose you,' he said. 'I never, ever, want to lose you.'

'You didn't answer the question,' Verity said.

'Look, I—' The doorbell rang, and Max exhaled in irritation. 'Who is that?'

'I don't want to see anyone,' Verity said with a sniff. 'Get rid of them.'

After Max had disappeared to answer the door, Verity crept from his studio to the darkness of the garden. The trees swayed and rustled beside her and she wanted to shush them. From here, she couldn't quite see the front of the house. If she strained, she could just about hear a voice. Frankie's perhaps? Why would she be here? Verity hadn't left Frankie and Red's house that long ago. Surely Frankie would be absorbed by being a parent now, picking up the girls and being spectacularly selfless and organised. After a few minutes, Verity heard the crunch of oversized tyres on the gravel. Maybe Frankie was worried about her. Maybe she'd noticed that Verity had nearly had a little outburst when Frankie had gone on about child-free time at New Year's. Why would Verity want time without Frankie's children? She adored them. And they were probably the closest Verity would get to her own, the way things were going. It was like Frankie and Red saw Verity as some child-disaster zone. *Don't let children near Verity. She makes them disappear. Poof!*

Max returned to his studio and held out Verity's bag. 'You left it at Frankie's house. She brought it back for you.'

Of course she did. Dependable Frankie with her shit together at all times. Sometimes Verity wondered if she'd be able to function without her. It was like having a mother and best friend rolled into one. She took the bag from Max and glanced inside it. 'Have you taken anything from it?'

'Course not. Why would I go delving in there? I'd never get out alive,' Max teased, although behind the cheer, Verity could see a little glimmer of nerves. He came over to her and squeezed her arm, then nuzzled into her, his lips on her neck. She wriggled away.

'What did you say to Frankie? About why I didn't come to the door?'

'I told her you were sleeping.'

Verity nodded. She could trust Frankie. But even Verity didn't know what she was dealing with after seeing that note, and she couldn't let Frankie see her falling apart. Correction: she couldn't let *anyone* see her falling apart.

She pulled the bag's contents out onto Max's huge oak desk. 'Maybe Frankie took something out? I feel like there's something missing from it,' she said, the thrumming of her heart starting up again. Makeup bag. Hairbrush. Phone: no messages. Purse and credit cards: everything there. She pulled at the strands of blonde hair that glistened between the teeth of the hairbrush and let them swirl to the floor. She glanced at Max, who looked at her with concern.

'Don't look at me like that,' she said to him.

'Like what? I'm worried about you. You seem a little tense. Do you think maybe you should start on the pills again?'

Pills, pills, pills. Verity had been rattling with them ever since her mum died when she was sixteen. She hadn't minded taking them so much to begin with. She quite liked the sense of detachment they gave her. It was like gliding around in a soap bubble. She'd had to stop taking them during the pregnancies, but for some reason she'd managed to hold things together. For as long as she was pregnant, anyway. Fake it till you make it. In between pregnancies, she'd stepped back into the bubble as though it was a princess carriage.

'I don't want anything to do with the pills. They might have been the reason I miscarried.'

Max sighed. *Not this again*, he was probably thinking. He opened his mouth and Verity didn't even need to listen to the words because she knew exactly what he would be saying. *'We've been through this, V. The doctors said it was completely unrelated. There was that peer-reviewed research, remember? No link. Nada.'* She usually laughed when he said 'nada'. Americanisms clung to him like little molluscs. He'd been the only one she'd ever told about the medication and her strange, unwieldy mind. When it started happening, she'd gone to the doctor alone, and it was only a few months after that when she met Max on that holiday in Chatham. She'd toyed with the idea of telling Frankie about how much she was struggling that summer, but although she had the odd little cry, the big words just wouldn't come out. She liked how Frankie saw her: impulsive Verity.

Perfect Verity. She didn't particularly want to draw over that satisfying picture with a new, disappointing scribble of herself. But with Max, the words slid out almost immediately, slippery as eels.

'Come on, Verity,' Max was saying to her now, ever patient. 'Maybe just speak to the doctor? You still drink alcohol, after all. Pills are no different.'

She shook her head tightly. 'Nope. Pills are different. Alcohol doesn't build up in your system like they do. It's completely different. These next few years are it. They are our last chance to have children. After that, I'll pop all the pills you want.'

Max looked like she'd slapped him. 'I don't *want* you to take anything, Verity. I want you to be okay. But fine, fine,' he said, holding his broad hands up in resignation. 'Let's forget it. Let's forget everything about this day. Let's go and pour a drink.'

'Not tea?' Verity asked. She needed more wine. She was at that horrible antsy stage of post-drinking. She needed the mellow stage back to be able to think through the letter, who it could be from and why they were trying to wreck her life. Who on earth did Max have secrets with? The thought made her feel like she might shatter into pieces.

'No, not tea,' Max said, scooping her up like he used to do when they first met, a million years ago.

'I believe you when you say you don't know who wrote the letter,' Verity said quietly, putting her arms around Max. The only way to not let people see her melt into a mess of molten anxiety was to not let it happen. People wouldn't see her fall apart if she didn't fall apart in the first place. She could feel herself trembling again, and she buried her head into Max's chest. 'I'm right to believe you, aren't I?' But her question was lost in the fibres of Max, his scents of oil paints and cigarettes and love, and so he didn't answer.

Then there were more. They arrived every few days exactly like an unwelcome, sudden gush of blood.

I remember it all, Max. Do you?
People talk, you know.

They were all handwritten, all anonymous, all posted with a local postmark, which meant absolutely nothing, because everyone around here knew Verity and Max Bentley. Whoever was sending them obviously meant them for Max but didn't care if anyone else – if Verity – saw them too. The post came in the late mornings, mingling with the scents of fresh coffee and Verity's favourite cocoa shower scrub. Even though she knew she'd be waiting for hours, Verity got up earlier and earlier each day to wait for the envelope to land on the floor, soft as a moth. It wasn't as though she needed to set an alarm.

'Who is it?' she asked Max daily. As they languished in bed together; as they ate dinner in their horribly tidy dining room that could belong to just anybody; over the phone during the day. She would keep asking and asking until he told her. Because he must know. If someone was sending you letters like that, it was because you'd done something that you and one other person knew about. So he'd done something, and there was one other person who knew.

'It's nobody. I don't know,' he'd say, in his stupidly irresistible drawl.

Well, that was two answers in one, wasn't it?

'You must know something.'

'I honestly don't, V.'

'So you have no idea?'

'Nope. None. None at all.' *Nada*.

Chapter Eight

VERITY

14 December

It was always going to reach some sort of climax. Verity felt the tension in her tighten each day, and it was inevitably going to snap. There had been the sour disappointment of stomach cramps, to begin with. Another chance gone. They had said they wouldn't do more IVF. Its emotional and physical toll shouldn't be underrated, Dr Brown had told her. But Verity didn't care. There would be no toll worse than her insides emptying themselves out every month in a slew of lost hope.

She'd managed to maintain the illusion that she was perfectly happy throughout the autumn. In the gallery and with her friends, Verity's *I'm Absolutely Fine!* performance went on successfully, day after day, the audience nicely persuaded after each show. Now that Frankie and Red had moved even closer, life even resembled happiness on some days. She and Max were always having Frankie and Red over, or they were hanging out at theirs, and when she was with Frankie, Verity felt as though things might be okay. Frankie made Verity feel in control somehow: she always had. And Maisie, Bella and little Harry offered painful solace, when Frankie would allow them in Verity's sight. (*Poof!*)

But then those dreadful letters began to slice Verity's nerves into shreds. Paper cuts were the worst because nobody else ever appreciated how much they stung.

'Who are they from?' she asked, she screamed, she cajoled, she flirted, but Max would let nothing go. His face might as well have been a sculpture for the amount it gave away. Perhaps he really didn't know. But he must!

'It's nobody! You don't even want to know!' he said on the day it all cascaded into some kind of madness. They'd just had lunch, looking out to the garden where a group of burly men were preparing for the felling of the trees a few days later.

'That's two answers,' Verity said, pushing away her salad. 'You always give two answers. You must know who it is, Max. Just tell me.'

He was looking slightly pale these days, like he'd just had a near miss in the car or heard a piece of terrible news.

You'll struggle to conceive naturally, Mr and Mrs Bentley.

'Because I'm guessing, V! I don't know. I mean, really, out of a whole village, a whole country of people who are jealous of us, who stalk me on Instagram and tell me I'm talented, or talentless, or gorgeous or stupid, it could be literally anybody.'

'But you just said I don't want to know. What don't I want to know?'

Max was silent. Verity puffed out a sigh of frustration and opened the bottle of Pinot Noir for a top-up. It was 2 p.m., but really, who was clock watching? It's not like she had anything to be sober for.

'Jenny's at the gallery today,' she told Max, who was looking at the wine in that judgy way he had lately. He never used to look at her like that. 'It doesn't need two of us there.'

'You've been going to the gallery less lately. Is everything okay there? Do you still like it?'

'Oh, yes. I like it. Selling other people's paintings. It's a riot.' God, if she could watch herself back; if she was someone on one of those reality TV programmes Frankie always got hooked on, she'd hate herself. # *Veritytoleave*

'Well then, why don't you do some of your own work to exhibit? We could build you a studio next to mine.'

Verity pictured it. A stack of canvases, splodges of oil paint, music drifting through the air. She could do it. She used to do it, before.

But it wouldn't solve the problem of the babies, and of the letters, and of suddenly looking at Max like he was somebody she'd never even met before.

She had a gulp of wine.

'Max, if you're seeing someone else, or if you've had a little slip-up at some point, then please just tell me,' she said, watching as the men crawled over the huge icy garden as though it were a crime scene. 'It seems like if you don't, then someone else will. And I really don't want that to happen.'

Max sighed. 'Verity, I have never so much as looked at another woman since I met you. You know that.'

It wasn't strictly true. He'd looked at Frankie, and that was after he'd met her. Verity probably should have let Frankie have him. Frankie hadn't had anything, then. She hadn't even ever had her own *parents*, for God's sake. And her adoptive parents were no good, like two cardboard cut-outs with no kind of emotional range whatsoever; no capacity to live with a teenage girl. But Verity had been a mess that summer. It had only been a few months since she had lost her mum, a woman who'd been luminous with fun and life suddenly becoming a grey husk and then, even more suddenly, gone altogether. Verity had tried hard to be more like her mother that summer in a bid to keep her alive. She'd heaved around impulsivity and sunshine smiles with her everywhere she went. Boring things like loyalty and sensitivity didn't fit in with who Verity thought she should be.

And plus, it was *Max*. Achingly beautiful, clever Max with his cool eyes and stories of Picasso and Klimt, of scruffy, rich art students and galleries and exhibitions. Sometimes, when they were alone, Verity let her act go a little. With Max, she forgot to use the gestures her mother used to use. She was able to step out of the tangle of personality traits that didn't totally fit her and were difficult to walk in, and just be. Max made her emotions stir in the pit of her stomach the way they hadn't done since her mum's diagnosis a year before. Nothing and nobody else could do that to her. She couldn't give it up, even for Frankie. Even though she had told herself that Frankie was like a second chance at a sister: Max was too good.

'Nobody else can have you,' she said to Max now, suddenly aware that her glass was empty and that she'd spent longer ruminating on the past than she'd realised. Time was a funny little thing. 'I simply will not let them.'

'Let's go out tonight,' Max said. 'Let's forget everything and go out. Just you and me. We'll have steak at Parfait. I'll get us a table.'

Verity smiled at him, suddenly happier. Yes! They'd go out. They'd show everyone. Maybe he was telling the truth and the letters were just from children, or someone who was jealous. Maybe he really didn't know. And she'd be ovulating again soon, so she really needed to stay calm and keep her body relaxed. She filled up her glass again and jumped to her feet. 'I'm going to have a big bubble bath and then get dressed up. I can wear my new red Vesture jacket.'

Max smiled. 'Attagirl,' he said.

Verity laughed. 'I'm not a pony,' she said. 'Saying that makes me sound like a pony.'

Max leapt up from the table and chased her from the room, saying things about ponies and crops so that Verity laughed and screamed, and then there was the hot bubble bath that made her skin prickle: delicate froths of vanilla foam and candles and Max, all of Max making her happy, so happy. There was the mirror, and bright pink lipstick because she couldn't find her favourite Chanel Coco red anywhere. There was more wine, some champagne from which the cork flew from so violently it pocked the ceiling and they both clung to one another, still damp from the bath, and laughed.

And then there was the feel of something unexpected in her pocket: smooth as a bullet. She pulled it out. It slipped from her fingers and clattered down the stairs.

'Verity?' Max appeared at the bottom of the staircase. Or had he been there already? Verity didn't know. She was suddenly very tired, and things seemed to have a weird Wonderland quality to them: upside down and inside out.

She motioned to the lipstick that had fallen to the bottom of the staircase, not wanting to go near to it or touch it.

Max bent and picked it up. He inspected it. 'Is this the red one you were looking for?'

Verity nodded. 'Coco.'

'Told you it'd turn up.' Max handed it out to her, smiling. That smile, those teeth, his lips. She knew them so well. Didn't she?

You can't keep secrets forever, Max, the last letter had said.

'But it was in my pocket. Did you put it in my pocket? I've never, ever worn this blazer before.'

Max laughed. 'Why the hell would I go around putting your own lipsticks in your pocket? Diamond earrings, maybe.'

He was talking about a time when he'd done that once. It was when they were first married and she thought she was going to have every single thing she wanted. He'd slipped a Tiffany box into the pocket of her coat.

But that was then, and it was a gift, and this was now.

And Max was looking at her with a sad expression, as though he was worried there was nothing he could do to reach her or help her. It was just like his miscarriage face. She closed her eyes briefly to try to shut out the horror of everything. What a phrase to think of. *His miscarriage face.*

'If it wasn't you, then who was it?'

Max sighed. 'Maybe you did it and you forgot?'

'Put a lipstick in the pocket of a blazer I've tried on once and never worn out? With no memory of it?' Her words ran together, blurring and merging like watercolours. Max's concern upped a notch, his smile fading completely.

'Come on, V. Let's not let a lipstick ruin tonight. Let's go out to dinner and forget about it now.'

She wavered on the last step. She could quite easily go upstairs and submerge herself in the bath again, or burrow underneath her soft, warm duvet and not come out.

'Come on,' Max repeated, coaxing and soft.

She took a shaking step down and reached out for the lipstick.

'That's it. Attagirl,' Max said carefully and for some reason, it made her want to cry this time. This was how things were, these days. Crying... laughing... There was sometimes very little between the two.

He kissed her and she felt the tension soften slightly. But then she opened up the lipstick and there it was, the crimson tip squared off like a severed finger. The floor seemed to quiver beneath her.

'So I suppose I did this by mistake, too?' she asked. She dropped the lipstick again, and it lay at her feet. Max stared down at it.

'Someone is messing with me, Max. Either you tell me who it is and what they want, or I'm going to go completely crazy.' She bent down and picked up the lipstick as he had and then she flung it across the hallway so that the blunt end smeared the edge of the wall. It looked like someone had streaked blood over the cool grey tones they'd chosen so carefully together. 'You can't tell me that I did these things, that I cut up my own possession like some kind of madwoman, and then forgot!' She was screaming now, totally out of control. It was as though she was floating above, watching herself like a spirit. Maybe a part of her had died and was floating around the fancy ceilings of their house. Or maybe she had gone mad: old-fashioned, electro-shock, lobotomy mad.

Max put his arms around her. 'Verity,' he began. 'Let's just have dinner.'

She went to bolt up the stairs, towards the bath, her bed, darkness, but he tried to keep her from going, and the wine had made her so *dizzy* and her legs tangled beneath her.

'Get off me, Max!' she shouted. 'Let me go! Your fucking dinner plans and your secret letters and your charm and your smiles. You're not being honest with me! You're hurting me!' The anger roared inside her, unexpected and red hot. How was she so furious with Max: her darling Max? Where had it come from? She flailed about, catching his cheek so that her ring scored his skin in an angry red line.

'Verity!' He was shouting now, and she was pushing him away, but he was too strong for her. What, she thought vaguely, if someone were to come to the door now? What if Frankie made one of her trips?

But nobody came to the door. It was just Verity, and Max, the perfect golden couple, grasping at each other's bodies like lions fighting for land until one of them, Verity, sailed down and hit the ground with a horrible defeated thump.

Chapter Nine

VERITY

16 December

The bruise flowered over the next few days. Seeing it made Verity feel strange, as though she were looking at an unflattering photograph of herself. It was the day that the trees were coming down. Max was lecturing at some London university and wouldn't be home till late.

Verity pulled on a long-sleeved jumper and headed to Frankie's.

'Come in,' Frankie said, ushering Verity into the kitchen, which smelt of vanilla and butter. 'I'm just making some shortbread petticoat tails.'

Verity grinned. 'Of course you are.' She didn't even know what the hell shortbread petticoat tails were, let alone be able to make them. She rubbed little Harry's delicious head, and he offered up a toy mouse from his highchair tray with a smile of pure delight. Shortbread, gorgeous children. No end to Frankie's talents.

'I'm thinking of painting again,' Verity said, the words surprising her. She hadn't taken Max's suggestion seriously at the time but perhaps she should think about it. Perhaps creating something in some form would help her. Perhaps it would relax her a bit. God, she needed something to relax her.

'Really?' Frankie said, sounding surprised. 'Harry, Verity doesn't want your mouse. Leave her alone. That's exciting!'

'Max said he might build another studio,' Verity explained as Frankie swiped the mouse from her and plonked it back on Harry's tray.

'It's a brilliant idea. What kind of stuff would you do?'

'Oh, I don't know,' Verity said, waving her hand, then remembering the bruise and putting her arm by her side. 'The opposite of Max. I wouldn't want people think I was trying to copy him.'

'You were into art way before you married Max. You have your own style,' Frankie said, bending down and staring into the oven. 'You should stick with it.'

'Thanks,' Verity said. She loved how *nice* Frankie was. There weren't many straightforwardly nice people these days. 'Frankie?'

'Hmmm?' Frankie said, taking her tray from the oven.

Tell her, Verity told herself. But it was complicated. Opening up to Frankie about how much everything hurt Verity these days – how one day she felt as though she could explode with feeling and the next like a hollow shell –

would change things. Frankie would look at her differently, less like she was the best thing she'd ever seen, and if she were brutally honest with herself, Verity didn't know if she could handle that. *You're kidding, right?* Max would say. *You could murder someone with an axe and Frankie would still adore you.* But he didn't know that. Their friendship had been this way since Verity's mum had died, since they had got together with Red and Max. Frankie was the one with the cosy home life and the kids they both wanted, and Verity was the one who didn't overthink or worry, who took fun and champagne everywhere she went. If that was taken away, what would be left?

Sadness, madness.

Frankie had placed the biscuits on a cooling rack and was waiting for Verity to speak. Harry banged his mouse on the plastic tray of the highchair and the cartoons blared from the huge television. The washer and the dryer thumped around and around in the utility room next door. It was all so *Frankie*, so colourful and familiar.

Maybe Verity would begin by telling Frankie about the lipstick and see how that went. Maybe Frankie would even smile and clear it all up somehow. Maybe Verity had sliced the top of it off in some kind of drunken error, and once Frankie had told her, Verity would remember. Yes, she'd tell Frankie, and everything would be alright.

'I—' Verity began.

And then the doorbell rang.

Verity felt the whip of cold air from the open door snaking its way into the kitchen. She heard voices, and then footsteps. Frankie appeared in the kitchen with a woman about their age. Verity was quite sure the woman wasn't from White Fir Lake from her outfit alone. She had cropped hair as though it were still the 1990s and a fresh, makeup-free face, like something from a soap advert.

'Verity, meet Alice,' Frankie said. 'She ran into some black ice on the bend and had a bit of a bump. She's in need of strong coffee.'

Verity offered her brightest smile. 'Alice, gorgeous name,' she said, making Alice look pleased. 'That bend is an absolute bugger. I nearly crash into that damn wall every time I come round here.' She held out her hand to shake Alice's hand, but as she did, her sleeve slid up her wrist a little, revealing her ugly bruise from the other day.

'Oh, V! What did you do to your wrist?' Frankie asked, and Verity had to stop herself from snapping at her to be quiet. She pulled her sleeve back over the bruise, then wished she hadn't. What was wrong with her? Trying to cover it up, being defensive, was the worst thing she could do. 'Slipped the other day. On the ice, actually. So you're not the only one slipping all over the place,' she said to Alice, trying to get the subject away from her horrible blue-green wrist.

'Thanks, that makes me feel a bit better. I'm normally a pretty good driver. Fifteen years no claims,' Alice said, her breezy tone in stark contrast to Frankie's worry, making Verity want to throw her arms around this new person in gratitude.

'Do you want some ice on it?' Frankie asked. Honestly, couldn't she just let it go? 'It looks sore.'

'No thanks. It looks worse than it is. Fifteen years no

claims, really? You've got about fourteen years on me,' Verity said to Alice with a laugh.

'Driving isn't Verity's favourite thing to do,' Frankie explained to Alice.

'Well, it's so bloody boring. Look at this, check that,' Verity said, relief washing over her as she threw herself into this nice new harmless topic. She was always scraping their Range Rover on walls, gateposts, other Range Rovers, or whatever else might suddenly appear in her way. What was it like to be someone like Alice, someone so vanilla, who washed her face and didn't then cover it in makeup, and wore plain jeans and had one accident every fifteen years? 'Who's interested in all those rules, really? I just want to get where I'm going. If people are in my way sometimes, that's their problem.'

They carried on chatting politely whilst Frankie made coffee. Verity glanced at the clock. She could really do with a glass of something. Frankie bustled around, dealing with Harry and drinks and wall-crushing visitors as though it were all nothing.

'Alice has just moved here, Verity,' Frankie said as she plucked Harry from his highchair and popped him down beside them with a little range of toy animals.

'New blood is always good round here,' Verity said, peeling her eyes from Harry. She meant it too. Perhaps Alice, an injection of something fresh, might help Verity claw her way back to who she used to be: someone who was always meeting new people, gushing over their names and telling them to come to her parties. She'd done less of it lately. Perhaps that was the problem. 'Where from? Have you come far?'

'We've come from London,' Alice said. 'That's probably why I'm not used to country roads. My first mission here is to find my daughter Luna something to focus on for the next few months. Just a little part-time thing. She's really into art, and we're looking at colleges for her, but for now, I think it'd be good for her to have a bit of world experience. She's not very confident.'

Verity looked at Alice curiously. She couldn't be much older than thirty, and there's no way this woman was the Botox type, or even the kind of person to use eye cream. 'How old is she? You don't look old enough to have a working-age daughter! You must use bloody good cream!'

Alice hesitated before answering. *Perhaps she had more than one accident every fifteen years after all*, Verity thought, then caught herself. Why was she such a bitch? Perhaps as a way of apology, she found herself offering Alice's daughter work experience at the gallery. Max wouldn't mind, she told Alice, who was beside herself at the mention of his name. He was a very good citizen, Verity explained.

'Oh, he is,' said Frankie, her face pink with pride and delight as she told Alice all about how long she'd known Verity. *Best friends*, Frankie always said, as though they were eight years old. Verity grinned along, already feeling a little more like herself. She used to do socially responsible things like this a lot, but lately, she'd found herself too tired, too prone to odd little outbursts for it all. Perhaps Alice was a blessing, she thought, downing her scalding coffee so they could get on with opening the wine, sent to remind her to get a grip and carry on being *the* Verity Bentley.

It was only a few moments after that the trees began to fall, and Verity gathered at the French doors with Frankie and Alice to watch. Patches of her house became visible like pieces of a jigsaw and seeing it here, from Frankie's kitchen, somehow made her feel safe, as though she was never going to be alone. 'Now there'll only be the lake between us,' she said to Frankie. 'We'll be able to signal to each other like people in a film! No secrets,' she added, although she wasn't quite sure why.

The ground churned, the trees fell like giant soldiers and her house was revealed one white square at a time, each as bright as a star.

Chapter Ten

VERITY

30 December

'What do you think this one means?'

Verity looked over at Luna. Alice's daughter was different: there was no denying that. She didn't make much eye contact, and Verity often found herself wondering where to let her own gaze settle as they talked. She wore strange baggy clothes, clearly hadn't had a haircut in years (couldn't stand the salon, Alice had said) and dipped her head down low all the time as though she was hiding from someone or something. The first time she'd come to the gallery, Max had been there and had pulled her out of her shell a little bit, even made her talk. He wasn't here today, and Verity had worried that she might not be enough for Luna. But actually, Luna was holding her head a little higher than Verity had expected her to and was talking quite animatedly about each painting in the gallery.

'What does "Lupercalia" mean?' Luna asked, looking from the label next to the painting, back again at the violent crimson swirls. It was one of Max's most popular pieces.

'It's a festival,' Verity said. 'A ritual of fertility.'

Luna stepped back and squinted at it. 'Oh.'

'Max painted it about ten years ago.'

Luna nodded. 'I like it. It looks kind of sad.' She turned to Verity with an unexpected wide smile and tucked her mousy-brown hair behind her ear so that, for a minute, she looked like a different girl. 'I can't imagine Max Bentley being sad. But that's a stupid thing to think, isn't it? Everyone is pissed off sometimes, I suppose, even famous artists. The only difference is that everyone is watching if you're famous. Is it hard?'

'Is what hard?' Verity busied herself behind the counter, putting pens in pots, opening and closing the till. But she knew what was coming.

'Everyone watching you both all the time. People are so nosy. They try to know everything about famous people, don't they? And you have to pretend you're okay with it. I'd hate it.'

'Oh, there isn't really any pretending at all,' said Verity. It slipped out nicely, all tied up in a bow. 'We're really very happy and lucky.'

Luna turned back to the painting, the bloody swirls that could mean both the end and the beginning. 'Mum said that you're lucky too.'

'Did she?'

'Yep.' Luna smiled again. The second time in one visit.

'Well,' said Verity, 'she's right.'

'I'd love to be an artist,' Luna said.

'Are you going to study art at college?'

It was like watching a crab retreat to its shell when you'd poked it. Luna's shoulders hunched again and her gaze dropped. 'I don't know,' she said.

'Why not? There are some great ones round here. I know your mum said you're going to wait until September, but I'm sure you could enrol after the Christmas break.'

Luna was silent, staring at the painting.

'Well,' Verity said, wondering what on earth was up with the girl. 'It's up to you, obviously.'

'I just...'

Verity waited.

Luna turned towards her again, but her gaze flitted around the gallery to the other paintings. 'I kind of didn't get my GCSEs.'

'Oh. Okay. I didn't know.' This was surprising: Luna came across as quite bright. Wasn't there some kind of grade inflation these days that meant everyone passed?

'I didn't even take the exams,' Luna said. 'I was meant to, but I didn't go. I couldn't go,' she said quietly.

'Can't you take them at college, and just do an extra year?' That's what Verity had thought she might have to do. Her mum had been ill when Verity had taken her exams at high school and she'd barely picked up a book throughout the whole thing. She'd managed to scrape some passes and somehow get through it all, probably because Frankie had sat up with her all night before every single one of Verity's exams, testing her on photosynthesis and World War II and Seamus Heaney. Frankie had all of her own revision to do, too, but she focused on Verity, because that's the kind of person Frankie had always been. And Verity let her, probably because that's the kind of person *she* had always been.

'I don't know. Mum doesn't think any of the colleges will want me,' Luna said.

'Why?'

'Oh, just stuff.'

'Stuff?' Verity laughed. 'Don't worry. You don't have to tell me. I always try to find out people's secrets. It's a weird habit I have. But I shouldn't be doing that with you.'

Luna took a few minutes, then a deep breath. 'It's okay. I want to tell you. I was excluded from school, actually. Permanently.'

Verity imagined Luna at school: uncool backpack slung low, lank hair hanging over her face, barely making a sound. 'I can't imagine you causing trouble. What happened?'

'Someone set me up.'

Verity could believe it. High school could be brutal for some people, and Luna just screamed, *Set me up! Mess up my strange life even more than I could myself!* 'How? What happened?'

'They put a knife in my bag.'

'What? Did you tell the teachers that it wasn't you?'

Luna shrugged. 'I tried. But nobody believes the weird

loner. Not even the teachers. *Especially* not the teachers. Even Mum doesn't believe me.'

Verity frowned. Luna wasn't bad. She was just completely lost. She didn't deserve this.

'I really can't wait to see Max again at your party.' Luna had moved on now, to another topic and the next painting in the gallery, a slightly boring landscape on canvas that Max's lecturer colleague had asked them to exhibit. It had been there for years, showing no sign of ever leaving. 'I was a bit star-struck when I first saw him, you know. I think Mum will be too when she meets him.'

'You do?' Of course she would be star-struck. Now Max had gone mainstream, even people who didn't know art knew Max Bentley.

'You're going out with my mum tonight, aren't you?'

'Yes, we are,' Verity said. She'd said to Frankie, in one of her more jubilant moods, that they should have drinks at GLASS with Alice. Frankie had a thing about people being left out and seemed pretty attached to the idea of including Alice in their lives. Verity had obviously invited Alice to the New Year's Eve party because she always invited everyone to that. But Verity had decided that it would probably be a good idea to vet her a bit first if she was going to be a regular in their story. She'd also been keen to fill her time: they'd seen Frankie and Red a lot over the Christmas holidays, but there had been a definite sense of something lacking in her own home. Max had bought her a beautiful diamond necklace, which came in a little red box. She'd bought him a set of his favourite cigars. Ava, their housekeeper, had cleared away the short section of red ribbon within seconds. And that had been that. No messiness, no raucous joy, just endless empty rooms.

'Mum barely ever goes out. But when she does, it means I get the television to myself,' Luna said, interrupting Verity's thoughts. 'Late-night gaming. Nachos for dinner. She might even let me have a beer if she's in a good mood.'

Verity smiled. Luna was nothing like any teenage girl she'd ever met, but there was something about her that she quite liked. Her straightforwardness, perhaps, when everything else seemed to be so hard to work out.

'You know, Luna, Max probably knows people at some of the colleges round here,' Verity said. 'I'm sure he could put in a good word for you with the heads. I'll ask him about the ones with the best art departments. We'll get you in.'

Luna took a step towards Verity, her expression puzzled. 'Why would you do that for me? You barely know me.'

Verity grinned. 'Because I'm fabulous. And I think you are, too.'

Luna gave her a small smile and stood awkwardly with her hands hanging down by her skinny waist as a voice in Verity's head whispered to her: *It's not because you're fabulous. It's because you feel guilty about Betsy.*

It was after Luna had left that Verity saw it, and her heart went cool in her chest. The post had arrived at the gallery that morning, hours before. There had been nothing of interest, just a few leaflets. Some customers had been in, and Verity had held the door open for them as they'd left. It definitely hadn't been there then. So it must have been in the last half-hour since she'd locked the front door.

She knew what it would be as soon as she spotted the envelope on the mat.

It was a plain white envelope. No bear, no heart, no address this time, just her name and not Max's.

Hand delivered.

Verity clutched it as she ran down the street to where she'd parked, and she flung it onto the seat when she clambered into her car. She locked the doors and sped towards home.

Max was in his studio.

'Was this you?' Verity asked, holding up the lipstick. 'Did you send me a new one? Please tell me that you did, Max.' *Please*, she begged silently, *tell me it was a weird romantic gesture.*

He shook his head and took the lipstick from her. He opened it.

'This one isn't sliced in half, at least,' he said. He put it down and moved closer to her, putting his arms around her. She let herself be pulled into him. 'It wasn't me. You know it wasn't me. I'll sort it out though,' he said. 'Let me sort it out.'

Verity pulled away. 'How? We have no idea who it is doing all this!'

Perhaps nobody else would have seen it, but Verity did. It was a tiny flinch, but it was there. 'You know who has sent the letters and threatened you, don't you? And that means you know why!'

Max pulled her to him and was too strong to resist. She beat against his chest with her hands again and again. That rare, strange urge to hurt him was back: she wanted to take chunks out of him with her hands, to shovel the lies from him so that they were out in the open.

'Verity, I don't know why this person is terrorising us. I really don't. I don't know what the letters mean. You've seen them – they're totally cryptic. And I don't know why someone's trying to frighten you. But I will sort it out, somehow. I promise. It's really important that you don't get upset over this and make yourself ill.'

He pushed her hair from her eyes and she looked at him. She'd never, ever not trusted Max before. And the way he was looking at her now, was that not real?

'Nothing makes any sense anymore,' she said, her voice hoarse from shouting.

'We make sense,' Max said.

'Do we?'

'We do.' He kissed her, his lips hard against hers, and pulled her so close again that she felt her bones against his. 'I don't want to ever lose you, Verity. I don't ever want to lose any of what we have. We can't carry on like this.'

Verity sniffed. 'Well, what do you propose we do?'

Max thought for a moment. 'We could move away. Start again.'

'Leave White Fir Lake? Are you serious?'

Max shrugged. 'Why the hell not? You're suffocating here, Verity. And we could live anywhere in the world. Somewhere where people don't send us hate mail and mess with your stuff when you're not looking. Somewhere where nobody knows who we are, and nobody is jealous of what we have. You could start painting again somewhere else, I know you could.'

Verity thought for a moment. She imagined a villa in the middle of nowhere, huge bold paintings, their own vineyard. No letters, no appearances in newspaper articles, no peering over her shoulder or finding weird, beheaded lipsticks in her pockets. 'I always thought I quite liked people being obsessed with us,' she admitted. 'But now, I wonder if being anonymous might be better.'

'We'd never be anonymous,' Max said with a grin. 'But the balance might be better if we lived on an Italian lake, or in a chateau in France. Imagine it, V. Just us.'

Verity closed her eyes. More and more lately, she'd had the miserable sense that although people in White Fir Lake looked up to her, they were also waiting for her to trip over in her designer heels and flail to the floor. How satisfying it might be to march away from them all.

'What about Frankie?' Verity asked. 'Could I really just leave her and move that far away?'

'Frankie would be out staying with us half the time,' said Max with a laugh. 'You think you could get rid of her and Red that easily?' He tangled his fingers with hers. 'A change of scenery might be good for you. I've read about couples who make big moves and then get pregnant. It's a healthier way of life, and you'd be more relaxed. Maybe we both would.'

Max more relaxed? That was barely possible. He was just trying to make her feel like she wasn't the only anxious mess. 'You seem to have this all planned out,' Verity said.

'I do, because I think it'd be good for you.' Max kissed her again, then rinsed his brushes and put them away. 'Why don't we get takeout tonight? That new little Indonesian place is meant to be awesome.'

Verity gasped and looked at her watch. 'No, I can't! I'm meant to be at Frankie's right now. We're going out with that new woman tonight.' She took her phone from her pocket and tapped out a message. 'I'll just tell her I've been held up. I'll meet them later.'

Max pulled her close to him again. 'Food with me first? I'll order it now. It really is meant to be the best cuisine in the country.'

Verity kissed him, caution making her pull away again. 'Okay,' she said. 'You choose the food, and I'll get ready while we're waiting for it.'

Max was right: the food was delicious. But there was way too much of it and Verity just wasn't very hungry. The thought of moving away and the thought of staying both kept sending jolts of nervousness through her blood. They ate in the front lounge where their largest Christmas tree twinkled with the lights that Ava had painstakingly wrapped around and around it. Max lit the fire. The flames flared in the corner of her eye, and Verity pulled on the neck of her black dress as she felt tiny pearls of sweat bead down her spine.

'I suppose I'd better call a cab,' she said. 'They'll be wondering where I am.'

Max popped a prawn into his mouth. 'I can drop you off.'

'No. I feel like if you drop me off there, I won't want to get out of the car.'

Max looked at her, concerned. She didn't want him to be concerned about her. She wanted him to see her as someone strong. She wanted to be able to pretend with him, with Frankie, with them all.

'I just feel a bit on the edge,' Verity explained, talking slowly and carefully so that she was in full control of each of her words. 'Like I might end up losing it.' She picked up a spring roll and inspected it. She wished she hadn't suggested going out. It was bad enough feeling like she might let herself go in front of Frankie. The thought of slipping up, of melting into a mess, with Alice there, the night before their big New Year's Eve party, was unbearable. It was handing her nervous breakdown, or whatever this was, to Alice on a plate for her to share around like a line of canapés.

'Losing it in what way?'

'Oh, I don't even know. Crying to them about babies or telling them about the letters. And I don't want to do that. I bet you don't want me to either,' she said, watching Max carefully. Their image was as important to him as it was to Verity. More important, probably, because he had his big, galloping career to think about, not just a pretentious little gallery to open and lock up every few days.

Max seemed to think about it carefully. 'I don't think Frankie would judge us. She has our back. She adores you. But this new woman... I don't know her. You don't know her. We don't want people gossiping at the party. Maybe give tonight a miss if you don't feel up to it. Just tell Frankie you'll catch up with her at a different time when it's just you two. She'll get it, I'm sure.'

Verity put down the spring roll and wiped her hands on a napkin. 'Don't be ridiculous. Frankie will hate that I'm not making an effort with someone new. It goes against her code. I'll just tell her I'm not well.' She closed her eyes and felt the tightness spread from her chest through her body. A shudder of tears ripped from her and escaped her mouth in an embarrassing little yowl. Jesus, she sounded like some kind of puppy. So much for strong.

Max pushed away his plate, then sprang up and came over to her, hugging her tightly. 'You need to go to the doctor and get something, V. This isn't right. Feeling like this isn't right.'

'No!' Verity shouted, surprising herself. 'I'm not going on medication! I've told you that. I can't.'

She heard Max sigh: softly, kindly almost. But he was obviously tired of all this too. 'It might just settle your nerves a bit.'

'I have wine for that.'

'Verity, come on.'

'No. Even if they don't affect getting pregnant, if I did, then I'd have to come off them. Then what?'

Max shrugged. 'We'd deal with it when it came to it. Or there could be something else they could do to help you. Therapy or something.'

'It didn't work, Max. Some old woman telling me to talk about my dead sister and mother is the last thing I need.' That's what had happened last time with the counselling the doctor had set up. *Do you blame yourself for the death of your younger sister, Verity?* Well, duh, yes, she'd wanted to say, because it was my fault. I'd promised her that I would play with her in the pool and I didn't, did I? I stayed in my bedroom painting my nails.

One nail pink, the next nail blue. The blue was too thin and she'd needed a third coat. That was a good enough reason to barely notice muffled cries for help, wasn't it?

Do you think you grieved properly for the death of your mother, Verity? Hmm. Let me think. Does sleeping with my dad's friend count as grieving? Nope? How about trying to *be* my mother? Watching videos of her to perfect her hair flip and her laugh? Does that count? No? Then no, I probably didn't. She hadn't said any of that, obviously. She'd flipped her hair and smiled and said no, of course she didn't blame herself for Betsy; yes, of course she'd grieved properly for them both.

'Go and have a bath,' Max said, 'and an early night. I'll message Frankie for you.'

Verity nodded, her head leaden, and pushed her phone towards him. 'Make it look like it's me messaging, remember.' He probably wouldn't. He was terrible at pretending to be something he wasn't.

She went to sleep easily, but then woke suddenly, the breath whipped from her in a gasp. Her mind stumbled behind her body, which was already alert, sitting up.

Someone was at the door. She heard Max's low tones, and then the soft close of the front door. Verity jumped out of bed and went to the window on the landing. She saw a figure retreating from the house, but her eyes were blurred from sleep and the light that flooded from the chandelier. It was a woman, perhaps, although it was even difficult to tell that.

She leaned against the wall and waited for Max to come upstairs and tell her who it had been. But she heard no footsteps on the stairs, just the murmur of the radio turned up in the kitchen. He probably thought she was still asleep. She considered going downstairs, but the conversation she knew they'd have – a ping pong of 'Who was it? / Nobody / Tell me / It's nothing' – stretched before her like a long road to nowhere.

She padded back to bed and slipped into the silky covers, but she knew that sleep was impossible. Her heart was still tight in her chest from waking up so suddenly. She took her phone from the bedside table. It was just after midnight. She opened Instagram and scrolled through her pictures. She liked looking at her own profile, to try and see what other people saw. Flawless, happy Verity. Laughing whilst blowing a dandelion; hand on hip holding a bottle of Veuve. Touching the tip of Max's (@themaxbentley) nose with a paintbrush and a flirty smile. Happy, happy, happy. Like, like, like. It was addictive seeing yourself from the outside rather than from the darkness of your own mind and making sure what you saw was perfect. Some brands even sent Verity things sometimes. Frankie liked to tease her and call her an influencer. What a term that was. Controlling what people did when you'd never even met them.

Verity scrolled down and down. She'd seen most of the comments on the older posts because she checked them regularly. But then a new one that she had definitely *not* seen before caught her eye. It was below a photo that was one of Verity's favourites, taken on a lazy August evening in their garden when Frankie and Red had been there. The light of the photo was mellow and golden. Verity was wearing her Dior straw hat and Max was lifting it up so that he could kiss her forehead, which she'd had Botoxed that very morning. Frankie had taken the photo and Verity had made her send it to her so that she could post it on Instagram immediately.

#lovehim

She'd even considered getting it framed.

So why, why, why, was there a week-old comment from Verity herself, that said:

Shame I can't trust him.

Feeling sick, Verity threw her phone down on the bed. Then she scrambled to find it again amongst the covers and got up. But as she moved toward the bedroom door, she faltered. Would Max really believe that Verity had absolutely no memory of making that comment? Her name was right next to it. Surely that would hurt him. Max could deal with absolutely anything, but Verity knew that his kryptonite was her. If he thought that she'd ever doubted him so publicly... She flung herself back down on the bed and opened Instagram up again, and there it still was.

Either she had been hacked, or she was going even more mad than she thought.

She flicked Google open and typed quickly. *Is memory loss a sign of madness?*

Her chest contracted and she closed her eyes, but the search results imprinted on her brain.

She was fine, and her phone had been hacked, she told herself calmly. Some weird boy with ugly glasses and bad teeth halfway across the world. She opened Instagram back up and swiped the comment.

Delete.

Then she read through the comments on her other photos, her eyes poring over every word. There was another one too, made a couple of weeks ago, slicing through her heart as she read it.

He really doesn't deserve me.

Verity's breathing became chaotic. Delete, delete, delete.

But what if it was too late? Max can't have seen the

comments. She would have known if he'd been upset with her, and anyway, Max didn't go on social media much. He was above all that: he only had accounts because his agent told him it was necessary. But other people might have seen them. They'd probably taken delight in them. *We knew they weren't that perfect!*

Verity had been hounding Frankie to get on Instagram for ages now, but Frankie was more of a Pinterest person, saving pictures of children's birthday cakes, hacks for organising toys and boards of hairstyles she'd never dare get. She posted pictures of her children on Facebook too, but she didn't have the stamina for Instagram. Thank God. But what if Frankie's friends from the school had seen it and told her? Or what if Alice was on Instagram, or Luna? Something like this was bound to cause a wave of rumours that Verity definitely wasn't strong enough for at the moment. What if someone passed it around at the New Year's Eve party tomorrow night? What if Mike Dawson, the reporter who was coming from *Hills Daily*, heard them? What if someone took a photograph of her looking tense and frightened?

Verity drew in a shaky breath. Maybe the way around all this was to make a little joke of it, just to get the word out that it was a game between Max and Verity. That would cover her and put an end to whatever people might start saying. Better to do that than deny it, or worse, admit she had no memory of doing it if someone brought it up. She pictured herself with a wicked grin as she told some carefully selected guests about a new game they played where she and Max pretended to snipe at one another.

Injecting some drama. A little role play. It's all about the making up.

She lay back on the smooth pillows, still clutching her phone. Her breathing slowed a little and eventually the songs drifting upstairs from the radio danced into her dreams.

the New Year's Eve

Chapter Eleven

FRANKIE

New Year's Eve

E very single year, Frankie woke up at 6 a.m. on New Year's Eve to make mini Yorkshire puddings filled with sirloin and horseradish, mini blackberry cheesecakes, mini everything. Verity always told her not to, and would be getting ridiculously extravagant catering in for the party, but Frankie knew that really Verity liked Frankie's canapés adding a touch of something extra to her parties too. It was a tradition.

So Frankie was meant to do the same today, like every New Year's Eve: get up early on the last day of the year, put on some fresh coffee and stir, pipe, roll and simmer until the kitchen smelled delicious and the windows steamed up with the promise of warm treats. Today, though, as her phone alarm battered its way into Frankie's consciousness, she felt as though it was vibrating right into the tissue of her brain. She whacked her phone with her fist to stop the noise and kept her eyes closed as she carefully revisited last night. A tight feeling in her stomach told her she'd done something that she wished she hadn't. It was only a few seconds until she remembered: using Verity and Max's keycode for the gate; demanding to know where Verity was. Wanting to push her way into their lives in the middle of the night. What was the matter with her?

She groaned and rolled over to where she expected Red to be, but the bed was cool and empty. Straining her ears, she heard the chatter of the girls, a wail from Harry. She managed a tut. People were never up before Frankie on New Year's Eve. She took a deep breath and sat up in bed. Red had placed a cup of coffee on her bedside table and she drank it down in thirsty gulps. That was a bit better.

Once she'd made it downstairs, she saw that the children were dressed, and that they were eating crumpets smeared with sticky chocolate spread.

'How's the head?' Red asked with a grin.

'Oh, not too bad, actually. The coffee helped, thanks,' Frankie said. She wouldn't tell him the price of the bill last night. Maybe by the time he saw the credit card statement, she'd have thought of some job she could get, or perhaps he would have realised he'd made more money than he thought he would from the church project. 'Have you been up long?'

'An hour or so,' said Red. 'I'm going to set off soon.'

'I don't want to go to Grandma's. I want to go to Verity's party,' said Maisie.

'You can't,' said Frankie as she put two crumpets in the toaster for herself. 'But you'll have so much fun at Grandma's.' Perhaps she should call Verity and ask her to come round for a bit of a pre-party. Red would be out all day: his parents always had some odd jobs they wanted him to do, and they always cooked him a meal, too, even when he didn't want one. Frankie could make some cocktails, and she could mention last night to Verity, make sure that it didn't look like Frankie was hiding anything. It had seemed odd to Frankie that Verity was awake last night when Frankie was at the door talking to Max, that she hadn't come straight down to see Frankie. But now, it was obvious: the noise of drunken Frankie turning up in a taxi like some kind of maniac had woken Verity up. She wouldn't have known it was Frankie from the window either: the pretty lights nestled into the ivy at the front door weren't bright enough for her to have seen that.

She took her phone from her dressing gown pocket and tapped out a message:

Missed you last night! Want to pop round lunchtime-ish? We can write our resolutions together! Xx

Should she have mentioned Verity's mystery illness? She was about to type another message but then her crumpets popped up merrily and her phone lit up almost instantly:

Definitely. Missed you too xxxxxxxx

She took the raspberry jam from the fridge and breathed a sigh of relief. It was going to be a good day, and an amazing night.

'Right!' she said brightly to the children. 'Time for Mummy to do some baking! Who wants to help me do my biscuit base before you go with Daddy?' She smiled as the girls leapt from their chocolate-smeared places at the table and ran to her. It was their favourite bit of Frankie's baking: bashing the living daylights out of bags full of digestive biscuits for her cheesecakes. She had to admit, it was one of her favourite bits too.

When Verity arrived, she held up a bottle of champagne, the bottle encrusted with little gems.

'Tacky, I know,' she beamed. 'But I couldn't resist!' She popped open the cork there and then in the hallway and bubbles flew down the sides and foamed onto the floor.

They settled themselves at their usual place on the breakfast-bar stools and Frankie put out some testers of some of the things she'd made so far: the miniature cheesecakes; tiny doughnuts rolled in cinnamon sugar, and some filo and mozzarella creations she'd seen one of her favourite chefs make on TV a few weeks ago.

'So how was the night with Alice? I'm so sorry I couldn't come,' said Verity, taking a doughnut and picking at the tiny grains of sugar.

'Oh, it was fine. Alice is nice enough. Did you see me at your house?' Frankie said, her words rushing out.

Verity frowned. 'I saw someone, but I didn't know it was you.'

Frankie felt a blush creep up from her neck to her cheeks. This was ridiculous. Verity was her best friend! Was there really any need to feel this awkward? 'Yeah, I just... I kind of missed you, and I wondered why you hadn't joined us, and I felt... I don't know. I was drunk and I wanted to see you. I felt a bit worried about you.' Frankie had been gazing at the mozzarella oozing from the pastries, but now she glanced at Verity. She'd thought out what she'd say, and she had known how Verity would respond: she would put her hand on Frankie's and her touch would be cool and delicate. 'Frankie, don't *worry* about everything so much,' she'd say, and then they'd both laugh and top up their drinks.

But there was none of that. Verity put down her doughnut on the worktop and stared at Frankie. 'What made you worried?' she asked.

'Well, the fact that you didn't come out with us. And...' There was a brief pause as Frankie chewed on her own doughnut, wondering what else to say. 'I just missed you,' she said again in the end.

Verity grinned. 'Well, you'll see plenty of me tonight.' The crack in her voice was small and the grin only wavered slightly, but Frankie noticed, and rushed to put her arms around Verity, who gripped Frankie so tightly that she could feel her friend's delicate bones and bra straps beneath her wool sweater.

'What? What's happened, V?'

'Oh, Frankie!' Verity said, her words muffled in Frankie's shoulder. 'I feel like I'm going mad!'

'But why? Tell me why, and then we can do something about it!'

Verity pulled back. She shook her head and wiped her eyes. 'Nothing's *happened*. I've just been feeling strange lately. My memory has been a little off and I've been doing weird things. And I feel like there are rumours.' She downed the last of her drink and motioned for Frankie to top them up.

'Doing strange things? What do you mean?' Frankie asked as she emptied the champagne into their glasses. 'And what's made you think there are rumours?' She thought of Alice last night, and her story about women in the coffee shop talking about Max.

'Oh, I don't know. New ones.' Verity waved her hand about, as though the rumours themselves were floating around in the air of Frankie's kitchen, mingling with the scents of cheese and cinnamon, roasting beef and berry coulis. 'I know people are always talking about Max, and his work, and me. It's never really bothered me before. It's part of who we are. But I just suddenly wonder if people are a bit *too* interested in us.'

'Of course they are!' Frankie said. Verity had always loved it. She lived for it. Max too. 'Everyone here adores you both, that's why.'

'Ha,' Verity spat. 'Do you really believe that?'

'Yes. And you should, too. You saw how excited Alice was when she found out who Max was. And look at Luna, and how going to your gallery has changed things for her already! People round here think you're like royalty. All the mums at school are dying for tonight!'

'But everyone knows our business, everyone can see our house, our comings and goings. They don't love us, Frankie. They're out to see us fail.'

'Well, that's just—'

'Max says we should leave. Start again somewhere else. Italy, France, anywhere but this place.'

Frankie felt hot fear rush through her. 'You'd leave?'

Verity picked up her glass and took a sip. 'I thought, when we bought our place, that I would have gorgeous kids running around it, wrecking my white furniture and wearing cute Dior dresses to my parties and piling into our bed at the weekends. You know,' she said with a shrieking laugh, 'it never occurred to me that I might not be happy, that I might not get what I wanted. What a fool.'

'You can still be happy,' Frankie said, not even bothering to keep the desperation from her voice. Max gone? Verity gone? A life with just Red and the children: no best friend, no thrill from the kisses on her cheek from Max? She and Red had saved so hard, spent so hard and planned so much to reach White Fir Lake. Living opposite anyone else instead was unimaginable.

Verity sighed. 'I don't know. It might be nice to go somewhere new and start again. Maybe a change might kickstart my crappy ovaries.'

Frankie was silent. The grenade. She couldn't deny Verity a chance for a baby. She needed to think about what Verity needed, not herself.

'Anyway,' Verity said, suddenly breezy. 'That's

something for another day. For now, let's think about tonight.'

'Yeah, you'll show everyone tonight that there is nothing for them to be talking about other than how fabulous you and Max are!' Frankie said, false cheer and determination oozing from her voice and making her feel a bit silly. It had to be a good sign that Verity could move on from the idea this quickly. Maybe it meant that it wasn't an actual possibility. There was obviously a lot she hadn't even considered. Verity never thought things through properly. That was her appeal.

'You're right. It'll be the best New Year's Eve party we've ever thrown,' said Verity.

'I don't know about that. What about the year you had flamingos?'

Verity laughed. 'That year was overrated. There was bird shit everywhere.'

'Well then, there you have it.' Frankie squeezed Verity's hand. 'Best year ever.' The party would get Verity through today. And then Frankie would have to pull something else out of the bag after that: something special.

The morning was one of those unruly ones that wouldn't behave and went this way and that without warning or permission. Frankie's mini sausages had burned at some point; she couldn't even work out when it had been, but the results were sooty black sticks that made them both hoot with laughter. Next, Frankie and Verity heard the key turn in the lock, the busy footsteps and chatter of Maisie and Bella. Frankie stood up, feeling the daytime fizz rush to her head, and met Red and the children in the hallway.

'What's wrong?' she asked. 'Why have you come back?'

'We went for some breakfast and then Daddy felt poorly,' Maisie explained importantly. 'He thought he might get better but he didn't, so we stopped for a bit but it didn't help, so he phoned Nanny and—'

'Nanny said we should go back home,' Bella finished, ignoring Maisie's high-pitched protests at the hijacking of her story.

'I just felt really light-headed,' Red said as they all piled into the kitchen. 'I thought I might pass out, so I had to pull over.'

'That's when we went for some breakfast,' Maisie explained, kicking her trainers off.

Frankie helped Harry out of his duffel coat and hung it up on the overcrowded coat stand. There had been one day about two months ago where Red had collapsed whilst on a building site, and since then Frankie had wondered if he really should be working so hard and so high.

'Yeah,' Red said. 'I thought a muffin and a coffee would help, but it didn't do much.' He nodded at Verity. 'Hey, V. Sorry to crash the party. I didn't know you'd be here. I'll have a rest for a bit and then see how I am later.'

'No way,' Frankie said. 'You're not driving today, after this. Not in this ice.'

'I might be better in a bit.'

'Nope,' Frankie said, holding up her hand. She found herself doing this sometimes: being protective and slightly bossy with Red, as though he were one of her children. It was like motherhood had quietly tipped over and leaked into all the other parts of her life without her noticing.

'You could take them up to my parents' instead, if you wanted to?'

'Sorry,' Verity said, holding up the empty champagne bottle. 'I've had my wicked way with her. No driving for Frankie, not for a few hours at least.'

'So we can come to the party!' Bella shouted with glee, jumping up and down.

'Bella!' Frankie admonished. 'You haven't been invited! The party's for grown-ups.' She turned to Verity apologetically, remembering the promise that tonight would be like old times. 'We can look after them in shifts, or something. That's if Red even still comes,' she said, glancing over at Red as he stretched himself out on the sofa in the dining area. 'We don't have to turn tonight into a kids' party.'

'Oh, nonsense!' Verity said, pulling Bella and Maisie towards her. 'Apart from your daddy feeling poorly, this is actually quite lovely. I secretly wanted you two at my party,' she said with a tickle. The girls shrieked in excitement. 'In fact, you girls go and get my handbag for me. It's in the hallway, I think. We have a very special job to do.'

The 'job' was the tradition of writing out their New Year's resolutions. Bella and Maisie were just taking the pens and tiny cards with matching gold envelopes from Verity when Alice arrived.

'I hope you don't mind me coming,' she said, as Frankie ushered her in. 'I just need a bit of help deciding what to wear tonight.' She nodded to the dresses that hung over her arm like limp bodies. 'Would you have time?'

Frankie thought of Verity's tears before; of the children, who now needed lunch and baths and party outfits on; of Red, who lay quietly on the sofa; of the burned sausages that needed replacing. 'Of course!' she said. 'We're actually just doing some party stuff. You should join in.'

'Alice! Hi!' said Verity. Nobody would have guessed that only an hour ago she was weeping in Frankie's arms. Even Frankie wouldn't have guessed Verity had been crying if she hadn't seen it for herself. The thought made her feel unsteady on her feet. 'I'm glad you're here. We're writing down our resolutions!'

'Feeling better, then?' Alice asked.

'Oh, good as new,' Verity said, causally waving her hand. 'Sorry about last night. I absolutely needed to recover for tonight, you see. Here you go, take one of these, and a gold pen from Maisie.'

'She gets us to do this every year,' Frankie explained to Alice. *But what if next year she's not here? What then?*

'What can I say? I adore a tradition,' said Verity. 'We all have to write down what we want from the year to come. Not all the guests do it. Only the best ones. Once you've written it, pop it in the envelope, seal it and then give it back to me.'

'What do you do with them?' Alice asked, squatting

down next to where Harry was screwing up a blank card. She stroked his head and took it from him gently, making Frankie wish she'd done it first. 'Do you read them all?'

'God, no!' Verity put her slim hand to her chest in affront. 'If you want to share them at the party, then you can, but you don't have to. I give them back at the party the year after, if it's what you want. If not, we throw them on the fire and watch them burn. It's like they never existed.'

'So do you normally get yours back? Or do you burn it?' Alice asked Frankie.

'It depends if I've kept to it,' Frankie said.

'Frankie always keeps to them because she gives herself ridiculously easy ones,' Verity said with a laugh.

'I do not!'

'Oh, yes you do,' piped up Red from his sofa. 'Girls, can you remember what Mummy's resolution was last year?'

'No chocolate on Fridays!' Bella and Maisie both sang out.

'Exactly. In fact, wasn't it only Friday mornings?' Red said.

Frankie laughed. 'Giving up chocolate is not easy, even if it's for four hours a week.'

'Hmm.' Verity tapped her pen against her chin. 'Even so, I think I might suggest that we are all a bit more ambitious this year.'

'Are you going to be ambitious?' Alice asked Verity, and Frankie glanced across at her friend uneasily. Verity's resolution had been the same every single year for ten years. She never read it the year after.

'She doesn't need to be ambitious,' said Red. 'She has it all, don't you, V?'

'I suppose,' Verity said.

'You do. And more to come, I would think,' Red said. 'So no need to sweat about anything you don't have yet.'

'Red never writes resolutions,' Frankie told Alice. 'He's the only one brave enough to defy Verity's New Year's rules.'

'I don't believe in resolutions,' said Red, standing up and heading over to their drinks cabinet. He sloshed some whisky in a glass. 'I like to believe I'll get what I want, anyway. I don't think writing it down will change it. You need to just do it.'

Frankie looked across at him. Did he have what he wanted now that they lived here, or was he still pushing on, his eyes on some other prize? She didn't know whether to tell him later that Verity and Max were thinking of moving. He might rip into Max sometimes, but he loved Verity like a sister. He'd worked so hard for this life, risked his health to join the elite. If Max and Verity left, it would turn everything on its head.

'Oh, Red, you say this every year. Let me have my fun,' Verity said. She locked eyes with Frankie. 'Go on, Frankie. What'll yours be?'

'I don't know. Maybe less alcohol?' she said as Red knocked back nearly half the glass in one go.

Verity gave a delicate snort of laughter. 'O-kay. That one will be going straight in the fire next year. Alice? What about you?'

Alice closed her eyes, apparently thinking hard.

'Hmmm,' she said after quite a dramatic pause, her eyes flying back open. 'I have a few loose ends to tie up. But I think the main one would be to make things better for Luna and I. It sounds a bit cliché, but we've had a rough time and moving here marks a change to that. At least I hope it does.'

'We've done ours!' Maisie shoved envelopes full of scrawled pictures into Frankie's face. Frankie took them absently, the delicious feeling of having a secret flickering inside her. She'd had a sudden, brilliant idea, and it would change everything for the better. It would give Verity all she wanted, and it would make them all as close as they used to be, if not closer. It would make Max see her as part of their family. And it would keep them all close together in White Fir Lake.

Chapter Twelve

FRANKIE

New Year's Eve

'It's just jammed. It's the zip,' Frankie told Red. 'It does fit.'

'Oh, I know.' Red tugged the zip up gently. He should probably be trying to tug it down, but she didn't blame him for not doing it. She couldn't remember the last time he had done. Frankie was quiet as she counted the weeks, or perhaps months, since Red had taken off her clothes, or touched her or even shown that he might want to. She'd lost track. It was only the same as all married couples with young children, though, wasn't it? 'All done.'

Frankie brushed down the soft, dark blue fabric. It wasn't the most glamorous dress but it fitted (it really did, the zip was just one of those temperamental ones!) and it was good material. She'd worn a silver dress to the last party Max and Verity had thrown, and the photos had shown up every bump on her body. Dark blue was much safer.

'I got this in the sale,' Frankie told Red. 'It was half price.'

Red nodded. 'It's nice.'

It hadn't been exactly half price. More like thirty per cent off. But she'd remembered her better-wife promise and was trying to make him feel less stressed. It seemed to be working. He spritzed himself with aftershave, the same one Max wore. She couldn't remember who'd started wearing it first. Red always insisted it was him, but Frankie wasn't sure.

'Should be a good party,' Frankie said. She picked up her glass of cava, which, for the record, did not taste the same as champagne, like that money-saving article told her it would. 'Red, there's something I need to tell you.'

He nodded again. He obviously didn't think it would be anything big. Frankie never did anything big or said anything big. He probably thought it was about a Waitrose substitution in their online order or a lost school shoe or a new electric toothbrush she'd seen a review of. Or a swimming lesson. She swallowed.

'I'm going to offer to be a surrogate for Verity.'

His expression changed. He stared at her for a while: so long that Frankie wondered if he'd heard her.

'Carry her baby,' she prompted. Perhaps she'd

underestimated how big this would be for him. She'd been focusing on how it would keep their lives intact, not how it might come between her and Red. Frankie's body was his too, in a way, despite her zip being firmly up, not down: despite it being months, not weeks. How would she feel if Red was going to change something about himself? She probably wouldn't care if it kept Max and Verity here. *Try harder, Frankie. Be a better wife, remember.* 'I've done quite a bit of research,' she pushed on. 'And Verity's talked about surrogacy before, actually, but it was when I was pregnant with Harry so it wasn't an option for me, and I don't think there would be anyone else she—'

'Absolutely not,' Red cut in bluntly.

'It would solve all of their problems. They're thinking of leaving White Fir Lake, Red.'

'They'd never leave White Fir Lake.'

Frankie took a breath. 'I don't like the idea of them not being here. So I'm not being completely altruistic. I think it'd keep them close to us,' she admitted. 'That's important to you, isn't it? You love them. I know you moan about Max, but both of them are like… Well, they're our family.'

She'd said it. That word. She didn't use it often: just dragged it out on absolutely special occasions, like an expensive wine glass that nobody really dared use. She had her parents, of course, but they weren't her biological parents. Who knew where they were? Families were people who knew you inside out, who let you be who you were.

'Playing the family card? For this?'

Frankie looked down at her gold shoes. Did they really

match her blue dress? She didn't know. 'It's important to me.'

'Mummy?' Maisie appeared at their bedroom door. 'Bella put some of the red lipstick that Santa brought for me on Harry and it won't come off.'

Frankie closed her eyes for a moment, then opened them again. 'Use a baby wipe.'

'They could pay us,' Red said quietly, his tone a little brighter.

'Oh they can't,' Frankie said. 'It's illegal to pay people to do it. They could cover expenses, but that's all.'

Red laughed, more loudly than usual. It was like a bad actor was suddenly playing him. This had obviously been the wrong time to tell him. But she had to tell Verity at New Year's because it was Frankie's resolution. *I want to carry Verity and Max's baby.* It was already written, bound in its gold envelope, ready to change everything for the better. 'Like they care about legalities,' Red said. 'Frankie, you don't get a house like theirs if you are law-abiding. There'd be ways round it. They could pay.' His eyes took on a hazy quality. 'Imagine how much they'd pay for a baby. You could be onto something.'

'Red, you're missing the point! Money would change it all. It would make it look like we were doing it for our own gain.'

'Well, you are. You said this wasn't altruistic.'

'Because I love her! I want her to stay! I don't want her money!'

'But you want all this.' Red motioned around at the

room: their plush grey carpet and expanse of wardrobes stuffed with shoeboxes and dresses and matching handbags. 'Don't you?'

Maisie appeared again, eyes wide at the raised voices. 'I can't find the baby wipes.'

'Bathroom cupboard,' Frankie said.

They were silent, paused until Maisie was out of earshot. She'd be back any minute. They always were.

'You think it's all done?' Red said. 'You think because we have the house now, we've reached our target?' He laughed again, even though it was clear he didn't find any of this in the least bit amusing. 'We're so far from our target, Frankie.' His laugh petered out and to her horror, Frankie saw tears fill his eyes. She'd never, ever seen Red cry before.

Stress is certainly a key factor in symptoms worsening.

She was going to end up killing her husband at this rate. 'Let's talk about this another time,' she said. 'Don't worry about it now.'

'Don't worry about how you obviously want to sleep with Max?'

Frankie took a step back, held up her hands. 'No!'

Yes, yes, yes! What she wouldn't give to have Max's hands on her, those lips on her flesh. All these years of longing. It was exhausting, like being starving for her whole life and never having a meal. She always thought she'd hidden it quite well though. *Wrong again, Frankie.*

Harry appeared at their bedroom door next, his face a shock of glossy red strokes.

'Mate,' Red said to him, tension tightening his voice. 'Go and get the wipes. They're in the bathroom cupboard.'

Harry flopped down on the floor.

'Get up,' Red said, his voice rising to a pitch that Frankie didn't recognise. 'You'll ruin the carpet. It'll stain.'

Harry rolled over.

'Harry! Do as you're told!' Red shouted.

'He can't understand what you're saying,' Frankie said patiently. Her heart was doing little skips. She hadn't thought Red cared this much about her; hadn't thought he'd be so possessive.

'Course he can.'

'He's too little.' She went over to Harry and picked him up, plopped him down on the floor of the landing and shouted for Maisie, then returned to the bedroom.

'Anyway,' she said, trying to make her voice kind. 'Max wouldn't… It's obviously not what I had in mind. I mean test tubes and Petri dishes. You've got completely the wrong idea about all of this. It's not about money and it's not about Max.'

'Yeah, right.' Red wiped his eyes. It was the second time in a week she'd been transported back to those sharp-hot days in America where he was like a shadow beside them all, unsure and unhappy, burning in the blazing heat whilst everyone else went nut brown.

'Mummy!' shouted Bella, followed by a shout from Harry.

'Look, let's just forget I said it,' Frankie said. 'We'll speak about it another day. I was going to offer it to Verity tonight, but I won't. I promise.' Frankie headed for the bedroom door, feeling for the first time how restrictive her dress was. She wanted to tear it off, to put her pyjamas on, to watch the final episode of the new ITV murder mystery she'd got into. Was it the boring police officer with three cats and no social life who'd done it? Or the apparently trustworthy wife who never seemed to do anything but the school run?

You just never knew.

Chapter Thirteen

VERITY

New Year's Eve

Verity didn't think much of the doorbell ringing. Deliveries were arriving all day every day; had been for a week or so now. There were the giant black feathers, the crates of bottles, the glasses and flowers and hundreds of tiny golden bowls and napkins.

She was sitting at her dressing table, absently fastening pearls around her neck and thinking about that morning at Frankie's. Frankie's kitchen had smelled completely delicious when she arrived and Verity had felt a violent hunger throb inside her for the first time in ages. She'd reached for a little doughnut that Frankie had made. She couldn't remember the last time she ate a doughnut. Maybe if she picked the sugar off, she'd save some calories. But she'd ended up putting it straight back down as soon as Frankie told her she'd come to her house after her night out with Alice.

'I felt a bit worried about you,' Frankie had said, her kind, wide eyes concerned, and that's when Verity felt a small crack inside her: only a hairline, but enough for everything to loosen a little and then fall apart completely. Of course Frankie was worried about her, because she'd probably heard about the Instagram posts. Frankie had probably heard one of the mothers at school talking about the posts, or talking about Max, or even talking about some secret that he had that poor Verity didn't know. And then she'd gone out with Alice. As loyal as Frankie was, that didn't mean someone new couldn't make her feel special enough, and drunk enough, to let a few strands of gossip unravel.

Verity had let Frankie hug her, and she'd said something garbled about feeling like she was going mad, but then she had managed to pull herself together. It was no good getting worked up now, on the day of the party. Puffy eyes and Frankie's sad, secretive glances were not what she needed tonight. She had told Frankie that Max had suggested they move away, thinking that then Frankie might be the one to burst into tears, but Frankie had been still and quiet.

Perhaps she didn't care quite as much as Verity thought.

'Mrs Bentley? A guest for you,' Ava shouted to her now from the landing. Verity frowned into the mirror and yanked off the pearls before dumping them onto her dressing table. Smile fixed, she bounded down the winding staircase. Perhaps this was Frankie crying now, having some kind of delayed reaction.

'Oh!' she said, when she saw who stood at the front door. 'I wasn't expecting it to be you! The party doesn't start for another four hours, you know.'

Luna gave a small, awkward smile and her cheeks flamed. 'I know. I hope it's not weird coming here. I just thought... It's been pretty cool at the gallery. And I just wanted to pay back the favour by helping you get things ready for tonight.'

'Oh, it's no favour. It's been great having you at the gallery. You've been good company.' It was actually true to a point, Verity reflected.

'But still, I'd like to help you with getting ready for the party,' Luna said.

'That's really nice of you, Luna.' Verity smiled and leaned in towards Luna conspiratorially. 'But I have staff for that.'

'Oh, okay,' Luna said. She looked down at her scruffy shoes. Honestly, why was she wearing those chequered trainers? She looked like she had on the feet of some washed-up skater waster. If Luna was her daughter, Verity would dress her to kill.

'You could still come in though,' Verity said. Her heart stirred a little. She'd cancelled a night with Frankie and this girl's mother last night because she didn't feel like being around people before the party. Because it was too much of a risk. She'd had a near miss of a full breakdown at Frankie's only hours ago at the thought of Alice knowing her business. But Luna was just a child, Verity reasoned, and today was a new day. The house would be full of guests before she knew it anyway, so perhaps it was a good idea to warm up in some way. She gestured grandly for Luna to step forwards. 'You can help me test the canapés. I have a few to try. The rest are coming later with the caterers.'

Luna frowned. 'I'm vegetarian. Do you have vegetarian ones?'

'Oh, darling, of course we do.'

They wandered through to the kitchen and Verity offered Luna a tiny beetroot fritter from one of the mini silver platters. 'So do you have an outfit for tonight?' Verity asked Luna, trying not to look down at those hideous shoes.

Luna nibbled on the fritter and shook her head. Verity immediately felt calmer. A purpose made everything better. 'Well then, you come with me. I think we're a similar size and I have hundreds of dresses. Hundreds.'

Luna followed Verity up the stairs to her walk-in wardrobe. 'This house is enormous,' she said. 'Don't you get a bit lost here, just you and Max?'

It cut just a little. But it was obvious that Luna had no idea and meant nothing by it. 'Yes. I wanted a load of babies, to be honest, but I'm finding that the whole baby thing is easier said than done. For some people, anyway.' There. She'd come out and said it, and she wasn't sniffling or hysterical or even shaken.

Luna stared at her. 'Wow. Sorry. I thought you had everything you wanted.'

Verity smiled and felt herself snapping closed again. 'Oh, I do, really. Now' – she pulled out an extendable rail of dresses in hues of emerald green, deep blue and stark black

– 'take your pick.' She glanced at Luna. 'I think green would look fantastic on you.'

Luna stared at the rack of dresses as though it were a pit of snakes. 'I don't know,' she said, stepping back awkwardly.

'Oh, come on. You're almost a woman, Luna. Enjoy it. Make the most of it. You know, I was only a little older than you when I met Max.'

Luna's eyes widened. God knows what she was picturing. Teen minds were filthy. Verity should know. 'Really?'

'Yes. It's a great age.' Verity took the emerald dress from its velvet hanger and offered it to Luna. 'Try it on. You don't have to show me. Just do it for you, and if you never want to wear it again just take it off and we'll never talk of it again,' Verity said with a grin.

Luna smiled back. 'Okay.'

'I'll be in my bedroom.'

Verity turned and wandered down to her room. She felt a pleasant yet painful combination of motherhood and sisterhood descend on her when she spoke to Luna: two states that she'd never quite managed to keep hold of for that long. She closed her eyes and leaned against the wall for support for a moment.

Betsy whispered to her from somewhere above: *Verity, Verity, play with me.*

Verity shook her head. Betsy wasn't here. It was just a memory of her, which was something positive to be treasured. But it was no good. Now two voices mingled in the air like poisonous gas as she forced herself into her bedroom.

Play with me, Verity.

Betsy, no, get off. I'm busy.

She yanked open her drawer.

You're always busy.

'Stop it,' Verity whispered. 'Go away.' But that made her feel worse. That was the whole problem.

'Verity?'

Verity whipped around. Luna stood shyly next to Verity's chaise longue. The green dress clung to her tiny waist and the kind of brand-new, tight curves that only teenagers had. 'Oh my God! Luna, you look incredible!'

'You really think I can pull it off?'

'Think? I know it! That figure! The colour! Who knew you were hiding that body all this time?'

Luna's cheeks scorched red. It felt good to have her here, in her bedroom, looking up to her, wanting Verity's advice and borrowing her clothes. Pay it back. That was what you were meant to do, wasn't it? Verity had tried it when Frankie had first started school, and she'd hung off Verity's every word. Make it up to Betsy, be a sister to Frankie instead. But then she'd wrecked that, really, by taking Max when it was so obvious that Frankie wanted him for herself.

So now, she could do things properly.

'How about we sort your hair out later, too? My hairdresser is coming to do mine at six thirty. I'll get her to do yours whilst she's here! Yes?' Verity remembered that Luna didn't like salons as she spoke, but this wasn't some five-pound-cut place. This was different.

Luna shrugged. 'I don't think so. Anyway, how much does that even cost? Even if I wanted to, I—'

'Oh no!' Verity interrupted. 'It'd be my treat, obviously.' She stepped forward and put her hand out to Luna's hair. It was smoother than she'd expected and fell through her fingers like silk.

'I know it's bad,' Luna said, staring straight ahead.

'What is?'

'My hair. I don't do hairdressers. I've never really cared what my hair looks like.'

'That's because you've never worn a fabulous dress or been to one of my parties before.' Verity grinned and stepped back. 'Okay. You go and change, and I'll call my hairdresser and ask her to squeeze you in as well. She adores me, she won't mind.'

Luna stood awkwardly for a moment. 'Okay,' she said eventually. 'I'll go and take this off.'

'Yes. Hang it back up then be back here at about six,' Verity instructed, deciding as Luna left the room that she needed to find her some makeup to wear. Luna had great features when she smiled, and she only needed to be enhanced, not painted over. A coat of mascara, a sweep of bronzer and a neutral lip would do wonders.

Verity pulled open her dressing-table drawer and her chest tightened as it always did now, whenever she went in there. This had been the last place she'd seen her lipstick before it had been hacked at and left in her pocket. Whoever was messing with her had been in this drawer. An image of gloved police combing through it for fingerprints flew into her mind. No, absolutely not. That was never going to be an option. The press would be all over it. There would be questions and delving: the last thing they needed. Verity took a slow breath and forced herself to look closely at the contents. Everything was as it should be: her lipsticks in glossy black rows, ordered by label. The soft, pale lipstick she would give to Luna later, Evening Rose, was right there. Verity shut the drawer with satisfaction. With every tick that went by on her vintage Rolex without a letter or a random, intimate possession going missing, Verity's heart became a little calmer.

Chapter Fourteen

VERITY

New Year's Eve

O f course, it wasn't long until there was cause for
Verity's heart to quicken like the wings of a
butterfly. It was never long.

'The band are setting up,' she said to Max. He was just
out of the shower, wandering about the bedroom with that
delicious mix of damp skin and masculine heat. She
wandered over to him in her underwear and kissed him as
the dramatic gong of the doorbell sounded. 'I need to know
which shoes to wear. Have you had any thoughts on this? I
could wear the silver Westwoods or the nude Louboutins.'

'Nude?' Max grinned and came over and gripped Verity
tightly. She closed her eyes and breathed him in. She could
hear the rumble of anticipation below: voices, clattering

dishes, the door opening and closing and the patter of quick feet.

'You seem better,' Max whispered into Verity's ear.

Verity opened her eyes and pulled away from him to step into her dress. 'I do feel a little better. A party helps everything, you know that. So? The shoes?' she asked as she zipped it up. 'Any thoughts?'

Max laughed as they wandered out of the room to the adjoining walk-in wardrobes. 'I've thought of nothing else, and sadly have come to no conclusion.'

Verity laughed too. 'This is serious stuff, Max.' She watched him as he pulled on his black trousers. Full tux for the men tonight, of course.

'Verity?' The voice came from the bedroom. As Verity walked back into her room and saw the person standing next to her bed, she felt the horrible sense of blankness and confusion that she'd had a few times lately. And then, in a rush, it clicked.

'Luna!' Verity gasped, relief rushing over her. The confusion had been legitimate! 'Your hair... I didn't recognise you.'

'Do you like it?' Luna asked. 'I bought a kit on the way home from here before, on a whim. I don't know what I was thinking, really, but it's done now,' she finished quietly, her cheeks flaming red against her newly bleached hair. Verity stared for a moment, trying to think of the exact colour to describe it. It was all one tone, which was a shame. But the colour: foreign sand; vanilla ice cream; a lurid hint of butter, wasn't altogether terrible. From a distance, it would look like Verity's own £250-a-salon-visit hair.

'It's incredible!' Verity gushed, delighted to see Luna's blushes subside at her words.

'Hey, Luna,' Max said as he stepped into the bedroom from the wardrobe space. 'Almost didn't recognise you then. All ready to party?' He did a funny little sashay, and they all laughed. Like a family would, Verity couldn't help thinking.

'I suppose,' Luna said. 'I'm not really the party type normally. I'm not great with people.'

'You're fine,' Max said. 'We'll have a great time. Has Verity made you do your resolution?'

Luna nodded. 'I have it. But I'm not showing anyone yet. Not till midnight.'

'Verity wouldn't dream of letting you. She runs a tight ship when it comes to resolutions,' Max said.

Luna grinned at Max for a little longer than was necessary, and the blush bloomed again, this time from her pale chest up to her neck and cheeks. Verity felt her grip on things slide a little. She'd been stupid to pop Luna into a little sister box and try to create some kind of relationship with her based on warped, pocked, ugly guilt. What kind of a person *was* she? Panic tapped inside Verity's heart. Maybe she'd got it all wrong. Maybe Luna wasn't here for sweet compliments from Verity. Maybe she was here for something entirely different.

'Come on,' Verity said, stepping towards Luna and taking her by the wrist. Her skin was cool, and Verity felt the bone beneath, fragile as china. 'Let's get your dress.'

'I'll leave you guys to it, then,' Max said, an undertone of concern in his voice. *It's fine*, Verity told him with a look.

I'm fine. And she was, she decided as she yanked open her underwear drawers to find a bra that would fit Luna. She could see the worn straps of the bra Luna was wearing now beneath her faded vest, no good at all for under the dress they'd picked. She was fine because Luna was just a teenager, and it was normal for teenagers, as well as young women and middle-aged women and old women and God, men, so many men, to fall for Max Bentley.

'Are you okay?' she heard Luna ask, but the words sounded far away, as though Verity's brain didn't know quite what to do with them. She nodded, or at least she thought she did, as she rifled through her bras. There weren't as many in the drawer as Verity had thought. Maybe she'd thrown some out? She had one the exact green of the dress, where was that? Verity pulled open another drawer of thongs and searched until the lace and cotton blurred in a colourful tangle.

'I can't find a bra for you,' she said to Luna, and turned to her.

Luna shrugged. 'That's okay.'

Verity stood still for a moment, then turned to her wardrobe. 'Maybe I put some things in here?' But even as she spoke, she knew it was nonsense. Verity's wardrobes were immaculate: rows and rows of colour co-ordinated heaven.

'I'm sorry,' she said, as she glanced inside the wardrobe. 'I can't find it. But you can pick another if you like. I'll leave you to it.'

'Thanks,' Luna said with that rare smile that made Verity feel calmer somehow. 'I really am grateful for this.

I've been so excited. My mum has, too. She's going to be so happy to finally meet Max.'

Verity flinched. She wouldn't normally care if someone said something about meeting Max, but at the moment, everything seemed too intense. What would it be like to live in a place where people weren't so excited and googly-eyed about meeting her husband? It's what they'd wanted, what this party was all about. But now it felt dangerous, a Frankenstein's monster in a Westwood dress that could creep up and suffocate them as they slept.

'She's not even into art like I am, but yeah, she must be pretty into his stuff.' There was a brief pause. Verity heard the band warming up, pleasant single notes drifting upstairs like smoke. 'I found her looking at a load of old newspaper articles about him before we moved here.'

'Newspaper articles?' Verity repeated. What was Alice doing with articles about Max?

Luna looked down, saying nothing, and her hair fell into her face. Popcorn yellow, pale daffodil. She'd have terrible roots, Verity mused, suddenly feeling nauseous.

'Verity!' Max's voice came from the landing, blurred with the sounds of the band. 'The hairdresser's here!'

Chapter Fifteen

ALICE

November

For some people, life was smooth as a peach. For others, it was something jagged that snagged at them over and over again.

From the start, Luna's life was one of the jagged ones.

I didn't even know I was pregnant until a few months before she arrived. My dad was furious with me. We were moving from our old house anyway, and he gave me a deposit for a bedsit out of the crummy small change left over from his debts and all the divorce fees. My mum automatically cast herself in an opposing role to him and came to be with me during the birth. She brushed back my hair and smiled, but even when she was up close to me, letting me squeeze her hand, I could tell a part of her was kind of gone. It was as though this mess was another reason for her to run back to her new man, her other house, without a crying teenage mother who had no idea how to put on a nappy.

I was meant to be doing my A Levels.

I was meant to still live in the house I'd always lived in, with nice holidays to America and nice dinners and no debt or sad divorced father.

I'll be different, I vowed to little newborn Luna with her strawberry lips and inconceivably tiny hands. *I'll be a good parent.*

I tried. But I wasn't that different, and I wasn't a particularly good parent.

'Mum?' Luna came into the lounge, bleary-eyed. She hadn't been asleep, it was only 11 p.m., but she would have been in the semi-darkness, her room lit only by whatever grim computer game she'd been playing. 'What are you doing?'

I couldn't think fast enough what to say, so I didn't say anything. She squashed beside me on the lounge floor and stared at all the newspaper clippings.

'Who are these people?' she asked, picking up one about an exhibition of Max's work in New York. Max's face was grainy, his eyes bright, just as I'd always remembered them. She turned and stared at me. 'And why have you got a load of clippings about them?'

Honestly. She never came out of her room in the evenings, but the one night when I dragged all the clippings from their hiding place at the back of my wardrobe, here she was, cosying up next to me?

'They're not important,' I said as I brushed them all back into the shoebox I'd stuffed them in over the years. Luna shrugged and stood up, ready to go and fight whatever green zombie was awaiting her. A strange urge to pull her down close to me flickered and then died again. I'd watched enough mothers and daughters over the years to know that we were odd ones out. They all seemed to share their bodies in a way that we didn't have the craving or ability for. Toddlers crawling into laps as though they were trying to somehow get back inside their mothers, somewhere safe and warm. Even teenagers swatting away their mother's hand ended up in touching, a connection of skin. Luna barely wanted me to touch her from the start. What would she do if I tried it now?

She'd already gone padding down the short, dingy hallway to her bedroom. I put the lid back on the shoebox.

'Luna?'

She reappeared.

'What?'

'Do you want to move somewhere else? Somewhere new?'

She shrugged. 'Doesn't make much difference now, does it?'

'Well, no. You can forget all about what happened with school.'

There was a flicker in her eyes.

'Luna, you know, you can tell me the truth about what happened. I won't be mad.'

'I have told you. They pissed me off.'

'Plenty of people will piss you off in life, Luna. Will you threaten to stab all of them?'

She frowned. 'I wasn't *going* to do it.'

'You had a knife!'

'Because someone in my form put it there! I found it in my bag, so I called their bluff!'

'You expect me to believe that someone put a knife in your bag for no reason?'

She was silent.

This was how it was. This was how it had always been. One minute wanting to pull her close to me and start things all over again, to know what her skin smelled like and her deepest thoughts, the next wanting to strangle her.

'Anyway,' I forged on, my tone brutally fake and bright, 'to be perfectly honest with you, I was waiting to see what your grandmother would leave me. But she hasn't left me anything.' When my dad had died, ten years ago now, I knew there would be nothing. Our house had long been sold, and he was forever in debt. I'd missed him a little; even after what he risked and what he destroyed, there was a small nugget of love for him still inside me, hard and irremovable. I'd thought that my mum might have felt something similar for me. Even though I'd failed to turn out the way she wanted, I hoped for some kind of sorrow and reconciliation year after year. It never came. And now she was gone, her lungs black and decayed from all the smoking that started on our last holiday together. I hadn't been invited to the funeral; didn't even know it had happened.

Luna's eyes widened a little and she fiddled with the belt of her grubby dressing gown. 'I thought she was loaded.' Maybe Luna had been expecting something too. Guilt sprang from my pores, making my face hot. If I'd been a better daughter, impossible to not love, I would have been a better mother by default.

'Yeah. Well, her husband was,' I said slowly, trying to sound like I had it together. 'I got the letter today. Everything has gone to their kids. Nothing to me, or you.' I picked up my bottle of beer and took a swig. 'So I think what with her giving up on me, and school giving up on you, it's time to move on.'

'Where to?'

'A place called Lower Hill. It's near the Cotswolds.'

'Where's that?'

'A few hours away. It's super pretty.'

'Pretty?' She wrinkled her nose. Pretty wasn't cool.

'There are lots of little art galleries round there. Maybe you could try to find something arty to do somewhere.' I was a bit frightened by Luna's art. It was all aggressive darkness, reds and blacks morphing together in angry swirls. It probably said something about her lack of love, her odd little life with just me and no money. Maybe when we moved and our lifestyle changed, she'd be different and start painting dogs or jugs like a normal person. 'We'll live the life we were always meant to lead.'

She turned away, my words lost on her.

Chapter Sixteen

FRANKIE

New Year's Eve

'V erity! Only me,' Frankie said as she knocked on the bedroom door lightly before entering with Maisie and Bella.

Frankie hadn't been in Verity's bedroom many times before. It was just as you'd imagine: pure, immaculate luxury. Frankie and Red's bedroom was about half the size of this, and although they'd had plush grey carpets fitted before moving in, the kind your toes sunk into like warm sand, most of it was usually covered in naked dolls or plastic cars. Verity sat at the dressing table with her back to Frankie and didn't turn around.

'V, we're here,' Frankie said, louder this time, holding

one of the girls' hands in each of her own so that they didn't charge into the room uninvited.

Verity turned then, and Frankie saw that it wasn't Verity at all, but a younger version of her. The real Verity appeared from her walk-in wardrobe on the left, in the kind of glittering, skin-tight dress that could stop traffic.

'This is Luna,' Verity told Frankie. Luna gave the tiniest of smiles, her eyes downwards. Frankie glanced at Luna and Verity's matching hairstyles, at Verity's green dress on Luna. Verity had mentioned Luna a few times over the last week or so. She seemed quite taken with her. Verity and Alice had both made her out to be a mousy loner. This blonde girl was awkward and gangly, but prettier than Frankie had imagined, and looking right at home in Verity's bedroom. She kind of looked like she could be Verity's younger sister.

Frankie glanced at Verity. Did she find it soothing, somehow? 'Luna! Of course! I thought it was you at first, Verity. I didn't know you were getting ready together.' She thought about the resolution in her pocket. Her plan would give Verity what she really needed, not some random girl all dressed up like a mini-me. She stopped herself. She was still stinging from the argument with Red before she'd left for the party. There was no use in fantasies about Verity's happiness and new little children in designer dresses if Red was made horribly ill in the process. Perhaps Frankie could just tell Verity that she had an exciting proposition for her, and not tell her what it was. Verity would try to drag it out of her, but Frankie would say it was a surprise for now. Keep Verity here, keep Red calm. It was a tightrope, but

Frankie needed to try her best to keep her head up and not fall.

'Your hair is so pretty,' Maisie said to Verity, wriggling her deft little fingers from Frankie's and running over to Verity, so that Bella did the same and followed, leaving Frankie empty-handed.

'Thanks, Maisie. Luna and I have just had it done together,' Verity said, touching her complicated up-do carefully.

'I didn't see your mum downstairs, Luna,' Frankie said.

'No, she's arriving in a bit. Luna came a little earlier to borrow the dress and have her hair done,' explained Verity.

'Verit-yy?' asked Maisie once she'd finished twirling with Bella in front of the Hollywood scale mirror. 'Can I use your hairbrush?'

'Maisie,' Frankie began in a warning tone. This wasn't the kind of house where you could pick up and drop things in a trail of mini destruction. Everything was absolutely pristine and not at all compatible with little girls electric with excitement about a party. Thankfully, Harry was at home with Red, the faint remnants of red lipstick still mottling his cheeks.

'Oh, Frankie, stop it,' said Verity, gliding over to the dressing table to where Luna still sat, looking a bit uncomfortable with this sudden onslaught of new people. 'Of course you can, Maisie. You can use anything of mine, you know that.'

'But you do always need to say please,' said Frankie, hating how mumsy – how like her own mother – she sounded. She caught Luna's eye with a grin to try and show that she didn't mean it, that she was fun and ready for a party, but Luna didn't see her.

'Your dress is so sparkly, Verity,' said Bella, reaching out to touch the thousand shimmering sequins on Verity's silver dress. 'I wish I had a dress like that.'

Verity smiled at the girls. 'I'll get you one made, and Maisie too. It can be your New Year's present,' she said. She turned from her dressing table, to Frankie, speaking over the thrilled frenzy of shrieks from the girls. 'Did you see me put on my perfume?'

Frankie frowned, confused. 'What do you mean?'

'I just don't think I put it on yet, did I? I can't remember.'

Frankie shook her head. Verity always spritzed her perfume in a particular way. One behind each earlobe, one in her neat cleavage and a final spray in her hair. It was quite a performance and hard to miss. 'Definitely not.'

'That's what I thought. So why can I smell it?'

Frankie sniffed. 'Because you always spray it here? It'll be lingering, I imagine. Or' – she turned to her girls who were now jumping on Verity and Max's bed and probably a moment away from banging heads and staining the beautiful white sheets with blood from a bust lip – 'maybe Bella or Maisie sprayed it. Did you, girls? Did you pinch Verity's perfume?'

The girls ignored her, and Verity shook her head. 'No, I haven't seen them with it. In fact, where is it? Have you seen it, Luna?'

'No,' Luna said, shrugging. She stood up and moved

away so that Verity could move closer and search through the delicate glass bottles on her dressing table.

'It's not here,' Verity said. 'This is the kind of thing I mean. It's the kind of thing that I keep doing, and I'm—' She yanked open a dressing-table drawer and then banged it shut again, shaking her head. She brought the fabric of her dress to her nose so that it pulled up and up, revealing her smooth, tanned thighs. 'It's sprayed on my dress. I can smell it. Why? This dress is brand new.' She dropped the dress again and looked at Frankie. 'I must have done it before and forgotten. I suppose it's normal, isn't it? Forgetting things and making silly mistakes when you're planning a big party like this. Maybe I'm just distracted, and that's why.'

'Yes,' Frankie said in the soothing voice she normally had to employ for grazed knees and high temperatures. She glanced again at Luna, who looked down at the carpet. 'You've had loads to think about.'

Luna's phone buzzed then, and she swiped it open to read the message.

'Mum's here,' she said. 'I'll go down and let her in, shall I?'

'Yes, please. I'll be down in five.' Verity brushed herself down, even though she was immaculate.

'Can we go downstairs too?' Maisie asked. 'I saw a chocolate fountain when we came in and—'

'A chocolate fountain?' Bella screamed.

Luna laughed and smiled at them both. 'You can come downstairs with me if you want, if it's okay with your mummy?' She glanced at Frankie, some of her earlier awkwardness dissipating.

'Yes! Yes!' Maisie shouted.

Frankie looked across at Verity. 'Okay,' she said. 'I'll be down in a minute. Don't get chocolate on your dresses.'

Frankie waited until Luna had disappeared down the landing. 'How are you feeling now?' she asked, watching Verity carefully.

Verity smiled. 'I'm okay, I think. I can't be anything else now everyone's arriving. Nobody wants a freaked-out hostess.'

'Do you think...?' Frankie hesitated. 'Luna seems to have spent quite a bit of time in here today.'

'And?'

'Well, the thing with your perfume. I don't want to blame her but...'

'I've been with her the whole time. It's not Luna,' Verity said. 'What happened to the Frankie who always wants to see the best in people? And anyway, you've just left your children with her. You can't be that suspicious!'

'Well, I'm not. I'm just worried about you, and I—'

'Stop *saying* that.'

Frankie felt like she'd been slapped. What was wrong with worrying about her friend? Worrying was a nice quality to have, wasn't it? Concern for other people. She couldn't help it. And so what if she were trying to discourage Verity from having weird teenagers hanging around her bedroom? Was that really so terrible of her?

'Look,' she said, deliberately calm. 'I am all for welcoming new people. You know that. And it's nice that you have so much in common with Luna, with your art and things.' Frankie stopped. Verity hadn't said any more about starting painting again since that day when Alice had turned up after crashing into the wall. Or – a horrible thought struck her – maybe she just didn't talk about it with Frankie because she knew Frankie didn't understand art properly? The lack of measurements and timings, the wide strokes and representations of things in place of real things blew Frankie's mind, and Verity knew it. Frankie cleared her throat and continued. 'But at the same time, you seem a little on edge at the moment, and you're saying that things don't seem quite right. So you might need to just protect yourself a bit. That's all.'

'Luna wouldn't do anything weird. I think a lot of her. It's almost like she's...' Verity trailed off.

Frankie stared at her for a moment, wondering whether to say it.

'She reminds you of Betsy,' she said in the end. The words sounded peculiar, dug up from beneath twenty-odd years of soil. They hardly ever said her name. Even though it wasn't Verity's fault, and she was only a child herself when her little sister had drowned in the pool, Frankie knew from the little Verity had told her that she blamed herself. Frankie had met Verity after it had happened, and only knew the details because her mother told her. Ruth had blamed Verity's parents.

'Flighty, the lot of them,' Ruth had said, her voice bitter as grapefruit. 'They always left that girl in charge of her sister while they sat around drinking like lords. And now Verity's the same. It's in the blood,' she said, as though that phrase didn't cut right through Frankie's centre.

'No. I just like having Luna around,' Verity said now, obviously not wanting to talk about her lost sister. 'She's like my little project. But actually, there is something about Alice,' she added, her voice low and her eyes darting nervously.

'What?' Frankie asked. Maybe Alice had mentioned something to Verity about last night. She frantically tried to remember everything she'd said to Alice in GLASS. She'd let it slip that Verity was struggling to get pregnant, for one. Or had Alice guessed? The memories were blurred with champagne, like everything else these days.

'Luna told me that she had some newspaper clippings about Max.'

Frankie breathed a sigh of relief. That was nothing to do with anything she'd said last night. And everyone got a bit carried away with the Bentleys. It was just the way things were. 'Well, that's nothing to worry about. She said Luna liked his work. And they both seemed excited when you mentioned his name. Lots of people probably collect articles about Max. He's famous, Verity. And that's what fame's all about.'

Verity chewed nervously on a glittering nail.

'I can speak to Alice about it tonight, if you like,' Frankie offered. 'I'm sure she'll just confirm it's nothing to worry about.'

'No!' Verity's voice was panicked and sharp. 'Don't do that. We don't know how she'll react. Tonight's the worst time possible to stir everything up. People would love that.

And I can't handle it. This is why I want to move away, Frankie. I can't handle all these people watching me, waiting for something to go wrong.' Her voice became shaky, and Frankie reached out and touched her waist, the sequins sharp against the tips of her fingers.

'Nothing's going to go wrong,' Frankie said. 'Things are going to get easier, I promise.' Maybe she should give Verity her New Year's resolution after all. Or she could at least tell her she was trying to get Red to agree to it, to give Verity at least a glimmer of hope. She pictured Red at home, bending over Harry's cot, tickling him on his chin, then flicking through his phone on his own all night. No. She couldn't.

Max appeared at the door, looking like a film star, obviously, in his tux.

'Hey,' he said. 'The party's starting.'

Chapter Seventeen

ALICE

16 December

'They're more scared of you than you are of them,' Luna said quietly as I hurled a frying pan at a spider. The pan missed, and the spider ran under the fridge. Damn it.

The flat was full of them, scuttling out from all over the place, giving me a heart attack every two minutes. Luna didn't mind spiders. She'd always been weird like that, stooping to the ground all the time to look at bugs, carrying soft brown woodlice and gleaming beetles into her bedroom to keep as pets.

Luna pulled a strand of mousy hair from her face with long, pale fingers. 'They'll go back into wherever they were hiding soon. It's because we're disturbing their sleep by moving in with them.'

'Yuk.' I pulled a face at her. 'I don't want to think about spiders sleeping in our new place.'

New place. The words jarred as we stood in the freezing kitchen that had been left splattered with grease and thick with the smell of bacon fat. It felt old, stale, just like all the other places we'd ever lived.

'I'm going to my room,' Luna said, grabbing the noodle pot she'd just poured boiling water into and stalking out of the tiny kitchen.

Her room was also tiny and smelled of damp. I should have followed her, hung posters on her wall, chatting and laughing with her like other mums would have done, before pushing their sleeves up and getting stuck into making the place look better. But other mums round here would have nice husbands, or at least their ex-husband's money, and a belief that everything always worked out. Other mums round here wouldn't have cleaned and scrubbed till their fingers were red raw and their back ached.

I grabbed my keys and called to Luna. 'I'm going out.'

The snow had stopped for now, but the ground glittered with black ice. Darkness was already looming even though it was only the afternoon. Frankie would be going to get the children in about an hour. Maisie and Bella Redmond. Year two and reception at Middle Hill Primary School, uploaded in regular pickup photos at a rough time between 3.15 and 3.20 p.m. It was amazing how careless people were, putting every little detail on Facebook. There was just enough time before she went out to pick them up. When I was closer to Frankie, I'd warn her about her Facebook posts, although I wouldn't tell her how much I'd found out about her myself. I'd change the names, tell her a creepy story about someone I knew in London. That was what friends did, wasn't it? Told little white lies to protect each other.

I sat in my car down the road from Frankie's house, the fans slamming out red-hot air that made my cheeks burn. I needed time to build myself up. I didn't even know if I'd be able to go through with it. But there didn't seem to be any other way if I wanted to win over Frankie. The house twinkled with a thousand fairy lights in the shape of a ribbon. In the middle hung a gigantic red bow. Verity's house had the same on it, only there were even more lights and an even more gigantic ribbon. It must be hard for Frankie to always be second place. But then at least she was part of the race, and not sitting on the sidelines, waiting for a turn.

I'd been sitting on Frankie's street for around five minutes when I saw Verity's white Range Rover with its personalised numberplate whizzing down the frozen road towards me. I caught a glimpse of her inside: blonde hair, huge sunglasses. Music thumped inside the car. I watched as she sped towards Frankie's house and pulled up on the huge driveway. She clambered out, wearing brown leather boots and a cream wool coat. A gorgeous bag – designer, no doubt – was slung over her shoulder.

I hadn't known she'd be there too. It was even better than I'd imagined, but even so, a wave of sadness washed over me. I shouldn't have needed to do this. I should have been invited in a long time ago.

I started my engine, took a deep breath and then hurtled the car towards the wall outside Frankie's house. Five, four, three, two, one and smash! I was in their lives.

Chapter Eighteen

VERITY

New Year's Eve

Max appeared at the door just as Verity felt herself sliding into the version of herself she didn't want to be, especially not tonight. Frankie was trying her best to keep Verity calm, but for some reason, it just wasn't working like it normally would. Verity could hear the buzz of noise from downstairs become louder, like an approaching wasp. She reached for her glass of champagne but it was empty; she reached for the bottle that she'd brought upstairs but that was empty too.

'Hey,' Max said. 'The party's starting.'

Verity pulled him into the room and closed the door. 'Shall I tell him?' she asked Frankie.

'What's up?' Max was casual, as always. He wouldn't

care if she said nothing more, wouldn't try to force anything out of her. Sometimes he seemed like a different species altogether.

'Alice has a load of articles about you,' Verity told him, without waiting for Frankie's answer. 'Luna told me.'

Max shrugged. 'Luna's into art. She likes my stuff. Alice knows that.' Confidence ran through his blood like sugar. Would he still feel so calm if he saw those comments on Instagram? Verity tensed at the thought of them.

'But the articles aren't always about your art, are they? They're about you.'

Max Bentley and his glamorous wife attended the opening of the new Hatch-2 gallery in Notting Hill on Friday night. The fifty-two-year-old artist smouldered in a simple Prada shirt and sipped classic champagne through the evening.

'People like that celeb stuff,' Max mused. 'I don't think it means anything.'

Frankie nodded and smiled at Max. 'That's exactly what I said.'

'Great minds,' said Max. 'Are you both coming down?'

Verity nodded. She should have asked Luna how many articles there were, and which ones. 'Don't say anything to Alice,' she said to Frankie and Max. 'I don't want any confrontation. I just want tonight to be perfect.'

Max nodded as he opened the bedroom door. 'I don't even know who Alice is,' he said with a wave of his hand.

———

Alice was wearing a bright pink dress that was creased at the back where she'd been sitting. Verity had told her to wear the black dress, but obviously Alice had decided that she knew better. As she stood and chatted to her with Frankie, Verity drank her wine quickly and tried to push Luna's comments about the articles to the back of her mind. But as she spoke light words about skinny-dipping in the lake and Harry's swimming lessons, Verity felt herself move closer and closer to a kind of hysteria, a need to yell or cry or *something. WHY?* she imagined herself shouting at Alice. *WHY do you have articles about my husband?*

No, it wouldn't do to be standing here fighting urges to yell at guests. The photographer had arrived and Verity could hear the snapping of the camera: every click a warning for her to keep it together. She recognised this feeling of being on the brink of something horrible from the last few weeks. It felt like the hysteria was close to her, like a lion stalking its prey. She excused herself, wittering on about guava cocktails as soon as her wine was all gone. Luna was outside with Maisie and Bella, and Verity stepped outside to join them, the rush of frozen air a pleasant relief on her warm skin.

'Veri-ty!' Bella shouted giddily. 'We've been finding bits of tree!' She held up a severed green bough. 'It's like bits of Christmas tree all over!' Bella had a dark smear of mud across her cheek. 'I'm going to collect all the parts and make a whole tree all by myself.'

'Oh, Christmas treeee,' Maisie sang, dancing around with her bit of tree. Bella laughed giddily and joined in the dancing. Bits of churned-up ground flew around them.

Their squeaky-clean hilarity with its pure joy was the kind of scene that flipped Verity's stomach inside out; she wanted it for herself that badly. The girls' blonde curls flew behind them like ribbons and their peals of laughter scored through the freezing night air.

'They're crazy,' Verity said to Luna, laughing. When Frankie was pregnant, she'd longed for a girl, a small nose; a boy, green eyes, cleverness; another girl, blonde hair. Verity wondered what Alice had wanted or expected when she had Luna. Possibly not an awkward, lanky thing who got expelled from school. Verity would take anything. *Anything*.

She glanced inside to see if Frankie could see the girls. She'd probably disapprove of them getting covered in mud. But Frankie hadn't noticed them and was talking to Alice.

'You're getting all dirty out here,' Verity said to Bella and Maisie.

'But it's fun!' Bella said, a wicked grin on her face. She was a little daredevil. Frankie would have to watch her when she was a teenager.

Verity smiled at her and turned to gaze across the lake, where a flicker of movement in Frankie and Red's dining room caught her eye. She still couldn't get used to the houses being fully visible to each other.

'Verity, can you stay out here with us? Luna feels poorly, so she might want to go in.'

'Poorly?' As she spoke Verity carried on looking across the lake, where Red seemed to be gathering things together. She saw that he was holding something – Harry, perhaps? –

before the light switched off and plunged her view into darkness.

'I'll be fine,' Luna was saying. 'I can stay out here with them if you like. I'm just a bit tired, that's all.'

Verity looked at her watch, the numbers blurring slightly. 'It's still only ten-fifteen. Go and have a rest in my room, if you like.'

Luna shook her head, looking down, shivering.

'Come on,' Verity said, taking Luna's cool hand in hers. 'In.'

Chapter Nineteen

FRANKIE

New Year's Eve

'You've outdone yourself,' Frankie said to Verity when they got downstairs to the party. 'It's perfect.' Frankie looked outside at the enormous garden where Luna danced around with Maisie and Bella like a casual pied piper. She hadn't been in Verity's kitchen since the trees had gone. She couldn't really tell the difference because outside was pitch dark, eclipsed completely by the lights and fizz of people and decorations and smiling waiters in here. 'I'm glad the snow forecast has held off for now. The girls are having a great time out there.'

'There's so much more room out there now the trees have gone,' Verity said after downing her glass of champagne. 'It isn't actually much bigger by the square foot, but it just feels so much more *open*. We could have some skinny-dipping later!'

'Oh, I think it's a bit cold, and a bit early in the night to be talking about getting naked,' Frankie replied, feeling herself blush. It was alright for Verity to think of such things: she'd whip off her little silver dress and reveal a body smooth as a doll's. Frankie grimaced at the thought of the sight of herself if she took off her blue dress for all to see the secrets underneath. Pale, wobbling flesh laced with navy veins and silver stretch marks. A map of middle age.

'Have you had a swim in the lake yet?' Alice asked.

'Oh, no,' Verity said. 'It's shallow as a puddle in there. I don't think skinny-dipping is really an option, so you needn't look so horrified, Frankie,' she finished, making Frankie blush. 'That reminds me! How's the baby spa going?' She turned to Alice. 'Frankie has found herself the best place to take little Harry to learn to swim. It's like a little spa for children. Robes, smoothies, the lot.'

'It's really great,' Frankie said, then took a burning gulp of her drink. She'd tell Verity later that she'd forgotten all about it. Verity would find it quite hilarious, but it wasn't the kind of thing Frankie wanted to admit with Alice there. 'He's swimming well after only a few lessons.'

'Wow. Luna only ever went with school,' Alice said. 'She didn't learn till she was about ten.'

'Frankie worries about water. About everything, actually,' Verity teased. 'She won't settle for a couple of school lessons, will you, Frankie? Right,' she said, swiftly changing the topic. (Frankie couldn't blame her: swimming lessons hadn't held her own interest very well, had they?)

Verity clapped her hands together. 'Where are those cocktail waiters? They have the most delicious guava cocktails and I need at least seven of them!'

Frankie watched Verity as she weaved her way through the guests, who were beginning to fill up the enormous kitchen-diner. The expanse of worktop was taken up with miles of cocktail glasses and ice buckets; flickering tea lights; trays of matching food and vases of white roses. White feather decorations (*'Full Gatsby, remember,'* Verity had said) and silver lights hung from the dizzyingly high ceiling.

'We're having fireworks outside, later, aren't we?' said Alice to Frankie.

'Oh yes. Verity wouldn't throw a party without fireworks,' Frankie said. She took a little purple canapé.

'Back in a minute,' said Alice. 'Just going to grab a drink.'

Frankie nodded and glanced outside where Luna and the girls were still playing. Actually, she *could* tell that the trees were gone if she looked carefully enough. Once she'd adjusted her eyes, she could see the golden lights from her own house dancing on the water of the black lake.

'Back!' Alice said, with a little 'isn't this fun?' rise and fall of her shoulders. 'Talking about the party with you last night didn't prepare me for actually being here.'

Frankie smiled. 'Like I told you, White Fir Lake is known for its parties. It has Verity and Max to thank completely for its reputation.'

Alice nodded. 'I read about it a lot before I came. I

became a bit fascinated. You can fall in love with it all quite quickly, can't you?'

Aha! So this explained the articles. Frankie hadn't even needed to ask her: there was going to be no scene, no drama. Alice probably just collected a few stories about White Fir Lake, and those stories probably had Max in them because they all did. He was synonymous with this place. Perhaps Luna had embellished the story, as teenagers did. Maisie was already one of the world's greatest fabricators and she was only eight.

Frankie nodded and swallowed the smooth, rather bitter remains of the canapé. 'You certainly can.' Her eyes returned to the garden, beyond the girls. If she looked really, really closely, through the reflections and across the lake, she could see her own kitchen. It was only a small blur of light, but it was there. How funny. She'd find Verity, see if she'd noticed too. She scanned the room, but Verity's search for cocktails seemed to have taken her elsewhere. There was Max, but no Verity.

'Just a minute,' Frankie said to Alice. 'I'm just going to find Verity.' She set one foot forwards, and that's when she saw Max's expression. He wasn't looking at Frankie, but behind her. His expression was shocked, bloodless, horrified, as though someone had a gun to his head.

Chapter Twenty

ALICE

Chatham, Cape Cod, USA: seventeen years earlier

I noticed them on the second day.

On the first day, Mum smoked constantly. I'd never seen her smoke before: not like this. She'd smoked at parties, the odd cigarette here and there on a balcony with a glass of whisky, or in an armchair as she kicked her strappy shoes off at the end of the night. But this was different. Her unhappy mouth puckered around cigarette after cigarette, pulling the poison deep into her body. Her eyes were far away, somewhere entirely different to me.

'What's the matter?' I asked her.

But she just sucked, blew out, shook her head. She never told me much, so I don't know why I expected her to tell me this. Whatever it was.

Dad was silent. He didn't smoke, as I remember. He smouldered, too hot to go near or try to touch.

They didn't talk to each other all day, and that night I heard sharp snatched whispers. Normally when we were here on holiday, we went to Sailor's on the first night and my parents ordered oysters and cold white wine. The first night always smelled like the bottom of the sea and felt like a bright beam of promise.

This year, we didn't even eat.

'Alice?'

'What?'

'Don't say what, say yes.'

I rolled my eyes in the mirror. I'd put on a load of kohl eyeliner and the whites of my eyes were stark against my jet-black rims and lash line. I lifted up a finger and smudged it against my eyelids. *Make it look like you've slept in it to look* really *rock 'n' roll*, the magazine I'd read on the plane had instructed.

'Yes.'

'Come down here.'

I sighed and pushed the lid back down onto the eyeliner. As I reached the bottom of the wide staircase of our elaborate holiday home, I noted that my dad, whisky in hand, stressed expression across his face, had a suitcase next to him.

'What's going on?' I asked. My eyes felt gritty and I felt them begin to water.

'Ask your mother,' Dad said.

I glanced at her and raised my eyebrows.

'Alice, I'm going to take a bit of a break. Alone.'

'Oh, tell her the truth, for God's sake,' my dad spat. 'You're not going to be alone, really, are you?'

My mum sighed and squared her shoulders as if preparing for a fight. 'I have a new friend,' she began, as though I were six and didn't know she'd already been going missing in the night for weeks now and coming home reeking of a kind of salty, sensual guilt.

My dad snorted. 'A friend? Understatement of the century.'

'He... Well, I'm going to spend some time with him.'

'She's leaving us, Al. It's just you and me on this holiday.'

'I'm not!' My mum's jaw began quivering and she fumbled in her straw bag, taking out a packet of Marlboros. 'I'm not leaving you, Alice.'

'But you're leaving Dad?'

She stuffed the end of the cigarette into her mouth where it dangled sadly whilst she fumbled more in the ridiculous straw thing, presumably for a lighter. 'I can't stay with a liar just for you, Alice.'

Just for you. I put a finger up to my eye and jabbed it around, trying to source the little scratchy flecks of floating kohl. I brought it away again, my fingertip covered in black.

'I didn't lie to you, Ellen,' my dad said. 'I didn't want to...' They both looked at me as his words faded away.

'Well,' Mum said, coming over to me and kissing me abruptly on the cheek with her smoky, warm lips. 'I'll phone you later in the week. Go out, Alice, find some friends. It's going to be your last holiday here. Make the most of it.'

She thought I didn't know.

But it was her who was really in the dark. She didn't know about my weird habit, my peculiar fascination with my dad's accounts. I had a thing for his office at home with its order and files and fountain pens in little pots. When he was out, or before school when he was out on his run, I used to sneak in there. It was the darkest room in the house and smelt of leather and adults. I glanced over numbers and papers, adding and subtracting and multiplying them in all the ways I needed to so that I'd get my A in maths. I knew that if I got my A, my dad wouldn't mind me in his office. I was going to take over the company, eventually. It didn't matter that I was a girl, because I had brains and sense and worked hard.

Then one hot June morning, I noticed that some of the numbers had become smaller, less impressive than they used to be. I scratched my prickling head idly. The company was making less money. That was normal, I reasoned. Companies ebbed and flowed. Dad had mentioned a few months ago that another place was selling the same computer systems and internet phones as his company. He'd shrugged it off. Healthy competition. Nothing to worry about, he'd said. But was it?

June melted into July. It was my last term at school. Soon, I'd be at sixth form, learning more about numbers. Manipulating them, Dad said with a laugh that made my stomach churn. Had I really been that stupid? The figures in his office had become lower, but that wasn't even the main issue anymore. There were articles about his company too: misconduct, manipulation, false, misleading. All the words I would never have associated with my balding, suited, calm and successful dad and his colleagues.

I said nothing and waited. I waited to be told we were moving house, that the company was over, that our yearly holiday in Cape Cod that cost more than some people's homes wouldn't be happening.

But it did happen.

And now, here we were.

———

I lifted my hand to my eye again.

'Alice, there's some things you need to know,' Dad said, staring down at Mum's bag.

'Oh, I know them all,' I said breezily. 'Just because you decided to keep it all from me, doesn't mean I didn't find out. I probably knew before Mum did.'

Dad stared at me with his stupid wide eyes that I used to trust.

'Alice,' he said nervously, holding up his hands as if he were trying to calm a nippy little dog.

I'd always been close to him. Peas in a pod, Daddy's girl, blah blah. But when I realised he wasn't quite the person I'd thought, I'd started looking at my mum in a different way. She hadn't known about the money at the point I'd found out. It was obvious from the way she swanned about giving people air kisses and having manicures and drinking gin in

163

the day. When she found out, I thought, she'd snatch me like a protective mother snake and we'd head off together. We might live in a small flat, on top of each other but happy. We were better off without him, we would tell each other.

Just for you.

And now, here we were.

I strolled along the sand, kicking shells, hoping they'd splinter.

I'd left Mum and Dad to their bitter goodbyes. Why stay?

And that's when I saw them. I stood still on the sand and watched them as the waves licked my trainers.

They exuded money; every single one of them. Real, old money; not the type of money that would be lost in some seedy, secret scam. The kind of money people didn't even realise they had because they were so used to it that they smelled of it, slept in it and ate it.

There was one with a blonde ponytail and a loud laugh, bright pink bikini, and colourful bracelets lining her wrists. Another girl, curvier, had long black hair that she kept flipping over her shoulder as though she thought it made her look cute. And two boys. One was a man, actually. He looked older than the other three. The second guy was about my age, maybe a year or two older. He was pale with gingery blond hair and kind of cute in a lanky, freckly way.

He glanced my way, and I looked out to sea then carried on walking in a strange zig-zagging shape to avoid them.

'*Hey! Want to come and hang out?*' I imagined the words called out to me. I imagined blushing, but heading across the sand towards their smiles, telling them about my parents (my *parents*? As if!), being a part of their group and spending the rest of the holiday with them. Maybe the old one would adopt me. No – not adopt me, because I'd had it with being anyone's child. I wasn't a child, and I was sick to death of being treated like one. He could do that thing that rich people did – be a benefactor, because he saw potential in me.

My feet dragged on the sand, my brown hair whipping around my face and into my mouth, tasting of sharp salt. I knew I was being stupid. People didn't do that. They didn't invite boring girls to join them for no reason.

And they didn't. Of course they didn't. The words didn't come, even after what Max did, even after Luna, even after any of it.

They hung around the same bit of the beach every day. They were like a bad American film cast. Big white smiles to match their big happy laughs, frisbees and fun and kicking water at each other in the sparkly blue waves. They must have noticed me, but I was obviously so forgettable that every day when they saw me in the distance it was like the first time, like goldfish bumping into the glass again and again.

The summer thumped on. Raw sun that made my shoulders burn strawberry red. Lonely, long days. Silent dinners with my dad. Calls with my mum so tense that the phone felt hot. As bored as I was, I didn't want the end to come because the end would mean another sixth form instead of the one attached to my public school. A different sixth form would just be the beginning of the end of my best friend Roberta, who had white-blonde hair, a wicked sense of humour and a mocking hatred for people who had no money. It had never been a problem before.

But whether you want it or not, the end always comes anyway, and soon it was the last night.

'I'm going out,' I shouted to Dad. I'd taken some whisky from the cabinet, because who was going to notice now? Everything else was packed up. It would be something to tell Roberta, if nothing else. And I needed some courage, because I was going to turn up at their part of the beach and make them involve me. It was their last night too. I'd heard them chant it and whoop it yesterday. *'Last daaaaay!'* They were on the brink of their charmed lives: endings obviously seemed a million miles away for them.

Dad appeared, his cheeks red. Perhaps he'd been on the whisky too. He was holding a spatula. 'Where?'

I shrugged and looked down at my trainers, which blurred a bit. I looked back up at him. 'The beach. I've made a few friends the last few days.'

'But I've made crab pasta like I always do on our last night here.'

I sighed. Crab pasta was Mum's demand every single year. 'Do you even like crab pasta?'

He grinned as though he was six and I'd caught him stealing sweets. 'No, I kind of hate it, but it's our last, last night here and tradition overrules everything else. Come on. Have some overcooked pasta with me and then you can go and meet your friends.' He squinted at me. 'This is one of those moments you'll look back on, Alice, and you'll think, "I shouldn't have been such a misery. I should have put all the other stuff to one side for that night and just enjoyed the pasta with my dad."'

I laughed, surprising myself. 'Really?'

But he didn't even crack a smile. 'Yes. Really. It's an important night, Alice. We won't be here again. I don't want you to have any regrets.'

'Okay,' I said.

If only.

Chapter Twenty-One

FRANKIE

Chatham, Cape Cod, USA: seventeen years earlier

Frankie ran her fingers over the cool glass of the bottle as she queued. The guy at the counter was about a hundred years old. Surely he wouldn't have a clue whether Frankie was thirteen or thirty. Max had said he thought she was eighteen when he first saw her. He'd been surprised that she was sixteen. She'd bought some push-up bikinis from Topshop to wear (and hidden them from her parents, obviously). Maybe that was why.

She stepped forward in the queue.

They'd been in America for four weeks.

She'd hoped to have kissed Max by now.

She hadn't kissed anyone yet. Sixteen and never been kissed. Such a cliché, it was embarrassing. Verity had kissed a few frogs, as she called them. Frankie would always have settled for a frog before, just to see what the fuss was about, to feel like an adult.

She stepped forward again. Second to the front.

Max was always talking about art. He would love this beer with paintbrushes on the bottle. He obviously didn't care that Frankie wasn't into painting like Verity was. She smiled to herself. It wasn't painting that he wanted to do with her. She'd seen him looking at her more than enough times now to know she wasn't imagining it.

The old man served her, taking her crisp dollar notes without even glancing up. She strutted from the shop, flipping her hair over her shoulder and feeling on top of the world. The heat hit her like a wall outside the shop, where she stuffed the beer bottle into her woven rucksack.

'Frankieeee!' Verity flung her arms around Frankie, so tightly that Frankie coughed. 'Where've you been?'

Frankie disentangled herself and shrugged. 'For a walk.'

Verity pulled a face to show how boring she thought that was. Water glistened on her cheekbones and in her hair. 'The water's gorgeous today, isn't it, Max? We should go back in.'

Max's body was covered in little beads of water too. Frankie imagined herself licking them off. She put her rucksack down gently on the sand. 'Okay,' she said, whipping off her little denim shorts. 'Race you all!'

There was shrieking and sand flying and glittering

water like diamonds, and then the cool sea. She brushed Max's arm as they launched themselves in and glanced up at him. But he was looking in another direction, at Verity.

'He's obsessed with her,' a voice said from beside Frankie. She looked around, shielding her eyes from the sun. Red had burned his nose and it stood out from the rest of his pale face. She always forgot he was there.

She grabbed him and dunked him under the water, making him yell, making Max turn and look at them.

***

'So, Max,' Frankie said as she helped herself to another taco. 'Are you glad you met up with us?'

'Sure am,' Max said. As the summer had deepened, so had his tan. A faint line of stubble adorned his jaw. Frankie felt longing tug somewhere inside her, a place she didn't even know she had.

When Verity had told Frankie on the flight out that her dad's friend was joining them, Frankie had barely registered who it might be. She'd been thinking about how strange it would be in the enormous holiday home this year. Frankie had joined Verity and her parents for their annual summer stay in Cape Cod since they were twelve. This would be the first without Verity's mother, Maria.

'He'll never want a summer without us,' Verity said now. Her father had gone inside, to bed, and she stretched her long, caramel-coloured legs over Max's lap. She'd never do that with her dad there, but he was going to bed earlier every evening. Frankie knew it was cruel, but she would normally be glad of his absence. His despair and grief followed him everywhere and she couldn't bear to look at it. But tonight, she'd cope with it, if it meant that Verity sat a little further from Max.

'Last night tomorrow,' Red said, gulping down his beer and then burping quietly behind a freckled hand.

Verity wailed. 'Don't! I can't bear the thought of September.' She turned to Max. 'You need to come to England, help me get an A* in art.'

'I'm sure you can do that all by yourself,' Max said. Was that flirtation in his voice? Frankie looked across at Red, who raised an eyebrow. *Told you so*, the eyebrow said. *Obsessed.*

———————————

Frankie's ache for Max was like a toothache, or a stomachache. Something physical that Frankie's mum might write a note out for so that she didn't have to do PE.

So what Frankie was about to do was like a note, excusing her from further pain.

Taking part in Physical Education will cause Frankie further discomfort.

'Where are you going?' Verity said, her eyes bleary. They'd had a lot of tequila.

'For a walk.'

'God, Frankie, you and your walks. What are you, a dog?'

Frankie laughed. 'I'll meet you at the beach in a bit.'

Verity turned. That should have been it. Frankie should

have gone along with her plan and should have had Max for herself.

Seeing Verity and Max together will cause Frankie further discomfort.

But as Verity turned, Frankie saw a track of mascara down Verity's cheek.

'V? Have you been crying?'

Verity turned back. Tears filled her eyes. 'No.'

Frankie held out her arms and Verity launched herself into them. 'I miss her,' she said. She pulled back and pushed her hair from her face. 'I'm sorry. I'm fine. Go for your walk. It's just that being here is weird. I'm worried about Dad.' A shaky sigh released itself from her body.

'It'll get easier,' said Frankie, and Verity smiled as though she believed her.

But what did Frankie know about losing a real mother who shared your blood and eye colour and way of holding your head and saying hello on the phone? She clamped her fists around the straps of her rucksack.

'Frankie?' Verity asked, sniffing. 'Do you think Max is into me?'

'I think your dad would go mental.'

Verity laughed. 'That's not what I asked.'

'Aren't you worried? He's a lot older. And he's your dad's friend.'

'Mum was twenty years younger than him.' The past tense stung them both, and Verity hurried on from it. 'So he couldn't say that much. And anyway, would you tell your parents about a holiday romance?'

Absolutely not. Frankie wouldn't tell her parents

anything about any boy, ever. Not that Max was a boy. 'Probably, if it was a big thing to me.'

Verity laughed again and turned to go back outside. 'You're such a bad liar, Frankie,' she called, her blonde ponytail swinging merrily as she went.

———————

Frankie had told Max that they were all going down to the pier for a change.

'Meet us there at nine. We'll all be there.'

Verity was right: Frankie was a terrible liar because she usually always told the truth. It felt thrilling and dangerous to tell Max something that wasn't true so that she could get him alone. It was as though she was teetering on the edge of becoming the person she should be.

She had a speech prepared and had whispered it to herself in the mirror of one of the million bathrooms in the house.

I just wanted to give you the heads up ('heads up' sounded adult, like the kind of phrase the other art lecturers he worked with might use) *that Verity is feeling a bit uncomfortable. She sees you like a brother.* No, that wasn't right. Like an uncle? Maybe that would be better. *She doesn't really want to bring it up with you herself.*

I bought you a present. I saw it and thought of you. Yes, the *bottle has paintbrushes on it! Cool, isn't it?*

She was wearing her best black push-up bikini.

———————

Max was already at the pier when she arrived. He grinned at her.

'Hey!' He kissed her on both cheeks, taking her by surprise. He'd never done *that* before. Her heart soared as she smelled salt and alcohol: a whole new adult life. 'I knew something was up when you told me to meet you all here and Red knew nothing about it.'

Frankie stopped herself from rolling her eyes. Trust Red to nearly ruin it all.

'I just wanted to talk to you,' she said, brushing her fingers through her long hair. 'Alone.'

Max looked concerned. 'Is everything okay?'

'Oh yeah, yeah. It's just…' The words she'd known she was going to say stuck on her tongue. 'It's Verity,' she began.

Max's eyes became a little brighter.

She thought of Verity's tear-stained face just before, Maria's funeral only two months ago, where Verity had shaken as though she was freezing to death, even though the heat in the church was suffocating, and clung to Frankie as though she'd never, ever let go.

Frankie dug into her bag and took out the beer. The label had peeled a little in the heat.

'She bought you this. She likes you a lot.'

Frankie handed Max the beer, then took a step back on the soft sand, the waves lapping gently beside them.

Chapter Twenty-Two

ALICE

Chatham, Cape Cod, USA: seventeen years earlier

Dad let me have a small glass of wine with the crab pasta, because he didn't know I'd already had three shots of whisky. Or if he did, he didn't care. Something took over him that night. Something took over all of us, I suppose.

'I'll walk you to the beach,' he said, scraping pasta into the bin. I'd never seen him do anything as homely as that before and it was weird, like seeing him naked.

'No thanks. I'll be fine.' I tried to make my words short and snappy to hide the dizziness that was taking over me. I stood up, pleased that I didn't stumble, and headed outside into the balmy air.

Their area of beach was about a fifteen-minute walk away.

They weren't there when I arrived. Packing probably, getting ready to return to their nice, shiny lives. I stood for a moment, gazing at the sea and the other people who played and laughed on the sand. *'Time of our lives,'* they'd say when they got home. I turned around and headed to the pier end of the beach. The sun was heavy in the sky, casting everything in bronze.

I'd brought the whisky with me and swigged from it. I smirked and hiccupped. I was like an old tramp, wandering the streets with a glass bottle.

I continued past the pier with its happy people and stopped walking just as the sun was hitting the waves. The air was becoming grey now, the day lost in the blur of that summer. I sat on the sand, stretching my legs out before me. And that's when he came and sat down next to me.

He was nice at first. They always are; I know that now. But then, I had no idea. Not about any of it.

'Good sunset,' he said. He was wearing sunglasses and I could see two tiny versions of myself reflected in them. Two little Alices, trapped in black glass.

'Yeah.'

'You're not meant to watch the sunset alone, you know.'

I shrugged and looked away.

He shuffled closer to me. 'You know the sun's already gone?'

'What?'

'Sunsets are just an illusion. That there…' He pointed and I saw the strength in his arm, thought nothing more of it. 'It's a refraction of the sun. The light is bending, and the sun has already gone.'

'Oh,' I said.

'I bet you already knew that though. I bet you're clever as well as pretty,' he said, making my insides all liquidy. 'You want to walk with me?' He'd already jumped up and was holding out his hand for mine. When he took it, he held it tightly. His fingers were warm and pleasantly firm against mine.

'It's my last night here,' I said.

'Shame. I've noticed you around.'

Pleasure bloomed inside me. 'Really?'

He laughed. 'Why do you sound surprised?'

'I just don't think I'm the noticeable type.'

'Course you are.' His words grazed against one another a little, and I wondered if he'd been drinking too. I felt my bag for my whisky. It wasn't there anymore, and I couldn't think where I'd left it. Probably for the best. And anyway, I was feeling less like I needed it now.

'How old are you, anyway?' I asked, suddenly brave.

He smiled, showing cat-white teeth. 'How old do you think I am?'

'I can't tell, because of your sunglasses.'

He pushed them up on top of his head. His eyes were dark brown, almost black.

'Eighteen?'

'Close. Nineteen. You? I reckon seventeen. Sweet, sweet seventeen and kissed only a handful of times.'

I only hesitated for one second. 'Yeah. Seventeen. Good guess.'

'Let's sit again,' he said, pulling me to the beach. He

pulled his sunglasses back down over his eyes. 'Nice and quiet here. We can do what we want. I'm Jamie.'

He likes me. The thought was addictive, my mind running over and over it like a tongue over a wobbly tooth.

This bit of the beach was strewn with rocks and we picked over them, tripping a little in the rapid darkness to find a clear patch of sand. When we did, Jamie pulled me to the ground so that I landed on top of him.

'You smell good,' he said. He smiled and pulled me towards him. His lips were soft and warm, and I could feel his beating heart under mine. But then, as his grip around my body tightened, and his kisses became biting and sharp, I felt a tug of fear. I tried to pull away but that made him press harder against me. I thought of my dad and his pasta. I should have let him walk me here. I shouldn't have stolen his whisky. I should have stayed and eaten more pasta and packed my case like a good girl.

'Please,' I managed to say. He ignored me, bore down, his hands moving over my dress, pinching and pulling.

'Please, stop!' I shouted as hard as I could this time. It made no difference. His breath was like gas, smoky and smothering.

And then I heard it.

'Hey! Hey, stop!'

I wailed as loud as I could. Whoever was near, whoever I could hear shouting, could change the direction of this. They could swing my life back around.

But still, he didn't stop tugging at me, pressing into me.

I heard footsteps, running.

'Hey, stop it. She doesn't want you to do that!'

Jamie put his hand over my mouth, whipped his head round. 'Get out of here, pervert. It's not your business.'

I shuffled and saw a glimpse of my rescuer. He was coming closer now.

'It's my business if you're doing something she doesn't want you to do.'

Jamie let go of me then, pushing me back into the sand so that my arm grazed against a stone that was behind me.

'Look, I warned you.' The guy was striding towards Jamie. Jamie swooped low for a moment, picking up a rock.

'Stop it! Stop!' I screamed. I scrambled to my feet. Now that he was closer, I recognised the man who had just arrived. He was the older one of the group I'd been watching all summer. He was tanned, and anger scored his pleasant face. He held a bottle of beer with a picture of paintbrushes on the label. I remembered his name from the others in the group shouting it over and over for the last five weeks.

Max.

'Don't,' Max said, eyeing the smooth, heavy rock that Jamie was aiming at his head, ready to throw.

'Don't what?' Jamie's voice taunted, and he began to toss the rock from hand to hand. How was this the same person who'd sat next to me and gazed at the sunset? I moved towards him but he hit out his arm to stop me.

And then there was his hand, outstretched, the rock heading for Max's head.

It all happened so quickly, yet in slow motion.

Max launching forward and crashing down the bottle in

a split second of panic. The bottle smashing down so that glass glittered through the air.

Jamie's body thumping to the ground, his head landing on a rock and cracking like an egg.

The rushing of the tide and the blood and the fear.

Max stood, silent and white. The neck of the bottle remained in his hand and I pulled it from him gently.

'We need to throw it in the water,' I whispered. But this part of the beach was deserted. I could have shouted, and still it would be our secret.

I crouched down, nausea rising in me. Jamie's smoky smell was tinged now with salt and metal. His head lolled to the side, black blood seeping underneath him, his eyes staring straight ahead, glassy and fish-like.

'He's...'

'I know.'

We stared at one another. We glanced at the incoming tide. And then we ran.

Chapter Twenty-Three

FRANKIE

New Year's Eve

Frankie swung round to look at Alice, to try and work out what it was about her that was making Max look so terrified. But Alice was just Alice, holding a bottle of beer. Frankie narrowed her eyes at the label.

'That beer…' she said.

Alice glanced down at it. 'Oh yeah. Cool, isn't it? I brought a whole crate. I thought Max might like it.' She pushed the bottle in Frankie's face, and Frankie had to step back an inch so that the glass didn't bang against her cheek. 'It has paintbrushes on it, look!'

Frankie felt like she was falling, as though time and space had disappeared and she was about to land with a jolt in the shop in Cape Cod, with her flat stomach and mean plans. She'd wiped that beer from her mind, along with the things she'd been going to say to Max. He probably still thought now that it was Verity who had bought that beer for him. But why had he looked so horrified a few moments ago when he'd seen it? Or was it something else that had made him look like that?

'I didn't know you could get that here,' Frankie said. 'I've only ever seen it in America.'

Alice frowned. 'They sell it here. You just have to look really hard for it. Are you some kind of beer specialist?'

Frankie laughed, but the sharpness of Alice's words stung like lemon on a cut. 'Not really. I just remember buying some in Cape Cod, years ago.' She glanced around again, but Max had vanished.

'Yeah, I used to go there too. Every summer,' Alice was saying. 'I was probably there at the same time as you. Do you think I might have been?'

Frankie shrugged as a faint but definite sense of unease descended over her. Alice didn't seem the Cape Cod type. Even Frankie had only ever been able to go because Verity's family took her and paid for her. Her parents had hated the flaunting of money and she'd had to beg them every single year until they rolled their uptight eyes and said, '*Okay then, Francesca, but don't be getting silly ideas in your head about what is valuable in life.*' Whatever that meant. 'Possibly,' she said, continuing to scan the room for Max.

'Mummy! Mummy!' There was tugging on Frankie's dress. 'It's *so* cool outside,' Maisie said, her eyes bright and her cheeks red with cold. Bella and Luna stood next to her so that they were all in a row.

Bella nodded in excited agreement. 'The trees are all gone!'

'Thanks for taking care of them, Luna,' Frankie said, the feeling of unease shifting around inside her as something tried to pull itself up into her consciousness. She opened her shoulder bag and took out some wipes. She could hear a photographer taking photos. It would be typical if Frankie's children ended up in *Hills Daily* with smeared-soil faces.

Luna nodded, but didn't speak, just glanced at Verity, who had led them all in. Frankie turned to Alice to say something else about Cape Cod. She'd mentioned those holidays to Alice when they were in GLASS last night. The memory was hazy, but she was pretty sure of it. Why hadn't Alice said anything about being there at the same time then?

But Alice had gone now too. Frankie frowned. Either she'd had much more to drink than she thought and wasn't taking enough notice of things, or there was some kind of secret game of hide-and-seek going on.

'Go and have a lie down on my bed,' Verity said to Luna, her voice firm. 'I'll bring you some water up in a minute. Then you might feel better in time for midnight.'

Frankie and Verity watched Luna disappear out of the main lounge and into the hallway.

'Luna's poorly,' Maisie said with a little pout as Frankie swiped her face clean. 'But I want to go outside again.'

Bella nodded a little wildly, her eyes almost popping from their sockets. 'I wasn't even a tiny bit cold!' she shouted with glee. Frankie probably needed to watch her children's sugar intake for the rest of the night. Bella was a devil even after yoghurt and a banana. Who knew what she was capable of after a whole chocolate fountain? 'Can we go out again now? Can we?'

'No,' Frankie said as she squashed the damp wipe back into her designer handbag. 'Not where we can't see you. Verity, are you sure you should be letting Luna into your room without someone there to watch her?' she added, ignoring Bella's whimper of protest. 'I'm feeling weird about Alice. Like there's something she's not being honest about.'

Verity tensed. 'Oh, Frankie, please don't start this again. You were the one who said the articles were nothing to worry about.'

'Mummy, pleeeaaase can we go outside?' Maisie whined. 'You can see us if you just keep looking out of the window.'

'There's just something a bit off,' Frankie said. 'I saw Max and…' And what? He looked frightened? Of Alice? Frankie needed to pick her words carefully.

Verity waited. 'What? What did Max do?'

'Nothing. It's nothing. Just keep an eye on Luna.'

'I know we're not sure about Alice,' Verity said in a low voice. 'But Luna isn't Alice. She's a different person. And she's so non-judgemental. It's probably a New Age teenage thing. Gen Z and all that.'

'Well, you know Luna better than me.'

'I'm going to help Luna find a college,' Verity said, and it was only then that Frankie realised Maisie and Bella had gone outside again.

Verity noticed too and laughed. 'When people say you

can't take your eyes off them for a minute, they really mean it, don't they?'

They pushed past guests towards the garden, through a heavy haze of perfume and aftershave. Most of them stopped Verity to congratulate her on the party. Then a waiter stopped them to give them more champagne. By the time they reached the girls outside, Maisie and Bella were dancing around in a small pit left by the root of a tree. The black lake sparkled beyond them.

'Girls, I told you not to come out here again,' Frankie said. 'You need to be careful. We don't want you falling down a muddy hole, do we?'

'Like in *Alice in Wonderland*?' Bella's little features widened in excitement. 'I would love that. But I don't want to see that mean queen.'

'Well, then you need to stay nearby, girls. Maybe you should try out the chocolate fountain again,' Verity said. 'That's inside, nice and safe.'

The girls shrieked. 'Yes! Yes!'

'Maybe we could take some chocolate up to Luna to make her feel better?' Maisie said as they headed back towards the warm buzz of the house.

'That's a fabulous idea,' Verity said and ruffled Maisie's hair with a delicate hand.

'What's the matter with Luna, anyway?' Frankie asked Verity.

Verity frowned. 'I'm not sure. She just said she felt a bit dizzy.'

'She's like Daddy,' said Maisie, skipping ahead.

'Daddy?' Frankie repeated, as the vague, unpleasant

feeling she'd had for the last few minutes shifted into something more tangible. Alice's words returned to her again, as loud and clear as if she was right there in front of them.

I was probably there at the same time as you. Do you think I might have been?

'Yep.' Maisie stopped skipping and turned around, her green eyes round and cat-like in the moonlight. 'She has a poorly heart, just like he does.'

Chapter Twenty-Four

ALICE

Chatham, Cape Cod, USA: seventeen years earlier

Max and I parted without discussing it. He ran one way; I ran another. As soon as I saw people in the distance, tiny as ants, I slowed to a walk. I smoothed down my hair and my clothes. I went into a shop and bought myself a chocolate bar to make myself feel normal, even though I felt like I'd never want to eat again. And then I found myself drawn towards their part of the beach. Surely now he'd notice me and talk to me.

Old friends, he'd say to the others to explain how he knew me. *We go way back.*

They'd accept me because I'd belong to Max.

They'd know we had a secret from our glances at one another. He'd know that he could trust me, more than he could trust any of them. I held his secret in my heart. We'd go deeper, forever.

A small fire flickered where they sat on the tiny strip of sand left, throwing ghoulish shadows over them. Max sat slightly apart from them, staring out to the sea. Usually he was the centre of them all, and they all danced around him, but not tonight.

I stepped down onto the beach, my eyes fixed on the twisting orange flames.

Crack.

Crack.

Crack.

I stopped and covered my ears, squeezed my eyes shut, but the sound came from within me: the smash of skull on rock, over and over again. I opened my eyes again, my breath racing, and wondered if he was hearing the same thing.

You're the only one who understands, Alice. I had no idea where he lived, but we could write, couldn't we?

I got closer to them and could hear the words of the blonde girl swirling with the sounds of the tide.

'And I said to him that I was going to do art at college and he said, "What, like paintings," and I said, "Well, of course painting, what else can art be?" So then he says, "Well, music, poetry…" and I just—'

I cleared my throat, and she turned and glanced at me. Her face was the kind of face that you don't see often in real life: a flawless combination of symmetry and clarity.

She turned back. 'Well, I just felt so stupid!' she finished with a peal of laughter.

And then Max turned and saw me and in that moment something in me changed. It was like a piece of me fell away. I suppose you could say I've been looking for it ever since.

His face was pale anyway, ghostly so, and he sat far enough from the campfire that the warmth of the flames couldn't reach his skin, so it was blue-white from the moonlight, and the horror of the night. But when his eyes met mine, the paleness intensified so that he looked dead.

Dead. The word blared in my mind over and over like a siren. Crab pasta one minute, a dead man the next.

The only person who would ever understand this, understand me, was Max.

I glanced behind him, at the tide. There was barely any sand left.

'The tide's coming in fast,' I shouted, trying to be confident, failing miserably so that my words trembled like pink jelly.

Max's eyes widened and he stood up. The others turned to look at me like a pack of curious dogs, ears cocked, waiting to see what the weird loner girl would say to them next. But Max would sort that out. I wouldn't be the loner girl for long.

Everyone, this is Alice.

Alice, hey.

Max, you're a dark horse! You kept Alice quiet! Little holiday romance?

Would they say 'dark horse'? Probably not. They wouldn't say any of it. I knew that from the way Max was staring at me. Yet I couldn't help but hold on to the fantasy for a few more minutes, probably because I knew in a moment it would be gone.

Max was edging closer and closer, his jaw clenched and his eyes hard. The group had lost interest and were listening to the blonde girl again.

'Of course, I know it. I mean, obviously poetry is art! But it's a different kind of art. He had to admit that.'

My gaze moved from them back to Max.

'What are you doing?' he hissed as he approached me, the sharpness of his words slicing me in half.

I gawped at him silently.

'Go away,' he whispered. And then he turned around.

It was only afterwards that I realised how stupid my fantasy had been.

Everyone, this is Alice.

Yeah, right. Max didn't even know my name.

I didn't go. I moved so that they couldn't see me, and I waited. I don't think I even knew what I was waiting for. But I couldn't face going back to the house with its packed cases and my dad's apologetic face. I couldn't face the summer being over. The inevitable 'For Sale' sign up at our home, stilted phone calls with my mum, my friends finding out I had no money.

So I stayed, as if I could mould time like Plasticine.

They all scrambled away from the waves that swept across the remaining strip of sand, laughing as though the daily movement of the tide was hilarious, clutching flip-flops and Walkmans; tubes of Pringles and tangles of headphones.

Max, the blonde and the dark-haired girl all wandered away from where I lay on my stomach behind a grassy slope. Their words echoed in the night, bouncing from the moon and the sea and against each other. The boy who was younger than Max walked alone, towards me.

I sat still. If I didn't move, he wouldn't see me.

And I was going to stay there: I really was. I was going to stay and let Red pass me by and go back to the house with its packed cases and apologies.

I was going to try to move on from the *crack, crack, crack* and Max's face and their turned backs.

I was going to try and be normal: more like them.

I was going to buy a Walkman. With what money, I wasn't sure. Realism had never been my strong point.

But then he passed me, and he said something, not to me but to himself, or perhaps the world. His tone was angry and frustrated, and instantly mirrored something that I was feeling too. He even kicked a rock with his foot as he said it. What he said seemed to open the floodgates in me, and, I don't know, perhaps I thought I'd finally found some kind of kindred spirit. What he said was only one word but it was enough.

'Max.'

Chapter Twenty-Five

FRANKIE

New Year's Eve

F rankie loved shouting at the television when she was watching her murder mysteries. '*It's him!*' she'd yell with relish at the television. '*It's the father! It's the vicar! It's the piano teacher! He's the murderer! He's the one!*'

But in a television programme, the signs are lined up as neatly as ducks, debated cockily by writers over one-use coffee cups and sandwiches from Pret. This was real life, and the clues had been all over the place; easier to miss. They'd been there though, hadn't they? And Frankie's mind had been busy making the connections, joining the dots without her even knowing it. The dots were meaningless alone: Alice appearing in their lives, and Red feeling like he'd seen her somewhere before. Alice telling Frankie with a pointed stare that she used to go to Cape Cod too; that they were probably even there at the same time. But the others were more obvious, now Frankie thought about it. There was the genetic heart condition.

And then there was the row of bright green eyes: Maisie, Bella, Luna.

Chapter Twenty-Six

ALICE

Chatham, Cape Cod, USA: seventeen years earlier

I followed him. He was difficult to keep up with but I took off my sandals. I was going to dump them in a bin but then I realised they'd be crawling with my DNA, and that was something I was going to have to be careful of now. So I dangled them from my hand, the way I'd seen the girls on the beach hold theirs.

And then I fell.

I did it on purpose, obviously, because I couldn't think of how else to attract him.

It worked like a charm.

He turned round swiftly. A nice boy, Mum would have said. If she were there.

I swallowed. 'Ow!' The fall might have been

orchestrated, but I really had scraped my knee. Blood sprang from it, garish in the moonlight.

'Hey, are you okay?' He came closer to me, and if he recognised me as the weird girl shouting about the tide a few hours ago, there was no sign of it. I could tell, now that he crouched beside me, that their water bottles at the beach had not contained water. Of course they'd been drinking. I was so stupid.

'Are you okay?' he asked again. 'Can I get you anything?'

I shuffled into a more comfortable position. 'Yeah, sorry if I scared you. I'm fine. This happens a lot.'

His eyes widened and my heart skipped a little. To have my own fantasy world was one thing, but to have someone else believe in it was quite intoxicating.

'I'm diabetic,' I said, the lie springing to my lips quite easily and making him look concerned and caring. 'I need food, that's all. I was walking because it's such a gorgeous night, and I'm going home tomorrow, and I suppose I just left it a bit late to get something to eat. Which I can't really get away with. I'm sure I'll make it back, though. I don't pass out that often, so I don't think it'll happen tonight.'

'Pass out? Nah, we can't have you risking that. I have crisps?' He swung his rucksack, some sporty thing with lots of pockets, from his shoulder and unzipped it. 'Here you go,' he said, handing me the crisps. I tried to meet his eye but his were glazed over.

He sat on the ground with me as I crunched through the crisps. I tried not to think of Jamie's waxy face, his fish eyes staring up to heaven, as I ate. Even so, I could feel the food curdling in my stomach.

'I've seen you on the beach a few times,' I ventured. 'With Max.' I thought saying the name would give me something: a name of a mutual friend. But it sounded hollow, and Red didn't even pick up that I knew him.

'Yeah, Max,' he said, shaking his head and laughing, although I could see that he didn't think anything was particularly funny. 'Good old Max.' He stopped laughing and turned to me. 'Can I ask you something?'

'Course you can.'

'I know Max is fit. I don't see it myself, to be honest, but he must be, because she is *obsessed* with him. They both are.'

'Okay, so what's the question?'

'Do you think I am? Fit? Compared to him?'

I didn't know much about boys, but I knew that it took a lot of alcohol for them to talk like this. Alcohol and a whole summer of watching the girls you fancied flirt with someone else. I stared at him for a minute. His glazed eyes were quite a piercing green close up. His jaw was strong, and his skin was clear and littered with hazy freckles. His strawberry hair fell over one eye, giving him a boyband kind of vibe.

'Yeah,' I said, feeling the thrill that I'd been lacking before. 'I do. You're a million times better than Max.'

He rolled his eyes. 'Yeah, right.' He took a bottle from his rucksack and downed whatever was in it, then offered it to me. I swigged and felt the pleasant burn of alcohol scorch my throat.

'I'm telling the truth,' I said. 'I think you're good-looking, and I think Max...' I stopped, thinking of what I'd done for him, and how he'd looked at me: just like the clinger-on I didn't want to be. 'I think Max looks down on people. He thinks he's invincible.'

'He is,' he said, 'when it comes to girls.'

'Some girls,' I said. 'Not all.' I nudged his knee with mine, and gestured for him to give me back the bottle he was holding, and he did, and as soon as I'd taken a mouthful, he took it out of my hand and set it on the path beside me. Then he cupped my face in his hands and kissed me.

I should have closed my eyes, but if I did that, I would have seen Jamie's gawping fish eyes and Max's horrified face; my dad scraping pasta into the bin and my mum at the door of the holiday house, turning away from me and my dad and our whole life. So instead, all the way through, as he gently pushed at me, and touched me, and unfurled me in a way that meant nothing would ever, ever be the same again, I stared up at the bright white moon.

Chapter Twenty-Seven

FRANKIE

New Year's Eve

'Can you watch the girls whilst I go and check on Red? Just for half an hour?' Frankie asked Verity, who obviously hadn't clocked anything. Verity would rather die than watch a mystery series. 'I just want to go and check on Red. I could take the girls with me, but...' Frankie would never normally ask Verity to watch her children, but she could hardly take them with her to confront Red with this. Maybe the disappearing Alice had even beaten Frankie to it and was there right now, at Frankie's house, asking Red for money and commitment and to be part of their lives. Well, she'd be lucky to get money from them. They were apparently on a knife edge from having nothing.

'Of course I can!' Verity said merrily. 'We can go and find

Max, can't we, girlies? He seems to be hiding! Make sure you're back for midnight, though. It'll be here before you know it.'

'Of course.'

She strode long, purposeful strides towards home. Her mind raced as quickly as she did.

Did Red know? Surely he didn't. Surely he did. As she walked, and useless thoughts circled her mind, Frankie placed her hand against her chest. It wasn't thumping as hard as she might have expected, for such a peculiar evening. Perhaps she was in shock.

She tried to take control of her thoughts and pull them back towards her like little dogs on leads. If Luna really was Red's, and that's why Alice was in White Fir Lake, then they'd need to just accept it. There was no need for Frankie to be anything but sympathetic towards Red, *if* he hadn't kept it from her. It was a big if. And how things worked out for them now really depended on what Alice wanted. And what Luna wanted, Frankie supposed. She'd probably be glad to take up roots with them all, with Verity.

Oh God, Verity.

Frankie stopped on the corner of her street. A lone flake of snow drifted down in front of her eyes.

'She's like my little project,' Verity had said earlier.

And now Luna belonged to Red, and by default, Frankie.

If Frankie ever dealt the girls sweets or gave them

scoops of ice cream, she could guarantee that one of them would use some kind of ultrasonic vision to identify any kind of inequality in portion size, and wail about it like a banshee until it was rectified.

How was Verity meant to sit by while Frankie got dealt scoop after scoop?

Frankie started walking again slowly, picking up speed and going faster and faster so that by the time she got home, even though the air was damp and icy, she was sweating.

'Red? I've just popped back to...' Talk about your secret love affair with Alice.

The thought caught her off-guard. Was that something she really suspected, that something was happening *now* between Red and Alice?

Frankie pulled off her coat. There was so much about all this that she still hadn't processed.

It didn't seem like Alice was here after all. There were no voices, no extra shoes or coat in the hallway. Frankie wandered through to the kitchen-diner, expecting to see Red sprawled on the sofa. But the sofa was empty.

'Red?'

Silence.

If Red had gone out, perhaps to the party, then he would have taken Harry. She rushed up to the nursery and opened the door quietly.

The cot had in it Harry's sleeping bag with boats on and his little blue bear. But no Harry.

Frankie pulled her phone out of her coat pocket. A message, sent twenty minutes ago, waited for her on the screen.

Getting a cab to the party. I feel loads better and Harry won't settle anyway. We'll be there soon x

Red probably passed her in his cab, but he would have been thumbing through his phone. Emails, Facebook, Rightmove – anything but the world around him.

Frankie returned to the dining room downstairs. The house was strange with nobody in it. She felt like she'd walked into another life, or perhaps pressed pause on her own. She sat on the sofa, suddenly exhausted from the walk home, the shock of the evening.

Now she was here, with the comforting hum of the fridge, the sink of soaking bowls that she'd left behind from this morning's baking and the furniture she'd selected so carefully with Red, the fact that she'd bolted from the party seemed absurd.

Just because there were a few signs, did that really mean that Red had another child, that Luna was his? Maybe Frankie was jumping the gun a little. She needed to collect herself before she went back to the party. And that was what she meant to do when she headed upstairs: put a bit more powder on, brush her hair, take a few moments to settle down.

But as she passed Red's office door, she paused. She never normally went into Red's office. That was his domain. It was an organised mess of files, a ridiculous number of monitors (who needed more than one screen at any one time, really?) and papers. Nothing that Frankie needed to see.

Or was there?

She opened the door cautiously, quickly opening the top drawer of his desk before she could change her mind. If Red knew about Luna, or if Alice had been in touch with him before now, then surely this is where he would stash the secret. But there was nothing in the drawer other than all the things Frankie expected: sheets of figures, some in red; a stapler; biros and a few business cards.

She was being crazy, psycho, imagining things. This must be how Verity felt all the time these days. Maybe it was catching. Maybe they really did need to start keeping an eye on their alcohol intake.

Frankie pulled out the second drawer and wondered how much her offer of surrogacy could change things. How much might be changed if Red had another child. Fear pulled at her as her fingers sifted through the papers. They couldn't afford another child; a teenager who wanted to go to art school and wear expensive dresses. They weren't ready for that yet! Her fingers came across something other than paper, some fabric. Perhaps Alice would be fair. Frankie would need to warn her about Red's heart, and the impact of stress. But then, Alice might already know that because Luna had…

Frankie's thoughts stopped dead as she pulled out what had been beneath the papers.

Chapter Twenty-Eight

ALICE

Monday 16 December

As I sat in Frankie's kitchen that first time after my little *accident* with her wall, I felt like I was living some other life, or watching a Christmas film. Who knew that real life could be this Hallmark? Frankie's Christmas tree was like something from a department store, fully colour co-ordinated and regal in the corner. Candles were dotted along the wide windowsill, filling the kitchen with the smells of cinnamon and nutmeg.

Frankie had been kind to me when I appeared at her door, ushering me in as I hoped she would. It was like being welcomed into a celebrity's house; I'd dreamed of it for so long. Frankie obviously had no idea who I was. Harry, her youngest, gazed up at me with Luna's eyes. Luna's half-brother. He was so different to Luna at that age, sitting on the rug playing nicely with his toy animals and being so quiet that you barely knew he was there. She had no idea how lucky she was.

Verity didn't remember me either, even though she'd looked straight at me that night on the beach in America. I knew that was normal: you don't remember every person you look at. Still, every moment that ticked by in Frankie's cinnamon kitchen, I imagined her or Verity suddenly gasping and saying, *Hang on! You're the girl from that summer! Max always wanted to reply to your letters, but he never knew what to say!*

I'd first found Max and learned his surname and where he lived a few years ago, after seeing him in a magazine. I didn't even know he was still friends with Red then. I'd done some digging online and found Max's address. Then I'd started writing to him. I hadn't even planned on moving close to him at that point. I'd just been doing what I'd tried to do in America: join their group. I'd wanted it badly when I was a teenager, but I wanted it even more badly as an adult; as a mother to someone who didn't belong anywhere we went. I wanted Max to write back and to say, *No way, it's you! Long time no see! Yeah, we all still hang out. You should come over and stay with us.* I was friendly in the letters at first. I just said things like, *Dear Max, remember me? From that night near the pier in Chatham?* But he ignored my letters over and over again, so I'd had to refer to what he'd done, to make him think about me and what we'd shared.

I'd learned about secrets in one of my online courses. The burden of them could harm the health of the keeper.

They could lead to intrusive thoughts and constant rumination. That was all I wanted to tell Max. I was staying silent for him, but it came at a price for me. Perhaps I should have sent him the article.

I stroked Harry's little cheek and he gave me a grin and showed me a toy monkey, shoving it in my face. I smiled back at him.

'Who wants a little glass of fizz?' Verity asked, flinging open Frankie's fridge and revealing a colourful burst of food, wine and beer. It was like an upmarket supermarket in there. I glanced at Frankie to see if she minded Verity acting like it was her own house, but she didn't even seem to notice. I wanted that – people at my flat acting like it was theirs, as though they were my family. I'd have to upgrade the contents, of course. All my fridge had in it at the moment was own-brand butter and milk and a single can of cider.

'Sure,' Frankie said. 'What's the celebration today?'

'Our new friend Alice!' Verity said.

My heart pumped a little faster. 'Oh, don't open anything on account of me,' I said, after the cork had already been popped.

The champagne tasted of money and was the colour of pure gold. I drank it with Verity, staying in Frankie's house whilst she went to pick up Maisie and Bella. This, I thought, the bubbles floating pleasantly through my blood, was what life should have been like all along. If I tried hard enough, I could even imagine that this was my own house, Verity my own friend.

'I still think you're amazing doing all this on your own,'

Verity said to me, her eyes wide as though I were a rare and strange bird at the zoo. She topped up my glass. 'What happened with Luna's dad?'

'Oh, it's probably a story for another time,' I said, trying to judge how long I was going to leave it. Long enough for them to trust me; not so long that I would seem odd for not revealing it sooner. 'I will tell you though. I was just a teenager, obviously.'

'I bet you and Luna are more like sisters or friends than mother and daughter,' Verity said.

I sighed. 'Not really, to be totally honest. I struggle with her a bit. She's not your average teenage girl.'

'That might be a good thing, from what I've heard.'

'Not really,' I said, more sharply than I wanted to. What would it be like to be like Verity, everything threaded with gold and happiness? Verity looked taken aback at my tone, and I smiled my brightest smile at her, my heart banging.

Don't blow it now, Alice. You're almost there.

I'd taken Max's silence as a hint that he wanted nothing to do with me, but now I saw that he'd been frightened. Sitting in Frankie's kitchen, staring their addictive beauty and happiness in the face, I could feel how much he had to lose. But it was okay: I didn't need to frighten him anymore. I was becoming part of their world without him, and it was big enough for us all to share without anyone losing anything.

I'd wait a little longer. Then I'd tell Verity and Frankie

that something had pulled me here to White Fir Lake, that I had no *idea* Red lived here but that on some level I must have known. That I hadn't recognised him straight away, but as time went on, I put two and two together. Luna had her father back, I'd tell them. How could they all refuse a sad, lost girl the father she deserved? How could he say no when chance had brought them both together?

What an amazing story. *What a happy ending,* everyone would say as they sipped their champagne and clinked their crystal glasses.

Chapter Twenty-Nine

ALICE

30 December

'Well, if it isn't the wall woman,' Red said to me in greeting as he swung open his front door. He had a wide grin plastered on his face, although he didn't sound that happy. He didn't seem to recognise me, just as I knew he wouldn't. Red was so drunk and so young when we slept together: he probably wouldn't have recognised me the day after, let alone seventeen years. I couldn't even recall his face properly so had no way of tracking him down until about six months ago, when I'd found him hanging on to some kind of second-hand fame in one of Max's articles. Thomas Redmond, a well-known property developer, and his wife Francesca had bought the house across from the Bentley mansion, the article told me. They enjoyed frequent parties at the Bentley mansion and were lifelong friends with the Bentleys. Thomas Redmond. No wonder I'd never been able to find someone called Red before. It was like uncovering a treasure chest. I'd been able to find Frankie's Facebook page, their address, the colour of their daughters' uniforms and bedrooms, their school pickup times and the Google map of their street, complete with a little white wall on a tricky bend. It had changed everything.

I wanted to stare at Red as I stood at his doorway, but I hung my head. 'I'm so sorry.'

'Come in,' he said. 'Frankie says you're forgiven, and who am I to argue?'

I grinned at him as I shrugged off my coat, but it was difficult. *Forgiven!* I'd brought up his child on my own for all these years and he'd been oblivious, making money and marrying someone nice and having children when he was good and ready.

'Frankie's kind,' I said evenly. 'She's turning into a very good friend.'

The house was warm, and I could hear the children playing and stomping around upstairs. I still hadn't recovered from seeing them that first time at Frankie's house when I crashed into the wall. Now, just like that day, I had to stop myself from rushing up to them, touching them and asking how they'd feel about a brand-new big sister. They had to have a spare room here in this massive house. Luna could sleep over sometimes and eat popcorn with them, read stories to her baby brother whilst I hung out downstairs with Frankie and Verity, drinking golden champagne and letting their success rub off on me like expensive soap.

'So you're new round here?' Red took my coat from me to hang up and I did a mental check of anything I might have left in the pockets that would give me away. My last letter to Max had been in the pocket until a few days before when I'd posted it, but there was nothing else in there.

'Yeah. From London.'

'Frankie's in the kitchen. She's been baking figs all afternoon. You like figs?'

'Oh yeah. Love them,' I said, feeling my cheeks flush. I'd never even had a fig. He probably knew that.

'I'll head upstairs. In charge of bath time,' Red said with a slight roll of the eyes that managed to convey his love for his children and the boredom of his life all in one. Poor Frankie. I watched him as he turned and disappeared down their huge, cluttered hallway. The pictures I'd seen of him in sporadic articles and on Frankie's Facebook posts over the last six months had made him look completely different now to that summer, but now I'd seen him up close, I felt weak with anticipation. It was really, actually him.

'Hey,' Red said, turning back. A flicker of recognition crossed his face, and my heart stopped. Not now. I wasn't ready.

'Yeah?' I looked down again.

Red winked. 'Remind Frankie to go easy on the champagne tonight.' He rubbed his forefinger and thumb together. 'Doesn't grow on trees.'

Red's comment floated around in my mind as we sat at Frankie's huge breakfast bar and ate her ridiculously sweet fig canapés. He was probably joking. There was no way he could be worried about money. Still, my chest felt tight with unease as I sipped my cold wine and listened to Frankie talk about Verity and said things in response about how wonderful it was that she was running her own gallery. That still seemed to be the passcode for this world: *Verity is wonderful*. Some things never changed. But she was wonderful, of course, so I couldn't even fight it.

'How amazing that she runs her own gallery,' I said. 'I'd love to have a decent career. But kids ruin all that, don't they?'

I thought Frankie would agree, and that we might bond as women who'd been done over by the system, by patriarchy and inequality. But I should have known better. Frankie just shrugged and mumbled something about doing both. I couldn't stand that 'women can have it all' nonsense. They couldn't have it all if they had nobody to pick up their daughter from school, if their family were long gone and there was no nice, neat pile of money waiting to pay for clubs and childminders and freedom. It was really that simple.

We sat in silence, a far-off look on Frankie's face. God knows what she was thinking about. How wonderful Verity was, probably.

'Not that you lot need to work, do you?' I said loudly, making Frankie start a little, as though I'd woken her up. 'You're all living your best lives. Should have bagged myself a rich man. Rookie mistake,' I said, watching her carefully. I needed Red to be able to set me up here, to change my life and Luna's life. My funds were already dwindling. I couldn't stay here without him helping me out. I'd banked on it. What if he couldn't? Panic flared in me, but Frankie smiled and it calmed me a little.

'It won't be long before Verity turns up for drinks,' she said. 'Shall we finish the wine? Or head out to the bar?'

I could hear Red upstairs with the children. I needed to be away from him to think about this properly. It hadn't occurred to me that Red was anything but loaded. I'd assumed that taking on Luna would be small change to him. Maybe Red was just one of those rich but stingy husbands. This was how they rose so high. They weren't old money like Max, I reminded myself. They needed some kind of strategy, just like I did too. I grabbed another canapé and jammed it into my mouth to soak up the wine I'd knocked back. 'Out.'

I'd seen the bar we went to as I'd driven around town to get my bearings when I first moved here. It was one of those places that had gone way over the top with its theme of glass. People loved themes these days. Nothing was in moderation.

As the waitress opened a bottle of champagne, I felt a shot of nerves. If Frankie expected me to pay half, we'd have to move on to wine soon. Or tap water. But it was necessary, I reminded myself as Frankie asked me about Luna. I hadn't been out with friends for drinks for, well, ever. I'd never shared wine and stories with other women, because I'd always been working or in a flat with Luna. Even though she didn't need me there, I usually stayed in with her. But now, even though I was out, I was doing it for Luna. If I was friends with Frankie, she'd be more likely to help me out, to take on Luna as Red's, and by extension, hers.

Perhaps tonight would even be the night I told them, I thought with a deliciously sharp twang of anticipation. After drinks and bonding. Frankie was already talking about Luna as though she really cared about her.

I'd considered sending Frankie a Facebook message when I'd found her, before I moved here. I'd thought about telling her that way. But she would have been able to block me, forget about me and leave me behind yet again.

This way, I thought as I sipped my drink, was better. This way, I was already embedded in her life.

This way was going to work, and tonight was going to be the start of it all.

Excitement prickled my skin. But then Frankie's phone lit up.

Verity had bailed on us.

'She isn't well,' Frankie said, her face screaming something else, something that she wasn't going to tell me and was going to discuss with Verity in secret instead. I took a sip of my drink, feeling the despondency of being left out, of that summer in America all over again, of Red not being able to give me what I needed. I'd moved here on a whim, I saw now.

And as we talked, my otherness stood out. Frankie had

lived around here forever. I'd lived in London before here, I told her simply. I didn't go into just how many different areas of London.

The flat in Croydon with the stoned neighbours who played trance music all night long.

The bedsit in Dagenham near the first of many schools that Luna left as a stony-faced six-year-old who couldn't get along with anyone in her class.

The room with the stained toilet right next to the kitchen sink; the flat above the shop where I worked until Luna stole a chocolate bar and I got fired.

What was it like to be so firmly fixed in one place forever, feeling as though you belonged there, as though a hole would be there if you ever left, for people to stand around, mourning you?

'I'm really grateful for you including me in things here,' I told Frankie. If you wanted people to do things for you, you should say thank you to them before they'd even fully done them. This created an easy pressure. *You should include me!* I wanted to shout as I drank more and more champagne. *I was part of this world when I was young. I'm meant to be here. I deserve it just as much as you all do!* 'I hope Luna makes good friends too. She loves kids, you know,' I added as an afterthought. 'So if you ever need a babysitter, I'm sure she'd oblige. She's awkward as hell with her own age, and adults, but give her a few kids and she's a different girl.'

I didn't tell her about the knife. Obviously.

'Maisie and Bella would love that,' Frankie said. 'They think they're teenagers themselves, as you've probably noticed. And there are some other couples around with young kids too. Luna will make a fortune if she's up for it.'

The comment stung a little. Frankie probably wouldn't ever expect her kids to babysit to make money.

'I'm sure she will be,' I said. 'Except for New Year's Eve, that is. Luna is a bit taken with Max and his art. Verity invited us to their party, and Luna would rather die than miss it.'

As we talked about the party, I felt resentment trickle through me. I should have been going to these parties for years, with Luna.

'Do they do that to you, too?' I asked Frankie.

'Do what?' Her eyes were starting to go bleary, and her hair had gone a little bit flat. She didn't look so perfect and collected as she had done at the start of the night, and it made me feel as though I could start opening up to her a little bit. *I feel like second-best Frankie,* she might say to me. *We're very similar, you and me. I'm so glad you came here, Alice. Luna's part of my family? That's perfect! Come on in! Help yourself to our fridge!*

'Make you feel like you want to be their favourite?' I asked.

But Frankie laughed and her face snapped shut. 'A lot of people look up to them.'

A bubble of disappointment rose in my chest. It wasn't going to be that easy. I made up some rubbish about Max being gossiped about to make myself feel better. A little plaster over my wounds, or maybe, as my online course tutor would say, to try to gain control. But even though Frankie was so drunk by that point that she could barely look at me straight, she was stubborn as a child every time I tried to suggest Max was anything other than a saint.

'Oh God,' Frankie said when the bill came. Her flushed face suddenly went horribly pale. 'Red's going to kill me. I wasn't meant to spend this much.'

'*You* weren't? I'll have to tell Luna she can't eat for a week,' I said, laughing desperately to cover up my returning panic. 'But at least I don't have a husband checking my every move,' I added in a last-ditch attempt to find out more.

'He doesn't check my every move,' Frankie said, sounding guarded.

I sat back and crossed my arms, wondering if Verity knew about this limit to their funds. Probably. She'd know everything there was to know about Frankie. It was only me who had no idea about the details of all of their lives.

'He's just worried, that's all,' Frankie continued, trying to make it sound like nothing and doing a terrible job. 'We've spent a lot lately, on the house and moving across to White Fir Lake. Money doesn't grow on trees.'

That stupid phrase again. 'Interesting. I got the idea that it does round here.' I heard the bitterness in my words, but I didn't care. If Red was watching his spare change so closely that Frankie was worrying about a few bottles of champagne, and if Frankie and Verity weren't going to let me into their little clique as easily as I thought, then obviously my whole plan needed to change.

Chapter Thirty

VERITY

New Year's Eve

'Can you watch the girls? Just for half an hour?' Frankie asked Verity. They were outside again, although Verity couldn't exactly remember why and felt as though it was only a few minutes ago she'd tripped on her way back into the house. She breathed in the cold air and the earthy scent of the churned ground as Frankie said something about popping home to check on Red.

'Of course I can!' Verity replied. Frankie never left her alone with the girls, and Verity always wanted her to, but now probably wasn't the best time. The garden wavered a little as Verity tried to focus. She'd have to get Max to help her watch them. 'We can go and find Max, can't we, girlies?

He seems to be hiding! Make sure you're back for midnight, though. It'll be here before you know it.'

Max had been in the same area as Frankie when Verity had been outside, she was sure of it. But he wasn't there now. She went upstairs to her bedroom, where the sounds of the party faded as though they were a memory. But Max wasn't in the bedroom; Luna was. Of course Luna was. Verity had only just sent her up there. The teenager lay on the bed, unaware of Verity standing in the doorway. Her torso moved up, down, up, down, slowly and calmly. Her pale popcorn-daffodil hair splayed out over the silk pillow.

See? Verity wanted to tell Frankie. Luna wasn't in there poking about or moving things around. She was sleeping, just as she had gone up to do because she was straightforward and did what she said and nothing else.

'Hey.'

The voice was close to Verity and made her jump. She turned around to face Red, and confusion fogged her mind. Hadn't Frankie just gone to check on Red because he was at home?

'I've just got here,' Red said. 'The kids said you were upstairs.'

Kids. Verity hated that word. They weren't goats, for heaven's sake.

'Yes, I was looking for Max. But I can't find him.'

Red grinned and held out a bottle of whisky. 'Just us, then.'

'Yes, just us. Although,' she said with sudden alarm, 'Frankie asked me to look after your girls, so we should go and find them.'

Verity put her arm through Red's as they made their way back down to the party. Maisie and Bella came running over when they reached the kitchen, with Harry chasing after them.

'Ah! You brought him,' Verity said, remembering the lights in Frankie and Red's dining room snapping off before as she'd been gazing across the water. She scooped Harry up in her arms, pressing her head against his little tubby body.

'Down!' he commanded, wriggling and then sticking a finger in her eye.

'Sorry,' Red said, laughing and taking Harry from her.

'Don't be. I love it, I love them all so much,' Verity said, not even bothering to hide the desperation in her voice. She gestured for Red to sit on the sofa just behind them. She normally hated sitting at a party, and most of her guests were up, dancing and laughing and swiping colourful cocktails from trays. She should leave Red and his whisky here and go and join them; do what she'd planned and sprinkle into conversation her little story of role play. *We make out we're fighting so that we can make up! Aren't we enviable, with our little sexy games?* But Verity felt so horribly tired. She thought again of going upstairs and lying down next to Luna, their two blonde heads next to each other like matching dolls.

'I know you love them.' Red put Harry down and unscrewed the top from the bottle he'd brought. He swigged from it, then held it out to Verity.

She laughed. 'Oh please. Let me get some glasses, at least.'

'Nah. It can be like old times. We can be teenagers again.'

Verity rolled her eyes and watched as Harry raced off to join his sisters at the chocolate fountain. 'Old times indeed. People always have such an affinity with old times. It's not because old times were any better. It's just the temptation of something you know you can't have.'

Red shrugged, swigged from the bottle again, then held it out, pushing it into her arm so that she could feel the cool glass against her skin.

'You know, Frankie has gone home to check on you,' Verity said after a pause. She swigged from the bottle after all and the whisky burned in her blood.

'I messaged her. She'll turn back.'

'Daddy!' Bella appeared, chocolate smears joining the mud from earlier. These children were starting to look like something out of a Dickens novel. When Frankie was in charge of them, they were pristine. 'Do you want some of the chocolate fountain?'

'I'll have some later. You test it out for me first. And ask Maisie to keep an eye on Harry, will you?'

Verity followed his gaze. Harry was now running around the legs of a woman who sometimes came into the gallery and bought thousand-pound paintings on a whim. 'I'll grab him,' she offered to Red, but he shook his head as Bella disappeared off towards the fountain again. 'Nah. He's fine.'

Verity swigged more of the whisky. The woman who had Harry circling her legs cast a strange glance over in Verity's direction, which made Verity spring to her feet. 'I'm going to get us some glasses,' she told Red. 'The best crystal.'

When she sat back down next to Red with a bump a few minutes later, she noticed that most of the whisky had gone, anyway. Red put his arm on hers as she steadied herself on the sofa. 'Are you okay?'

She laughed. 'Of course.'

'Are you? Really?' Red stared at her. He used to do this all the time, Verity remembered with a start. He used to gaze at her like a lost puppy when they were teenagers. She'd forgotten about that. Once he had her gaze, it used to be quite hard to break away from it without feeling guilty, like she'd rejected him somehow. He hadn't done it for a few years. Or maybe he had, and Verity had stopped noticing. 'I know how hard things are,' he continued. 'Aren't you tired of it all? Don't you want to just do something new, something a bit dangerous, to try and get what you want?'

'Oh, here we go,' Verity grinned. 'Red the risk taker.'

'*It's how I built my empire,*' he always said at the end of dinner parties, bleary-eyed and proud of himself. '*Risks pay off!*'

'Well, risks pay off,' he said.

Verity had never really taken this seriously before. She'd never had to: she and Max had always had money – her parents' money, his parents' money. It seemed to breed. They'd never had to stake anything for it. But a baby! It was risk after risk, she realised now. *The IVF will begin to take a toll on your wellbeing, Mrs Bentley. There needs to be some point where you draw a line.*

Well, the line had clearly been crossed. She was going stark raving mad and still had no baby, anyway. So why not go a little madder, push the universe a little more to give her what she wanted? No, what she *needed*. Want was ice cream on a hot day or a holiday in St Tropez at the end of a cold winter. This was something entirely different, that came from within her bones, that was required for her very survival.

'What kind of risk can I take, though?' she mused aloud.

Red laughed. 'I'm pretty fertile. Harry was one shot, you know.'

Verity stared at him, hoping to see a flashing 'JOKING' sign on his face. But there was nothing, and he said no more, just stared at her again. She put her hand to her head. Where was Frankie, anyway?

Chapter Thirty-One

FRANKIE

New Year's Eve

There was a bra nestling underneath Red's papers. And it definitely wasn't Frankie's. It had neat little cups for one thing, not the unattractive hammocks that Frankie needed. And Frankie's bras were neutral beige, because beige went under anything, and they weren't underwired because since having the children and breastfeeding, she'd found that she just could not bear to have wire cutting into her skin, no matter how much it might perk things up.

She lifted the bra from the drawer, the deep green lace and tiny sparkling beads catching on her fingertips. She closed her eyes, her mind reassembling the life that she thought she'd had into something else, one where she found underwear hidden in drawers and didn't even know the man she'd married.

When she opened her eyes again, she saw the tip of something red, beneath where the bra had been. She parted the papers and picked it out.

The very top of a red lipstick, cut like the tip of a finger, its garish pigment bleeding onto Frankie's skin. Next to it was a bottle of Verity's Chanel perfume, the one Verity had been looking for tonight, the one that she knew someone had spritzed on her new dress and then hidden to play with her mind and make her feel as though she was going mad.

Either that was Verity's cover-up because she knew she'd left these things in Red's sad little office with its red letters and scent of stale alcohol, or Red was taking Verity's things and hiding them, touching them and making Verity feel as though *she* was the one with a dirty secret.

If it was a cover-up, it was an extravagant one.

And Frankie was rarely out without Verity, was she? How would Verity ever be here alone with Red?

But Red was at Verity's house enough to slip things out of her drawers, and he was at home quite often when Verity's bag was in the hall or her coat was slipped over their extensive oak bannister that they'd chosen together and spent twenty thousand pounds on. Often enough to take out lipsticks and cut off the part that had touched Verity's lips.

Frankie's blood seemed to cool in her body. She thought she might be sick, right there in the drawer, over Verity's things. She took a deep breath and drew the bra up to her nose, smelling deep musk, a scent that made you feel as though Verity were right next to you, close enough so that you could feel her breath on your skin.

Frankie threw the things on the desk and turned, slamming the office door shut behind her.

Frankie never ran. She didn't have the body for it and there was always too much jiggling of everything. But tonight was different. She felt as though something, a different life, was hurtling towards her and that she needed to pick up speed to beat it.

She ran as fast as she could back towards the party. She supposed she could have called a cab, or even driven Red's car and ignored the rules about drink- driving, because what rules mattered when your husband was obviously harbouring some sort of creepy obsession with your best friend?

All this time, Frankie had lugged around her guilt about loving Max like it was another child, one yanking her in a direction she didn't want to go in. She'd carried the guilt of it around with her to pick the children up, to bed with Red, to bars and restaurants and Max's front door.

When she'd stumbled down the stairs from Red's office to their kitchen-diner, she'd collapsed onto the sofa. Red's sofa, where he lay every evening, gazing out of the French doors and drinking whisky. She'd gazed across the lake herself, to Verity's house, straight into Verity's bedroom.

Verity never closed her curtains.

'*The trees aren't under a preservation order,*' Red had said not even a month before, eager for the trees to be gone. He'd looked into it, encouraged Max and Verity to do it.

How stupid *was* she?

And how dangerous was he?

She ran and ran. Her shoes sliced into her heels, and the hard ground slammed the fibres of her body together.

All this time, what else had he been stealing from Verity's private drawers? What else had he sniffed and kept and done God knows what to?

The words thumped in her mind, in time with her heels on the ground.

All. This. Time.

226

Chapter Thirty-Two

VERITY

New Year's Eve

'Frankie isn't into me. Never has been,' Red said eventually.

Verity looked around. People would be listening, even if they didn't look like it. They always were. Even though a part of her was nicely oblivious because of the alcohol she'd had, there was always a small piece of her dedicated to ensuring that things didn't go too awry. A little stumble or slurring was okay. But conversations like this? Absolutely not.

'I think I'd better…' She started to stand, but Red pulled her back down.

'Don't you see it?' he asked in a low voice. 'Frankie and Max?'

'Daddy! Maisie said I can't have any more chocolate. She's being a bossyboots.' Bella appeared again, outraged. 'Verity, where's Luna?'

'I think she's still asleep,' Verity said.

Bella yawned, revealing a tongue tarry with chocolate. Verity looked away. 'So, can I have more, Daddy?'

Red nodded, and Bella grinned and weaved her way back towards the fountain. Verity thought about standing up again, but the skin on her wrist where Red had pulled her back down to the sofa was still smarting a little. He obviously really wanted her to stay and listen.

'Do you really think nothing has ever happened between them?' Red asked. His green eyes locked onto Verity's again.

'No,' Verity said. 'I don't.' Had Frankie told Red about the letters? Were the letters something to do with Frankie? Verity's head spun so violently that she put it in her hands.

'Well, at least one of us is convinced. Frankie doesn't want me, you know.'

Verity lifted her spinning head. Red wasn't looking at her anymore, but staring ahead.

'She never has,' he went on. 'It was always Max.' He shook his head. 'I can't believe you can't even see it. It's there. It's always there.'

'I do see it,' Verity said. Of course she did, but it was *Frankie*, and it was *Max*. Frankie thought she hid her crush on Max. Max knew Frankie adored him and promised her nothing. He never had. And Frankie wouldn't ever cross that line. She didn't even dare to get highlights! As if she'd dare to act on her crush and ruin their beautiful bubble.

And anyway, Frankie was happy with Red. Or at least Verity had always thought she was happy enough, because she'd never thought to question it. Frankie had never given her reason to.

'You're wondering now, aren't you?' Red said with a smirk.

'No,' Verity said. 'I'm not wondering.'

'Well, I'm just saying. They wouldn't have a leg to stand on. Not that they'd find out. Look at my kids,' he said, motioning with the bottle. 'They could pass for yours and Max's. Nobody would have to know. I know it sounds ridiculous,' he said, laughing.

Verity laughed too. 'It's so ridiculous!' Her words were loud, so loud that a man she recognised as a professor of modern art, helping himself to a guava cocktail, turned and glanced at her. 'So ridiculous,' she whispered, glancing at Red. He couldn't mean this, could he? What would it do to Frankie if she found out? The thought slashed right through Verity, and she stopped laughing.

Red yanked Verity up before she could pull away, his fingers pressing into her wrist again. He led her away from the people who were starting to look at them, away from the girls and Harry who were heading back to them, smeared in sickly sticky chocolate, away from the lights and the drinks and all of it. Verity caught a flash and a click. Photographs of this, ready to shoot out into the world for all to see. It was unthinkable.

'I need to watch the children,' Verity said, trying to pull away, trying to make her voice low and strong all at once. But Red ignored her, and they weaved their way out of the dining room, through the hall, then into one of the downstairs bathrooms. It was empty and smelled of vomit. Where were the cleaners she'd hired? Everyone kept disappearing tonight. Red shut the door behind them and stood in front of it.

'You can't say a word without people listening,' he said. 'They're vultures, V. All of them.'

'I know. And I can't stand it anymore. All of it. That's why we're going.' Verity pulled out her New Year's resolution from her bra, where she always kept it, every year. She never showed anyone. But this year it was a different one. She unfolded it and showed it to Red.

Move away. New Year, new start.

'Move from White Fir Lake? Ha. You'll never do it,' Red said.

'I'm deadly serious about it. You've just said yourself that people round here are vultures. They're sucking the life out of me. And you told me to take a risk, so I am.' Verity threw Red a triumphant glance.

'You can't leave me, Verity. We're the ones who should have got together. Me and you. All the others can go to hell.'

'Red, you're saying things you'll regret.'

'I'm not. I'm saying things I should have said years ago. It's me and you, V. You know today? When I came back home with the girls? It was to be with you. I knew Frankie was going to have you at our house and I couldn't bear it. I had to turn back to see you.'

Verity felt a creeping sensation all over her, as though a

spider's egg had exploded above her head. 'You came home because you felt ill,' she said firmly.

'I always feel ill. Every second of every day. But I can't say that because I can't deal with Frankie's worrying. She's unbearable. What if this, what if that. I don't know how you cope with her.'

Verity threw herself towards him and pummelled Red's chest with her fists. She'd never lost control with Red or even touched him before. Tonight was like a surreal painting, huge Dali strokes of madness and nonsense. 'Stop it! Stop saying such vile things!'

Red put out his hand and pushed her back. His strength was unexpected, and she was slammed back into the shower door, her spine banging against the cool glass.

'You know I never make New Year's resolutions,' Red said calmly as he reached into the pocket of his smooth black trousers. 'But for you...' He unfolded a piece of paper and she stared down at it.

Give V a baby.

He put his hand on her shoulder, the warmth of him soaking through her dress and into her skin. 'Everything I'm saying is for you. I care about you, V. I'm not stupid, I know you'll never leave Max. I'm just trying to give you what you want, to make you better. I'm not out to get you. I'm protecting you. From him, from all of them. Plus,' Red continued, on a roll, 'if the rumours are true, about what Max has done, and then you did get pregnant, then he couldn't really say much, could he? He'd have to admit he's been lying, which he'd never want...' Red's face fell as he saw Verity's confusion. 'Oh, I thought... Don't worry,' he said. 'I'm talking shit.'

'What rumours? What has Max done?'

'Nothing. I just, it's... it's... never mind. It's the whisky chatting. You know that.'

'Red, what rumours?' He was messing with her. This was all a weird joke, made all the more weird because she was so, so very drunk. But even if it was a joke, she needed to be far away from it. She needed to go, as soon as possible. She couldn't have people even joking about this kind of thing, about Max keeping secrets from her and doing something so destructive.

It couldn't be true. She took a deep breath and put her hand out to the doorframe to steady herself as Red began talking.

'Someone I've been working with on the church apartments... his wife is a receptionist at some clinic.'

Verity nodded, her body tensing. Fight or flight, they said. She'd been willing to fly with Max, to fly straight to a villa in France. But on her own?

'Apparently, Max had a vasectomy a while ago. After the last time you...'

Verity nodded again and put her hand up. She didn't need Red to say the bloody, hideous word. Miscarriage. Like she'd been pushing something along merrily in a fancy little carriage and then the wheels had fallen off.

Verity stared into Red's eyes. They were hazy with alcohol, but she could see real concern in them too. Maybe he really did care about her. Maybe he cared about her more than Max did, or Frankie, or any of them.

'So if I got pregnant, he'd know it wasn't his,' she said, as Red pulled her a little closer towards him.

He gently pushed a piece of hair from her face. 'He'd have to tell you his secret for you to tell him yours. Or maybe he wouldn't. Maybe he'd just go along with it. And then you'd have everything you wanted.'

Verity closed her eyes. Maybe Red, the one in the background, had been the one she needed to trust all along. Maybe Frankie and Max should just have each other, and this was what she should try instead of flitting off to France or Italy with lying, heartbreaking Max and his blank shots. Maybe, maybe, maybe.

Her eyes were still closed, the gleaming ceramic of the room too bright and blurred to cope with. But she felt Red come closer still, his sharp breath on her face, until his lips brushed hers.

Chapter Thirty-Three

ALICE

New Year's Eve

I had wanted to arrive at the New Year's Eve party with Luna, but she'd spent over an hour in our tiny bathroom and then disappeared from our flat without even bothering to say goodbye to me or tell me where she was going. By the time we needed to call a cab, she still wasn't home. She obviously hadn't bothered with the Bentley party. Maybe she wasn't so impressed by them after all. She'd seemed to adore Verity since her couple of trips to the gallery, but maybe now she was experiencing what I had as a teenager and found herself unable to penetrate their glossy bubble. A sense of satisfaction warmed me as I waited in the cold. I might tell Luna about America. Not everything, but enough to make her see that we were similar after all. Then I could reassure her that I'd almost managed it now. I'd had to do a last-minute change of plan, but we could stay here. I could get us both in, I was sure of it.

I dumped the crate of beer I'd brought on the front step and pulled my phone from my old black handbag so that I could message Luna as I waited for someone to open the door of the mansion. If she knew I was here, maybe she'd be more likely to come and join me later. Or if she didn't want to come, I could leave early and celebrate the New Year with her, in our flat. I could surely sneak out a bottle of Verity's champagne for us to share.

I imagined us clinking glasses. *Happy New Year! Our first of many in White Fir Lake.*

This might be our year after all.

I was still looking down at my phone when the door swung open, and at first I didn't even register who was standing there.

But then, I saw everything all at once.

'Luna?' I asked, even though I didn't need to. Here was my daughter, with her hair bleached a cheap version of Verity's, her body flaunted by a dress that was probably worth more than our flat.

'Hi,' she said breezily, gesturing for me to go in as though she owned the place.

'How have you done it?' My words spluttered out. How *had* she? How had she managed to slot in with these people without even trying, when I had made it my life's work and had only just edged open the door to their world? Tears of frustration filled my eyes, which I had tried so hard to line with a cheap kohl liner for the first time since I was a teenager.

'A home dye kit. It was pretty easy.'

'No, not your hair,' I said, rolling my eyes. It was clear how she'd done that – hours in our tiny bathroom without even bothering to tell me, then racing around here to show Verity the second it was done. Verity probably hated it, because it screamed cheap, but Luna wouldn't see that because she'd be so dazzled by them all. 'Being here, with them.'

Luna looked around and shrugged. 'Verity invited me here to get ready together. She let me borrow a dress. Why don't we put your beer in the kitchen?' Luna beckoned me to follow her as she tottered across the enormous hallway to what was less a kitchen, more a place where royalty might hang out and let chefs cook them tiny portions of ridiculous food. Even in my early life, when my parents were together and money floated around like bright autumn leaves, I hadn't ever seen a house like this.

I put the box of beer down amongst some weird feather decorations and expansive gold trays of cocktails in fancy glasses. I'd spent the early hours of the morning googling the particular beer brand because I didn't know the name of it, I just remembered that the label had paintbrushes on it: bright, primary school paintbrushes completely at odds with the contents of the bottle and everything about that night. Once I'd found out what it was called, I'd called twenty-nine niche alcohol stockists to find out if they had it. Then I'd driven two hours south to pick it up at the only one that did.

It was perhaps extreme behaviour. I knew that, of course I did. But I needed a way in other than Red now that I knew he was a dead end. I'd struggled and flitted for long enough, and this was where I belonged.

I'd listened to my favourite psychology podcast in the car on the way to buy the beer.

Fear, Dr Chander had explained to his guest, motivates people more than anything else.

'He's swimming well after only a few lessons.'

Frankie was telling me about a fancy baby spa she was taking Harry to, and as I nodded along at her, my vision moved slightly to the left, and that's when I saw Max.

He didn't notice me looking, so I was able to study him. I'd only seen him printed on paper for so long. In real life, he was slightly shorter than I'd always imagined him and his face was more lined than I thought it would be, although he was still red-hot beautiful. His voice carried slightly across the room, that drawl I had thought of for so long. The sound of the tide rushed in my ears. The crack of a skull. The taste of horror and fright.

I forced myself to turn away from him, to listen to Verity and Frankie talk about the spa. Luna had always wanted to go swimming when she was little. She'd never wanted dolls or little pink prams. But she liked crayons, and she liked water. I loved the idea of her in a pool, her lank hair transforming into mermaid waves and her awkward limbs suddenly balletic. But I couldn't even afford to take her to the grimy public baths.

'Wow,' I said. It was no wonder Red had no money left. 'Luna only ever went swimming with school. She didn't learn till she was about ten.'

'Frankie worries about water. About everything, actually,' Verity said with a wide and sisterly smile. 'She won't settle for a couple of school lessons, will you, Frankie?'

Inadequacy puddled in the bottom of my stomach. I hadn't wanted to *settle* for that either. I worried about everything too, actually; about Luna being so pale, so odd compared with the other kids at her school; about loving her properly and enough and being clever and charming enough for us to fit in wherever we moved to next. But nobody saw that, did they? They only saw that you cared if you had a nice husband and enough money for your children to wear soft white robes and a garden big enough to throw parties with a sky full of fireworks.

I looked away from them all, to the expanse of garden and lake outside. I could see Luna, her yellow hair shining in the moonlight. Her features were animated, not like they ever were when she was talking to me. Maisie and Bella stared up at her as though she were a celebrity, or an influencer or whatever the cool people were called these days.

Come on Luna, I could say to her. Pack up. We're leaving. This isn't the place for us.

But then what?

I was hovering around my overdraft limit already. If I wanted to stay here, time was running out.

Fear is a bigger driver of behaviour, both planned and instinctive, than most people are aware of, Dr Chander had said.

I had to go through with it.

There was no other way.

'Back in a minute,' I said to Frankie, who was eating canapé after canapé. 'Just going to grab a drink.'

Some invisible staff member had put my beers in a gigantic cooler for me, and as I took out a bottle, a pretty young waitress came over and zapped off the top without me even asking. I was back with Frankie within seconds, and looked beyond her, where Max still stood, holding court with some of his guests. I waited until he glanced my way, and then I met his eye as I took a slow swig of the beer.

His expression was even more intense than I'd imagined it to be; definitely fear, and perhaps a little anger too. But how could *he* be angry with *me*? His cool blue eyes bored through me, and I tore myself away from them to look at Frankie, who was saying something to me. I had to force myself to listen.

'That beer,' she was saying, staring at the bottle.

I smiled in what I hoped was a casual way. 'Yeah, cool, isn't it? I brought a whole crate. I thought Max might like it.'

'I didn't know you could get that here. I've only ever seen it in America.'

Was there really nothing about Max that Frankie didn't know? I looked to the side. He was still there, still staring at me.

'They sell it here,' I said to Frankie. 'You just have to look really hard for it. Are you some kind of beer specialist?' I couldn't help adding, my heart racing. Tonight was the night everything was going to change.

Frankie laughed and mumbled something about Cape Cod. So she'd had the beer there too. I should have known. She didn't dream that I'd been there with them, watching them, sleeping with Red before Frankie got him for herself to share a life of figs and nice clean bubble baths for their pretty, fortunate children. She didn't consider that I'd been there with him, creating Luna's very first cells under the white moonlight.

'Yeah, I used to go there too. Every summer. I was probably there at the same time as you. Do you think I might have been?' *Go on, ask how on earth my family afforded it*, I willed Frankie. But she didn't, because she was too nice for that. She just said 'possibly' and stared at the fairy-tale party around us. I glanced sideways but Max had vanished now, leaving me to deal with it alone yet again; the flashbacks of Jamie's fish eyes and the fear and the crunch of bone on rock. Nausea pushed its way through me, and I ran from the room, feeling the weight of people's eyes on me as I went.

I was always sick when I remembered it all. I always wondered if Max was too. After all, some of his fear must be the same as mine: a police officer turning up with a grainy image of us on a beach or a shard of old glass and a stack of questions about what we were doing one August night seventeen years ago. I made it to one of the downstairs toilets and heaved out acid and horror, then splashed my face with cold water and stared at myself in the mirror. My eyeliner had curdled in the corner of my eyes and smudged onto my cheeks. I shouldn't have bothered wearing it. I'd never bothered with it since that night in Chatham. I blamed makeup and a short denim skirt for everything that happened that night. Since then, until tonight, I'd lived in cardigans and washed my face with plain supermarket soap so that no man would even look at me or give me sinister chat-up lines about sunsets or drag me off to deserted places.

I patted my face dry with a soft white towel and left the bathroom to make my way back to the party, pushing my way through people and cutting through their conversations.

'Oh, and then the patio! Did I tell you about the patio? It's really a—'

'To be perfectly honest with you, I didn't think she'd ever pick up the violin again, but here we—'

'Of course you can tell! We're talking twenty grand's worth of surgery!'

And that's when I heard my name.

Verity had her back to me, and Frankie was flitting between talking to Verity and turning to Maisie, who obviously wanted her attention. Maisie was so pretty, so feminine in her little pink dress, so *normal*. Luna never wore a dress, never wanted to come to a party with me, never wanted my attention. Even tonight, she had slunk out on her own.

The band were playing out in the giant hallway. It was a slow, tinkling song that did nothing to cover up conversations.

They really should have gone for something louder.

'I'm feeling weird about Alice,' I heard Frankie say as there was a lull between notes. She didn't see me standing there. Her voice was conspiratorial, like it always was when she spoke to Verity.

Maisie said something then, about going outside. Frankie ignored her and said something else, something about Max, but I couldn't hear what it was over Maisie's voice and the band starting a new song.

I turned around. I'd heard enough anyway.

Chapter Thirty-Four

VERITY

New Year's Eve

'No!' Verity yelled, her eyes springing open. What was she *thinking*? Red jumped back and frowned, looking like a little boy.

'V, come on. I've explained to you everything you need to know; the way things really are. What Max has done... What Frankie has done. They're out to get you.'

Verity shook her head, her brain banging against the sides of her skull like a tennis ball. 'No.'

'Look,' Red said, his voice low. 'Frankie told me that you haven't been yourself lately. You're confused, and forgetful. It's the stress. Wanting and wanting, and never getting... it damages you, V. And you can have it! I'll give you what you want. You'll feel like a different person. You'll feel like everything makes sense.'

'You're the one who is confused, Red.'

He laughed, puffing out air that smelled of stale alcohol and smoke. 'How are you being so blind to this? Have you not seen the look in her eyes? She wants Max! So let her have him if he isn't giving you what you need!'

Verity suddenly, badly, wanted to see Frankie. She wanted to be in Frankie's gloriously full and busy kitchen. She wanted to try to ignore Frankie's delicious baked treats like she always did, to try and forget the wafts of cinnamon and sugar that floated past her starved senses. She wanted to ask about Frankie's marriage, about how Red *treated* her, for Christ's sake. They never spoke about Frankie's problems. Probably because it had never occurred to Verity before that Frankie had any problems. She'd always thought it was just Frankie, who had gorgeous children and most things she wanted, who admired Max from afar. And Verity had quite enjoyed that. She liked having something Frankie wanted. It felt like things were balanced out somehow.

'I'm a terrible friend,' Verity mumbled, her words horribly distorted, as though she needed to be tuned back in.

Red grabbed her arm. His hand was tight around her skin, his thumb pressing against her wrist bone. She expected to hear a snap, for her wrist to shatter into a hundred pieces of bloody bone china. 'You're an incredible friend,' he slurred. 'She's lucky to have you.'

'You're hurting me,' Verity said. If this were Max, they'd

be rolling around on the floor now. She'd be swiping at him, screaming at him with all the feeling and anger and love in the world. But with Red, she couldn't summon what she needed. It was *Red*, for crying out loud! Harmless, slightly tedious Red, still squeezing her poor wrist with his pale fingers.

Verity opened the door with her free hand, so that the sound of the party was suddenly loud. Someone said something about midnight, fireworks. There was a sharp crack of a broken glass and a spray of predictable applause.

Red still didn't let go of her wrist, even though people were close and might see him.

'Let go,' she hissed. 'I need to go and find Max.'

He let go then, throwing up both his hands and laughing. 'Okay, okay. Go and ask him about the rumours. Oh! And have this back, too. You really need to take more care of your stuff, V,' he said with a smirk as he tossed her phone towards her. She tried to catch it but missed and it clattered to the ground.

'You've had my phone?'

Red shrugged. 'No harm done. Just a bit of teasing on Instagram, that's all. People like the show you put on. And you shouldn't pretend you don't love being watched.'

Time seemed to stop. So it had been Red making her feel like she was going mad. Or making her go mad. She couldn't really tell the difference anymore.

'You wrote those letters, too, didn't you?' But the writing was always so feminine. She'd seen Red's handwriting a million times; blocky and unintelligent. 'Who did you get to write them for you?'

'Verity!' A guest had spotted her coming out of the bathroom. It was Georgia Bates, one of Frankie's mum friends from the school. She gazed past Verity to where Red was standing in the doorway of the bathroom still, inexplicably, hooting with mean laughter, ignoring her questions about the letters and her horror at what he'd told her.

'He's crazy,' Verity said to Georgia, crouching down to pick up her phone, all the blood rushing to her head. 'And I am going to find my husband.' She strode forward, but then her heel gave way and she stumbled.

'Are you okay?' Georgia asked as Verity straightened herself. 'We've been looking for Max but we couldn't find him. Or Frankie,' she added, her eyes wandering to Red again.

Vultures. Red had been right about that. But she had a point. Where was Frankie? Verity glanced at Red, too, who looked back at her smugly. She shook her head at him. No. Frankie had gone somewhere, hadn't she?

'I'm totally fine. Just a little bit too much champagne,' Verity said, taking exhausting care over her words so that they were carefree and tinkling. As she did, a satisfying memory slotted into her mind. Home! That was where Frankie was. Nowhere mysterious. Just home, to check on Red, because she had no idea he was here in the downstairs bathroom, trying to get Verity to sleep with him. 'Frankie popped home. She'll be back in a minute. And Max is probably in his studio,' she said. Damn. This woman would probably follow her there now. She gave a last smile and sped up.

'You're going to miss midnight if you don't hurry!' Georgia called after her.

The air took Verity's breath away as she headed out towards Max's studio. The light was on, so he was in there after all. She put her arms around her freezing chest and picked her way over the gravel. As she neared the door, she heard voices.

Was Frankie in there with him?

No. She was not. She would not be and could not be.

Verity swung open the door.

Chapter Thirty-Five

ALICE

New Year's Eve

A waiter passed me with a tray and I took two flutes of champagne from him. I downed them both, one after another, to try to mask the acrid taste of vomit in my mouth, as I listened to the chatter around me.

'The trees! They've all gone!'

'Oh, you must see it. Between you and me, those Bentleys are ruthless!'

'The lake is just right there!'

'Verity says it's not very deep at all. Imagine having your very own lake to paddle in!'

I'd thought I was so close to being their friend when I first arrived. But I saw now that I was nowhere near it;

never had been; never would be. Frankie's words would not leave my mind.

I'm feeling weird about Alice.

Frankie, who had normal daughters who'd probably curl up and watch films with her and tangle their limbs with hers and give her the odd hug, even when they were teenagers. She'd know how they smelt, their particular scents of sherbet lemon or coconut or strawberry or whatever they smelled of: nice girl fragrances. They'd tell her where they were going, text her about what they wanted for dinner and then turn up for it, perhaps with some polite friends who'd come round to do homework.

I didn't deserve this. I deserved to have the same things as they all did: nice homes where there were muffins baking and bright jumbles of expensive shoes at the front door; friends I could carelessly drop into conversation who would be there for me at the drop of an expensive hat.

When Max saw me with the beer, I'd imagined him pulling me into a side room and whispering to me and telling me, *Thank you, thank you, Alice, I'm so glad I could trust you. Yes, Alice, anything you need.*

But instead, Max had vanished.

And Frankie and Verity, my new *friends*, were judging me for not being able to afford baby spas, failing to trust me.

I crashed the glasses down on the piano in the hall and ignored the people looking at me. It wouldn't be me they'd be looking down their noses at soon.

I wouldn't cause any real harm.

I would just make them all see that these people weren't all that perfect. It wouldn't be very difficult.

I needed to find Luna, so I headed out to the garden. Frankie was nowhere to be seen, and Verity was floating around with Frankie's children in tow.

'Where's Luna?' I asked Verity. This house was too big. It seemed to swallow people whole like something from a horrible fairy-tale.

Verity batted her beautiful lashes at me slowly. 'Oh, she didn't feel too well. I sent her up to my bed a while ago. I wanted her to get a bit of rest before midnight.'

I spun around and left her. I didn't even know where Verity's bedroom was, but after what seemed like an age of tramping from room to room, I found it.

Luna was fast asleep, her newly yellow hair in its weird wedding pins stark against Verity's bright white pillow. I stood at the doorway for a time, just watching her.

When she was a toddler, I used to watch Luna sleep, amazed at how the lack of tension in her features made her look so angelic, so easy going. Now, I edged into the enormous room and gazed across at her, then sat down gently on the bed, moving so slowly and gradually that I was soon lying next to her without her even stirring.

She smelled of deep, musky roses, of black ink and a faint, sweet trace of ammonia.

I stood up again. I shouldn't wake her; shouldn't ask her what I'd been planning to ask her. Sleep was Luna's secret weapon. Her heart had been a challenge from early on, blighting us both. She'd been pale and dizzy for years now.

We didn't remember it any other way. Sleep was one of the only things that gave her a little more colour, a steadier step and a slightly louder voice. But she struggled to sleep in our flat with its noisy neighbours and hard bed.

If we only had a brighter home, a lighter existence. Maybe she'd be better.

Verity was going to get her into college, Luna had said the other day.

I watched her for a few more moments, and then left the room.

———————

I passed Red as I marched down the wide staircase. He barely looked at me, obviously preoccupied with something, or someone else. I glanced into the kitchen, where the children were at the chocolate fountain, watching in never-ending delight as thick chocolate tumbled down onto their marshmallows. Harry had chocolate all over his red trousers.

Nobody was watching them, except me.

I stepped towards them. Maisie glanced at me.

'Can you do something for me?' I asked, my voice hideously sweet.

Maisie frowned. 'Where's Luna? Is she still asleep?'

I nodded. 'Yes, and she wants you to help me with something.'

Bella held out a strawberry to me. 'White chocolate!' she cried in pure joy.

'Ooh!' I exclaimed. 'Bella, will you do something for me?' Maisie's eyes flitted from me to Bella, back to me, sharp with mistrust. She was like eight going on eighty.

'When Luna gets back,' Bella said, holding up a filthy finger to indicate that might only be one minute.

I'd been right with my original plan: Luna was the one they'd listen to. They wouldn't do anything I wanted them to. I pulled my phone from my pocket. I could still do it. It might show Max that his precious bubble wasn't so incredible after all; that if he was serious about ever being a parent, then he needed to surround himself with more responsible people.

I tapped out the message for Luna to see when she woke up.

I pressed send and then swung around, my eyes scanning the crowd.

It took me a long time to find him. But eventually, I remembered that he had his own art studio outside, in a separate building; big as a house itself. Of course he did.

My mouth went dry as I reached the doorway. I'd thought of this moment a million times in my mind, and in all of the versions I'd imagined, I'd known exactly what to say. Now, the words flew from my mind.

Max turned and stared at me as I opened the door. His eyes were hard, annoyed, just like they were when I turned up at the beach that night.

Go away.

'Why are you here?' he asked. His voice was neutral, as though he were speaking to a stranger. But I was no stranger. We'd shared a life-changing moment. He'd saved me. And then I'd kept his secret and saved him.

'Why shouldn't I be here?' I glanced around the room. Huge canvases were leaning against one another, splashed with the confident designs that I'd been following for years, first on his website, then in fancy, overpriced department stores and on Instagram.

He ran his hands through his hair. 'I don't know why you've never been able to just leave me alone.'

'Because I didn't want to.' He never asked any of the others to leave him alone, did he? Frankie, Verity, Red. They'd swarmed around him constantly and he'd never tried to swat them away. 'You could have just replied to me.'

'What would that have achieved? I wanted to move on with my life, not remember that night.'

'You've never told anyone, I gather.'

He laughed, threw his hands up in the air. 'Why? Why on earth would I have told anyone that? I know you probably don't go to many dinner parties, but believe me, it's not really the topic of conversation you normally get into.'

I stared at him, blood rising in my head. 'You're right. I haven't been to many dinner parties. I've been busy living in bedsits and cleaning other people's shit off their toilets to pay for it. But you wouldn't care about that, would you?'

'No. I don't care. Why would I? I barely know you. I

253

saved you, I did something terrible, and we both moved on.'

'You think I moved on?' I closed my eyes briefly and leaned against the door. That night returned to me yet again. Red's uncertain teenage hands on my body, his cool, pale skin against mine, his bitter jealousy of Max and search for satiation with a girl who said what he wanted to hear.

'You know that Luna is Red's child?' I said to Max.

Max stared at me, cogs whirring. 'What did you just say?'

I shrugged. 'It's pretty obvious, really. If you'd all noticed me on that holiday, really noticed me, and noted how much time has passed, and how old Luna is, you'd all have known straight away. But you notice nothing other than yourselves, do you?'

Max covered his face with his hands then dropped them. 'So why have you been writing to me? Why not Red?'

'I didn't even know who Red was until recently. But I knew who you were because you're all over the place, aren't you? I just wanted to be part of your life, Max. I wanted—'

Max stepped towards me so that I could smell brandy on his breath. 'What *did* you want?'

As I considered this, my phone beeped. It was Luna. I typed out a quick message back and then looked at Max again. 'I wanted to be one of you all. I was there too, that summer, but you never included me! I was falling apart, and you all made me feel worse.'

Max laughed. 'So why did you want to be one of us if we're so terrible?'

Could he not see it? The beauty, the easy touching of one another, the laughing and the money. 'I deserved it. My parents lost all of their money. I would have been there every summer after that if they hadn't. But I couldn't be. So I found you and wrote to you instead. I thought you'd want to hear from me. I thought it would make you realise we should be friends. We'd shared so much.'

'You should have just let it go,' said Max. 'Those horrible letters. I tried to hide them from Verity but she saw them. I won't have you making her ill. You need to leave.'

'I'm not making her ill. I brought Luna here. Verity loves her.'

Max's face fell. He knew I was right. I'd seen something that Verity needed, just like a good friend would.

'I've seen her with Frankie's kids. She wants her own. Luna is the next best thing. Like a younger sister and a daughter all rolled into—'

'STOP!' Max roared at me. 'You might have got away with hounding me, but you leave Verity out of this.'

'I've managed to make friends with Verity and Frankie,' I said, pushing the unease of Frankie's words about me away. 'Turns out I didn't need you for that. You're not as important as I thought. But I need money to stay here,' I continued, as though he hadn't just screamed in my face, even though I was trembling. 'Red has none, so that's a dead end.'

Max shook his head. 'You know that you sound like something out of a terrible film? I'm not giving money to some random woman.' He came closer still and set his hands down on my shoulders. His eyes were even more blue this close up. Oh, to be so beautiful. 'You need to stop playing silly little games, and you need to speak to Red about this idea you have about Luna being his, and then—'

'If you don't give me money, I'll tell them all,' I blurted out. 'I'll put it all over the internet. I'll tell Verity. Max killed a man.'

He stepped back.

'You can't,' he said. 'I can't have Verity knowing that. It'll crack her. She won't be able to take it.'

I shrugged. 'So then give me some money. I'll need enough for a deposit for a new place and then some help each month. I'll get a job, eventually. I'm going to be a counsellor.' I smiled at the thought. A plush office with a box of tissues on the table, talking people through their troubles so that nobody felt alone.

He was silent. We heard the distant buzz of the party: laughter, clinking, shouting.

I felt something behind me, a brush of a hand against my skin. I turned around and saw Luna.

'It's almost midnight,' she said. 'Do I really need to—'

I sighed. 'Go back to the house. I'll be there in a minute.'

She rolled her eyes and turned around. I watched her retreat, swinging her hips. She'd picked up Verity's mannerisms like viruses. She obviously wasn't going to do as I asked, then. I knew she wouldn't. She'd listen to other people in a heartbeat, but me: never.

'I'm going inside my house for New Year,' Max said. 'And you should go home.'

I stood across the doorway and crossed my arms. 'Forget

the monthly help. One lot to set me up and it can stay our secret. Luna's ill, you know. She needs a better life.'

'I'm not *doing* it!' he yelled.

'You know, I've done you a favour, keeping your secret for so long. I've carried so much for you.' I really had. Red's jealousy, wrapped up in a blanket, staring up at me with his eyes.

'*You* have carried so much for *me*? Are you joking? I did something that I've had to carry for all these years to save you. And this is how you repay me? I won't agree. Not to any of it. My money is Verity's money too. Giving even a penny of it to you would be a betrayal. I will never betray her, do you understand?'

'A betrayal worse than keeping a secret like this from her, for all these years?'

A countdown started from the house, carried over to us on the frozen breeze.

Ten, nine, eight, seven.

'I could even tell everyone that Luna is yours.' It was my last bullet, and I fired it casually, hoping to get him right in the chest.

But he dismissed it with a wave of his hand. Swatting me away yet again. 'Get out of my way.'

Six, five, four.

'It's easily done. A bit of your DNA on the test kit I have. Then you'd have to give me money all the time. It would be public knowledge, in all your magazines.'

'You'd do that to Luna? You're sick. You need help.'

I took the New Year's resolution from my pocket. 'Then I'll give this to Verity. I'll tell her everything.'

Someone cleared their throat behind me and I spun around. 'Luna, just go back in!' I yelled.

But it wasn't Luna this time.

Three, two, one.

'Tell me everything about what?' Verity asked as fireworks bloomed in the sky above.

Chapter Thirty-Six

VERITY

New Year's Eve

'Tell me everything about what?' Verity asked. Fireworks rumbled in the air. Damn. She never, ever missed their New Year's Eve fireworks.

Yet here she was.

Alice smiled at her: a pearly toothed grin so banal Verity could scream. Maybe she would scream, right now, at the top of her voice. Verity had braced herself for Frankie being in here with Max, even though she couldn't bear to admit it to herself. But she hadn't expected this. Max barely knew Alice. He'd never even met her before tonight.

'Verity,' Max said. 'There's nothing to tell.'

'Oh?' Alice raised one of her pale brows. 'Really, Max?

Because that's not how I see it. I think your wife should probably know what you've been hiding all these years, and what you're capable of.'

Verity felt sick. Why was everyone saying terrible things about Max tonight?

'Max?'

Max shot Alice a look of venom, a look she'd never seen on his face before. 'Verity, please. Don't listen to her. She's crazy!'

Crazy. That's what she'd just told Georgia Bates about Red. Maybe they were all crazy, and that was the problem.

'I think Verity can decide that for herself,' Alice said, her vanilla voice cutting through the mesh of thoughts in Verity's mind. She handed a crumpled piece of paper to Verity, and Verity stared down at it. 'I used my own paper, Verity,' Alice said. 'I wouldn't dream of taking something of yours.'

The words, which swirled beneath her eyes, said nothing special. Verity had seen lots of similar ones over the years.

Make a new life for myself.

No, the words themselves weren't important, or not that Verity could see. They were words that people said all the time, that she'd even said to herself lately as she imagined drinking red wine with Max in a chic French village. But the feminine handwriting, looping and curling, and the paper, with a fat little bear clutching a tacky heart in the corner, made Verity's own heart thud to the bottom of her stomach.

'I thought it was Red,' she said slowly. 'Red has been messing with my stuff. Are you in this together?'

Alice hooted. 'I wish!' she said.

'You need to go,' Max said. He gestured wildly as though Alice were a goose that might flap and bite. 'Out! Out!'

Alice didn't move but grinned at Verity. 'He wants me out because he's worried I'll upset your little apple cart. He's ignored me all these years and hoped that I'll go away. But someone should know what he did.'

Verity heard screaming, and wondered vaguely if it were her own screaming, only it was quieter than she would expect it to be. She put her hands up to her mouth and found it closed, her lips sticky with the gloss she'd applied... when? She couldn't remember.

Max frowned, and Alice stopped smiling her stupid smile, gazing past Verity, past the open studio door.

Fireworks popped and banged against Verity's mind.

And then Max was running, and Alice was following.

'Someone's in the lake,' Max shouted, his words whipping about in the icy night.

'But it's freezing,' Verity said, confused. 'Who would go into the lake in the freezing cold? We need to get them out!' She began to run too, her heels flying over the gravel.

'It's deep in there,' Max shouted from ahead, although Verity wasn't sure who he was telling.

'I thought you said the lake was only shallow?' Alice said as Verity caught up with her.

Verity thought as they approached the house. Had she said that? She had no idea. She said all sorts these days just to move time along and make people think she was okay. 'I don't know,' she said dumbly as Alice ran past her, pushing her out of the way.

Chapter Thirty-Seven

FRANKIE

New Year's Eve

F rankie reached the party just as the last firework bloomed in the black sky above the house. It was strange, Frankie thought as she huffed and puffed her way through the people in the kitchen, how it felt so different now. The party had a completely different atmosphere to when she'd left. What had seemed like an elegant build-up now felt more like a shrill buzz of hysteria. Her world had tilted and taken the party and everyone there with it.

But as she looked at more and more faces, all turned in the same direction, like a load of shop mannequins, she realised that it wasn't just her perception of things at all.

Something had happened.

She looked for Verity, for Red or Max or anyone who might tell her that what she had found at home had been planted there, that everything was okay. Verity might tell her that she left her bra there by mistake (In Red's drawer? Come on, Frankie). But none of them were there. Perhaps they were in the garden, where everyone seemed to be staring towards the lake.

'What's everyone looking at?' she asked a woman next to her who she recognised as Lucia, the hairdresser who had done her blow-dry yesterday. *This is like a dream*, she thought. Everything impossible yet possible; bizarre and familiar all at once.

'There are people in the lake,' Lucia said.

Frankie nodded, and relief rushed through her. Ah, so that was it. Verity had actually been serious about the skinny-dipping and people were watching her. *See*, Frankie thought, *you do love people looking at you, V.* Perhaps Max was out there too. But then, where was Red? And where were the—

'Children,' Lucia said. 'Up to their necks in that freezing water. Someone's gone in after them. I hope they get out okay. They've already pulled out a...' Her voice faded into nothing as Frankie ran past the crowd that had gathered around something in the garden. Someone shouted at her, and she ignored them.

Children up to their necks.

She ran and ran, the cloying scent of pine suffocating her. Pine was meant to smell of Christmas carols and happiness, not of black lakes and white-hot fear.

She ran.

There were barely any children at the party other than her own.

The water lapped against her feet.

'Don't go in there!' someone shouted. A lone firework popped over the lake, lighting it up so that she saw the scene perfectly for a split moment in time.

Alice in the water, a small body slumped over her shoulder, and Luna further back still, her face pale, dragging Bella – *Bella!* – Frankie's precious Bella, soaking wet and terrified, towards the shore. But then there was darkness again.

Frankie was propelled forward, wading into the water. It bit at her ankles, making her want to scream out in agony. Her breath was cut short.

'We've got them all! Go back!' Alice shouted. 'Frankie, go back!'

Another firework boomed in the sky, fragments of red showering down on them, illuminating Alice again and making Frankie scream as she saw that the body over Alice's shoulder was Harry.

But it couldn't be. Harry had been in his cot less than an hour ago. He'd had his blue bear and he'd been wearing his sleeping bag with boats on.

Except she'd seen the blue bear and the sleeping bag with boats on discarded in the cot. Red had got him up and brought him here. And now he was in the lake, his body limp. He was wearing his Ralph Lauren trousers, which Frankie had bought from one of the gorgeous little baby boutiques in the village the other day, telling Red they were a hand-me-down from one of the school mums.

But it could not be Harry.

Harry in the lake, Bella in the lake, Red God knows where. 'Maisie!' Her voice was warped with horror and cold. 'Where's Maisie?'

Chapter Thirty-Eight

FRANKIE

New Year's Day

Frankie couldn't remember when the ambulance arrived. She had no recollection of when or how she'd arrived at the hospital.

Words and faces swirled in her mind.

Harry swallowed a lot of water.

Secondary drowning.

Lungs.

I know this is a difficult time for you, Mrs Redmond.

Your husband has passed away.

His heart condition, combined with the cold water.

We'll never know.

Unconscious.

Some do make full recoveries.

It was as though someone had thrown a million-piece jigsaw at Frankie and she had to make sense of the fragments.

Alice, Harry, Luna and Bella in the lake.

Red lying on the ground with a soaking-wet Max and another man, whose name she couldn't remember, next to him, surrounded by a crowd so big that Frankie didn't even notice them as she ran past.

Red had already gone, Frankie. He went when he was in the water. There was nothing you could have done.

I could have asked him why Verity's bra was in his drawer, Frankie wanted to say. I could have told him Luna was his daughter. I could have asked if he knew. I could have told him I'd found out about his obsession with Verity, realised he lived for her and had stolen her things and made her think she was losing her mind.

One elderly party guest who'd obviously had a lot of cocktails had told Frankie that Red had dived straight into the water as soon as he'd seen Luna in difficulty. 'But he shouted, "Hang on, Verity!" – which doesn't make sense, does it?' The woman had paused, annoyed by this inconvenient, dangling thread in her story.

Frankie thought of when she arrived at Verity's earlier that night, finding Luna sitting at the dressing table with Verity's hair and Verity's dress. Even Frankie had made the same mistake. 'Oh, it makes perfect sense.'

Now, Frankie leaned over and touched Harry's hair, and her fingers slid across to the smoothness of his temple. His skin was so new, so untouched by life. But his lungs, his brain? Too early to tell the neurocognitive outcome, the doctor had said, as though Frankie might know what in the world that meant.

She'd turned to her side a couple of times to see what Red thought, to ask if he thought Harry would pull through, to see if he hated her for not being there when her children needed her.

But, of course, Red wasn't at her side anymore. There was just a hospital bay that smelled of sour hope and disinfectant, the constant scurrying and beeping of activity at odds with the silence of Harry.

She closed her eyes briefly as a tidal wave of emotion threatened to grip her and pull her under. No. She couldn't let that happen. Harry could wake up at any minute, and when he did, he needed to see Frankie in control. She couldn't be thinking of something else, like she always had been before. She needed to be different now.

'Any change?' Frankie's mum put a hand on Frankie's shoulder as she returned with coffees for them both.

Frankie shook her head.

'Your father's just phoned me. Maisie and Bella are doing okay. They're making him watch Cinderella.'

'How's Bella? Is she still...' Alive? Healthy? The image of Bella's little lips, tinged blue and juddering violently, kept returning to Frankie, even though the paramedics had assured Frankie that there was no damage, that hypothermia hadn't set in. She'd been very lucky, the male paramedic had said, judgement all over his face.

'Maisie knew best. Better than anyone,' Frankie said to Ruth. 'She was the one who told the adults that the others were in the lake, you know. If she hadn't done that straight away, then I...' She suddenly felt the urge to squeeze Maisie, her little know-it-all Maisie, so tightly that she could feel her heartbeat and the tiny hairs on her arms and smell her peach shampoo and sugary breath.

'Luna wanted us to go in,' Maisie had told Frankie.

Luna's a psychopath, darling.

As far as Frankie could tell from the scattered bits of story she'd been told, it had been a domino effect.

Luna had taken in Bella.

Red had gone in to save them.

Max had gone in to get Red out.

Harry must have followed Max.

Alice went in to get Harry out.

It was like a hideous nursery rhyme, up there with the worst of them: witches and goblins and trolls under bridges.

'Maisie has her head screwed on, alright,' Ruth said.

'I was going to tell her not to be such a know-it-all,' Frankie said dully. 'I got it all so wrong.'

'You didn't know.' Ruth handed Frankie her coffee, the smell curling into Frankie's nostrils and making her feel nauseous.

Tears threatened to overtake Frankie and she took a wobbly breath. 'I'm so, so angry with Luna.'

'We don't know what happened yet, Frankie, or why they were in there. Sit tight before you go blaming yourself, or other people.'

'Frankie?'

Luna stood nearby in a mismatched tracksuit, her hair

an unpleasant tone of yellow-green. 'Can I talk to you?' she asked quietly, her voice hoarse.

Frankie glanced at her mother. Ruth would get rid of her.

But Ruth stood up. 'I'll go and find us some sugar,' she said. 'This coffee's appalling.'

———

Frankie watched as Luna stared at Harry for a while.

'He might not wake up,' she said simply to Luna.

I'm sorry, Luna might say.

Please forgive me.

I never meant for this to happen.

Would Frankie forgive her? Could she?

Luna turned to Frankie, her eyes laden with misery.

This was it.

'Frankie… I…' She fixed her eyes on Frankie's. 'I don't know why you wanted us to go in the water.'

Chapter Thirty-Nine

FRANKIE

New Year's Day

Frankie had a sudden, crazed urge to laugh. She had to have heard wrong.

But Luna carried on, her voice barely there. 'When Mum said you wanted the girls to go in the lake in the freezing cold, I thought it was weird.'

'I didn't want them to go in!' Frankie said, cold horror creeping over her skin. Were these more lies? She couldn't keep track of what was the truth anymore. *I'm not sure about Alice,* Frankie had said to Verity. *'Don't let her in your life so easily. Don't let Luna into your bedroom, because do you really know her? No, you don't.'*

But then Frankie had gone and left her children alone with Luna and Alice.

272

Clues everywhere, and she'd missed them after all. She wasn't as clever as she thought she was.

'I had to go home,' Frankie told Luna. She stared at Harry as she spoke. An oxygen mask covered most of his face. His eyes flickered and her body tensed. 'I had no choice. There was something important to deal with.' It occurred to her that Luna might know about Red being her father, that Frankie might be the last to find out. But she couldn't take that on now. If she carried one more thing, she'd drop it all.

'I was trying to find you,' Luna said. 'I looked everywhere. Mum had sent me a message to say you wanted me to take Maisie and Bella into the lake, and I wanted to check with you first.'

'Why would she do that? What was she trying to do? Was she trying to harm us?' Frankie stood up as another chill ran through her. Alice was probably behind this little visit from Luna too. Some psycho plan to pull out Harry's wires or poison Frankie. It was frightening. 'You shouldn't even be here, Luna. You need to go.'

Luna stared up at her with sad, red eyes, and Frankie realised that this was just a child, possibly Red's child.

But Red wasn't here anymore.

If Red wasn't here, then why had Frankie torn up her New Year's resolution? Perhaps she hadn't ever wanted to be a surrogate for Verity, because if she had and he was gone now, why wasn't she jumping at the chance? Frankie's mind worked slowly, pulling pieces of wreckage of the last day together to try and make some kind of recognisable shape. But it was impossible.

Frankie sat back down and put her head in her hands. 'Your mum could be done for manslaughter, you know. If...' She motioned to Harry but the words wouldn't come.

'She didn't want to hurt anyone,' Luna said quickly.

'Well, what did she want?' Frankie's voice rose and she pulled it back so that her words ended up sounding strangled.

'I don't know,' Luna mumbled.

'You haven't asked her?'

'No.'

Frankie wanted to scream, to shake Luna by her weedy shoulders. She was so much like Red used to be. It was so obvious now. Why hadn't it been this clear straight away? 'So how do you know that she didn't want to hurt us?'

'In her message, she only told me to paddle a bit. Not go right the way in.'

'Show me her message,' Frankie said, holding out her hand. 'I want to see exactly what it said.' She felt like she was trying to extrapolate a true story of why someone got pinched or was crying or had a mountain of hidden sweet wrappers under their pillow or was still awake at 10 p.m. She hated doing that whole 'Who started this? Tell me the truth'; never had the time for it. Red had always been better at it than her.

Frankie had loved him. Hadn't she?

'I've deleted it.'

Frankie took her coffee from the little bedside table and stirred it. The police would be able to retrieve the messages if it came to it. Stay calm, Frankie.

'What did it say?' she asked again.

Luna looked as though she was going to cry. 'She just put something like, "Let the girls paddle in the lake, Frankie's orders." I couldn't believe it, so I replied and said that it was way too cold, but Mum said you'd be annoyed if I didn't do it.'

'Why on earth would I ask for my tiny children to be taken into a freezing lake? In the dark? Do you really think that's the kind of mother I am?' Oh God, but what kind of mother was she to invite Alice into all of their lives? She had made her coffee and given her wine and canapés; she'd showed off her dazzling life that she shared with Verity. She'd sensed Alice's envy, and she'd got off on it. Frankie always used to be the envious one. It was so nice to be on the other side that she'd completely missed what she was meant to be looking at. Maybe this was all because of envy: a feeling that Frankie had carefully watered so that it bloomed into a huge, ugly flower.

'Mum said it was part of a surprise, or something. And she said Verity wanted me to do it too. She said you were both going to be in there.' Luna's voice rose, and Frankie glanced at Harry. She didn't want him to wake up and see Luna, hear her frenzied words. 'She said Verity told her it was really shallow, so I didn't think it would be dangerous. I don't ever go to parties like that. I didn't know if it might just be some cool trick they were going to do. Like light up the lake or something. Some kind of a show.'

Frankie grimaced. So that was what their lives were: so grotesque and ostentatious that nobody knew what normal behaviour was anymore.

'Even when we were in there, and Red had been pulled

out, I thought you were going to pop up. I was so frightened.' Luna started rocking slightly now, backwards and forwards in her ugly plastic hospital chair. 'I was hoping and hoping that it was a joke, maybe, or a show, like I said. I thought Red might suddenly stand up in the water and laugh and be totally fine. But then I saw Max's face as he was pulling Red out with the other man. He was so horrified and frightened, and I knew. I knew how stupid I'd been. I didn't want Max to be upset with me.'

Frankie stared at Luna as she rocked, forwards and backwards again and again. Not another person obsessed with Max. Although really, could she blame Luna? Frankie would die if she thought Max was upset with her, too. She reached out to Luna. Her hand brushed Luna's bony shoulder, and the rocking stopped. 'Did nobody try to stop you going in?' she asked.

Luna sniffed: an ugly, waterlogged grunt. 'Nobody really noticed. I think they were all drunk. I couldn't see Verity anywhere either, but I thought she would appear to be a part of whatever you both had planned. So I just took the girls to the edge. Maisie wouldn't go anywhere near the water. She said she'd stay behind. So I took off Bella's shoes for her, because I didn't want to get them wet. And the water was so cold. But she didn't care. She just threw herself in, and I couldn't keep hold of her. I shouted at her to come back. I'm not a good swimmer, and she was so fast.'

'She's been to a lot of lessons,' Frankie said, almost proud, and then felt a punch to the gut as she remembered Harry next to her. Poor Harry, who hadn't been to a swimming lesson in his life. And whose fault was that? 'Go on.'

'I tried to keep up with her but it was so, so cold, and I started to panic. We were getting further out and it was getting darker and darker.' Luna put her skinny hands up to her face. 'I didn't know Harry was even at the party. I hadn't seen him before that point. But then I saw Red at the shore, and Harry behind him. Red told Harry to stay where he was, but Harry wanted to follow him. I could see it all as it happened, and I was trying to shout at the same time as catch up with Bella. Red wasn't even listening to me. He seemed so determined to get to me. I think he thought I was Verity,' she said, looking down and blushing pale red. She looked up again. 'He was shouting her name. But then he saw Bella too and that seemed to be when he started to struggle.' A low groan emitted from deep inside Luna and turned into a sob.

Intense emotions, such as fear, can trigger heart attacks, especially in those with genetic heart conditions.

The ward seemed to spin around Frankie and she thought she might be sick again. When they'd first arrived, she'd been sick in the corridor and it had splashed onto her ankles and her soggy, strappy gold shoes. She looked down. There were still yellow specks of vomit crushed between the straps. She'd have to throw them away. They'd cost a fortune. Red would go mad.

No, he wouldn't. Red wasn't here anymore.

Frankie swallowed down acid that had started to rise in her throat. 'What did you tell the police?' she asked. They'd been crawling all over Max and Verity's garden, and then they'd appeared at the hospital too. They'd asked her questions in between inane small talk, as though Frankie's husband hadn't just died and her tiny boy wasn't hooked up to a load of plastic tubes to help him breathe. 'It's always a busy one, New Year's,' the policeman had said in such a casual way that Frankie had wanted to kick him. But now she saw. They were hiding this from her in case she went after Alice. She could understand that, but they'd better be taking it seriously on her behalf; getting to the bottom of why on earth Alice had done it. She'd get a restraining order, at least, surely. There was no way Frankie could let that woman near her children, near Verity. She was probably being questioned right now. They would be making sense of it all, getting the answers that Frankie was so desperate for.

Luna looked frightened. 'I told them that I took them into the water because Bella really wanted me to,' she said, her voice low. 'It wasn't a lie. Bella did want to.'

Frankie stared at Luna, registering what she'd said before about deleting the messages. 'You didn't tell them what your mum did?'

Luna was silent and held her gaze. Harry's machine beeped and nurses laughed to one another at the station in the centre of the ward. A car beeped its horn outside and snow flurried against the window. The world carried on around them.

Chapter Forty

ALICE

2 January

I t had been nothing like I'd imagined.

When would I learn that nothing ever was?

The garden had smelled of rank water and dead pine. Max was already wading through the lake when I got there. He was with another man and they were pulling at someone, an adult. My heart stilled as I saw that it was Red, his head flopping forwards. Luna was further out in the water with Bella, and she was motioning to me, pointing to the shore.

'It's deeper than it looks,' a woman to my side wailed.

'They'll be frozen to the bone,' said her husband.

And it continued, on and on.

'Why on earth were they in there?'

'He looks like he's had some kind of fit or something. Unless he couldn't swim?'

I wanted to scream at them all to be quiet. Luna was too far away for me to hear her, and the lake was so dark. Nobody else had noticed, but she was telling me something.

Max was struggling with Red, and the water was rippling, silver and secretive.

And then I followed Luna's wild gesturing and saw an arm. A tiny arm, flailing and falling.

I ran and ran, and then I dived in, prepared in no way for the cold that was to come.

———

I'd imagined midnight as a flurry of fancy fireworks. Colours blooming in the sky. Luna at the sidelines, chewing her nails. People gossiping in that way they did round here.

'What are those children doing, paddling in that cold water without their parents?'

'Who are their parents?'

'Oh, Frankie and Red. But they're not here. They seem so perfect but…'

'It's rather dangerous. Someone should be watching them.'

'It's partly Verity and Max's fault that the children have ended up in there, don't you think? They chopped down the trees.'

'You'd think there'd be a barricade, wouldn't you?'

'Or a responsible adult.'

And so it would go on until I arrived, and saved the children from anything terrible happening.

'Alice is the only sensible one out of the lot of them,' they'd all say. *'She might have saved their lives.'*

'They're so lucky to have her.'

'You did as I said,' I told Luna. 'I didn't think you would.'

We were sitting in Luna's bedroom. I'd never sat in there with her before. It was neat, because she didn't have many belongings: a few short piles of art magazines, the odd dirty sock. A crisp packet on the bedside table. We'd left Verity and Max's mansion days ago, but it seemed like only minutes. People had clapped me on the shoulder as I left.

Red was dead, and people had clapped me on the shoulder.

I was a hero.

'You never do as I say,' I told Luna. I let out a sad little laugh. 'What a night to start listening to me.'

Luna glowered. 'Red died because of me. Harry might die. He's just a baby. And you're laughing?'

'Harry will *not* die! And it was not because of you, Luna!' I shocked myself with my shouting. Luna looked at me, wide-eyed and taken aback. I took a breath. 'None of this was just because of you,' I said more quietly. 'You know that. Don't you?' My Luna. My little shock daughter, who had stared up at me with so much newborn faith that it made me want to run far, far away. The trust had been too much in those early days when she seemed so embryonic that she was barely human, but it had slowly ebbed away so that I hadn't thought any of it was left. Luna never did as I said.

Sometimes, Dr Chander said on his podcast – in fact, oftentimes – people have much more control than they think they have. Ah, I'd thought. But I don't! Not me. Not Alice, at the periphery whilst other people have fun and fortune. No, there was no way I had more power than I thought.

Red was dead. Gone.

His heart could have done this at any point, the doctors had told Frankie, who had told Luna, who had told me.

And Harry would simply have to wake up. He would wake up. He would wake up and everybody would be so thrilled about that, they'd all forget why he was even in the water and who pulled him out. There would be nobody to blame and no heroes.

Luna sipped the cup of tea I'd made her. She was silent.

'What did you think of him?' I asked her. 'Of Red, I mean.'

She wrinkled up her nose, implying my stupidity.

'Did you like him?' I offered.

She thought for a moment. 'I barely knew him.'

So she hadn't guessed, then.

'For the best, I suppose,' I said.

Luna yawned and flopped back down on her unmade bed. Her limbs, suddenly so adult these days, folded beneath her.

'Luna,' I began. She didn't move, just lay staring at the ceiling. 'The police. Have they... have you...'

'Bella wanted to go in the lake,' Luna said immediately,

sitting up. Her cool green eyes pierced mine. 'That's what happened. So that's what I told them.'

'And Frankie?'

She looked down. 'I told her about the messages. But I told her they'd been deleted. I would deny it if she tried to tell anyone that's what happened.'

'But why?'

She shrugged. 'Because. If I tell them the truth, what then?'

I stared at Luna. She'd probably be taken in by Verity, or even Frankie if she knew the truth about Red. Perhaps Max had already told Frankie. She'd probably be safer than she'd ever been before: cared for, surrounded by art and money.

'Yeah,' I said. 'What then?'

Chapter Forty-One

VERITY

2 *January*

'Verity? What the hell are you doing?'

Verity didn't turn around but instead carried on scrabbling in the mud. She'd bought the little trees from the nearby garden centre. She'd never been there before. Why would Verity Bentley ever have been to a garden centre? She and Max had gardeners, and anyway, she wasn't a boring old person. The garden centre had been closed on New Year's Day, so she'd had to wait until this morning. She was their first customer, the man opening the doors had told her with a smile, as though the world hadn't just crumbled down to the ground.

'Are you... do you know what you're doing down there?' Max asked now as he reached her in the garden.

She squinted up through the weak sunlight. 'How hard can it be? We should never have chopped them down. None of this would have happened.' *Hills Daily* had forgone the collage of photos they'd normally include in a feature about a Bentley party for a rather grim headline: *LAKE HOUSE OF HORRORS*. She hadn't dared read it and Max had swiped it away, never to be seen again. But it was out there, circulating, seeping into people's days and conversations.

'Verity, I'm not sure they are the right kind of trees,' Max said patiently. 'And you're filthy. I think you need to come inside. I'll run you a bath.'

'Harry could die, Max. It was our fault. And you think a bath will solve it?' She didn't mention Red. There was too much to think about where he was concerned. She didn't even know what had happened and what she'd dreamed or hallucinated, maybe. Frankie had been at the hospital this whole time, so Verity hadn't seen much of her to talk things through. She needed to be there for her more, to do more for her best friend. She was going to visit Harry this afternoon, and at least she'd be able to tell Frankie that she'd planted some trees.

It won't happen again, Frankie! None of your other children or husbands will end up drowning in my garden, thank goodness!

Max took a deep breath and then exhaled a little cloud of silver air. He'd told her it wasn't their fault a thousand times, but it was, it *was*! 'I'm not going to London tonight.'

'You have to. The whole exhibition is about you.' They'd all know, of course. They'd all be talking about him, whispering about irresponsible partying and people dying in open water and all sorts. No wonder he didn't want to go.

'I need to be here for you.'

Verity sat back on her heels and arched her spine. 'I don't need you. I have plans.' Max would never agree to Luna coming to the house. He wanted to wash his hands of all of them. Of course he did. She looked down at her own hands, which were black with soil. Out, damned spot!

'You need to rest, V. Come on. Come in.' He put his hand on her shoulder so softly that she could barely feel it. She flinched, and he took it away again.

'I don't want to come inside with you,' she said. The words she wanted to say rose up in her throat. They'd kept getting stuck there. *You told me about Alice, and the man on the beach. You told me you burned all of her letters. You told me you never, ever replied to her.*

'But you didn't tell me about your other secret, did you, Max?' She hadn't realised she had spoken out loud until she heard her words.

Max shook his head. 'I have no other secrets from you, Verity.'

'Red said you had one more. A big one.' *You ended one life and now you're preventing another. Do you think you're God?* Maybe it was Verity's fault. She'd acted like Max was God since the day she'd met him. They all had. Maybe he'd taken the deifying a little too seriously.

'You said yourself, Red had big problems. He was a pathological liar. He tried to sleep with you, for God's sake.' Verity had apparently told Max this at the end of the night, but she didn't really remember it clearly anymore. She only remembered that Red had told her something awful, too awful, about Max.

'But you kept one secret from me. Why not another?'

Max sighed but didn't answer. They hadn't really got anywhere since before the party, had they? Pinging and ponging, backwards and forwards. Both equally good at the game.

'I was there,' Verity said next, digging deeper, cool, grey stones snagging against her trowel and jolting her whole body. She kept doing this: jumping from secret to secret. It would go on and on forever. 'I was there that night, in America, when you did it. You could have told me then. You could have let me in. But you didn't. You kept it from me all this time.'

'Verity, I've told you why. I didn't want you to have to carry it for me. It was so long ago.'

'But we're meant to carry things together. I told you about Betsy straight away, didn't I? I never kept that from you. I couldn't, even if I'd wanted to.'

She remembered that night in America, leaning against his broad chest, telling him about the pool they had when she was younger. Telling him that it was her fault, that she ignored the splash and the cry and then was suddenly doing a reading at her own sister's funeral.

'That was different,' Max said now, his voice as beautiful and patient as it had been then.

Verity thought about this. Perhaps it was. She had been neglectful, but she hadn't smashed Betsy's head with a rock. 'I don't know how you kept it from me.' Back and forth, back and forth, a pendulum of doubt.

'We can save this,' Max said quietly. 'We can patch it up.'

Verity stood up and dropped her trowel into the mud. She'd never been one for make do and mend. She was more the 'Oh, just buy a brand-new one' type of person. But now?

Her beautiful Max.

A secret keeper.

A murderer.

Chapter Forty-Two

VERITY

2 January

'These are for you,' Verity said as she passed a pile of
sympathy cards to Frankie. People had been
dropping them through her door to pass on to Frankie since
the night of the party. The hospital bay smelled sour, and as
Verity moved closer to Frankie, she realised that it was her
friend who smelled; bitter sweat, stale breath.

'No change,' Frankie said, without even looking at
Verity and dumping the cards on the little table next to her.

'Well, that's not a bad thing,' Verity said. She pulled her
wool scarf up to her nose and breathed in Chanel. 'I've
planted some more trees. Where the others were. We should
never have chopped them down.'

'Everyone feels so sorry for me,' Frankie said, Verity's

words drifting somewhere over her head. 'I've had so many messages and cards. They think I've lost a perfect husband. And I keep forgetting. How can you forget something like that?'

Red's voice came back to Verity, close to her, like it was on New Year's Eve. It kept doing that, sentence by sentence, popping back into her mind with no warning, making her feel quite delirious. What she'd told Max about him offering to sleep with her was true after all: she remembered now. *'I'll give you what you want. You'll feel like a different person.'*

Verity wasn't going to tell Frankie about what Red had said. What would be the point when she'd lost him anyway? *I know your husband is dead, and that's a shame, but I think he was actually a psychopath, so things aren't as bad as you think.*

'It's the shock,' Verity said. 'The same thing happened to me.' When Betsy died; when Verity's mother died; when she'd lost all of her babies, she'd kept forgetting all about it: just for a split second. She'd think, *Betsy's not been quite as annoying as usual today,* or she'd pad down the hall to her parents' bedroom to tell her mum something. She'd put a gentle hand on the smooth skin of her belly and think, *Hello, little one.* And then she'd keep being catapulted into the horrible present so hard that her whole body hurt. All that grief, over and over again. It was torture. No wonder she was losing her mind.

'No,' Frankie was saying. 'I keep forgetting he's not here, obviously. But I also keep forgetting that he wasn't really who I thought he was.' She finally turned to Verity, so that Verity could see the terrible black bags under Frankie's eyes.

'Did you know?' Frankie asked.

'Red was very drunk at the party,' Verity said, unsure what Frankie wanted her to say and waving her hand as though that covered everything nicely. 'He was behaving a little strangely. But it wasn't a big deal.'

'I'm not talking about the party,' Frankie said. Her words were coming out in an odd way, as though someone had their fingers around her neck. 'Remember you told me that you thought you were going mad?'

Verity laughed. 'Oh, we're all going mad, Frankie. You know that.'

'You weren't going mad at all. I'm so sorry, V. I should have noticed. But I never did. Honestly, I never had time! I was always picking the children up, or making dinner and sorting out things for school, and trying to keep things together, and I—'

Verity stood up and went over to Frankie, draping her arms around her awkwardly and holding her breath. 'Shush,' she said. 'It's fine. You're fine.'

They stayed like that for a minute until Frankie pulled away. 'I need to tell you,' she whispered, glancing at Harry as though he might be listening. If only. 'I didn't know anything until the party. Red hadn't been on top form, but I just thought it was his heart and his workload. He'd been quite distant. We hadn't really had...' She lowered her eyes. 'You know.'

Verity knew. You could see from a mile off the couples who didn't touch one another anymore. She could see it in

Frankie's face, in the way she looked at Red, in the way she wore her clothes, for God's sake. But if she knew, why had she never asked Frankie about it? Why had she never asked if Frankie was okay?

'I know,' Verity said quietly.

'And we are always so busy. Were.' Frankie reddened at the correction and gave a weak smile. 'Did it again,' she said.

'Go on.'

'I honestly didn't suspect anything like this. On the night of the party, something made me... Well, I went home—'

'Oh yes! Why did you go home? Ah,' Verity interrupted, another memory slotting into place, 'to check on Red?' She frowned. 'But Red wasn't there.' Oh no, he had been with Verity, telling her things about Max and his secrets and offering her a baby. A baby! Like a fifty-pound note or a scarf on a chilly night.

'I didn't know Red wasn't there. He'd left for the party, but I didn't get his message in time. But yeah...' Frankie hesitated, then carried on, full steam ahead. 'I went home to check on him. And for some reason, I went into his office.'

'Why?'

'I don't know. I just did. Maybe I was looking for something. I can't really remember. Anyway, I found some things. Your things.'

Verity waited. Another memory, harder to reach for, dropped into her mind. Something about Red taking something of hers. Oh God. He'd taken her phone. It was him making those comments on Instagram from Verity's account. Her stomach tipped over and she brought her scarf up to her nose again. She took a deep breath of rose and amber.

Frankie cleared her throat. 'He had a bra. It was yours. He'd taken it and hidden it, V.'

Shit. Her green bra that she couldn't find for Luna. Verity thought about when she'd last seen it. Sometime before Frankie and Red were round for dinner a few weeks ago. Even though they had lots of downstairs bathrooms, Red always used the one upstairs. Verity had always put it down to him wanting to feel like more than a guest, like a member of the family. Verity had always been quite happy with that. But now her skin went cold. 'What colour was the bra?'

Frankie closed her eyes as though she couldn't bear to look at Verity any longer. 'Green.'

Verity nodded. 'And your first thought was that Red stole it? Jesus, Frankie. You didn't suspect me leaving it at your place?'

Frankie shook her head, her face collapsing and her eyes filing with sudden, violent tears. 'No. I knew you wouldn't even look at Red. Or do that to me.'

'Okay.' Verity breathed out. 'Good. That's good.' She wanted to leave this room right now, with its creepy stories about Red and her private things being stowed away in his sinister office, and bury herself in Max's arms: the old Max, the Max who hadn't murdered a man and kept it a secret. The one she knew inside out, who would keep her safe and make her eat even though she didn't want to. *Just a bite, V. Come on, it'll do you good.* Where had that Max gone? He'd still be there if she let him, but she couldn't let him now. She ached to tell Frankie about what Max had done, to lay her cards down on the table and let Frankie see her properly, for real. Verity put her hand up to her head.

'There was a lipstick too,' Frankie said, sniffing. 'Not the whole thing, though. Just—'

'The tip,' Verity finished.

'How did you know?'

'I...' Verity recalled the lipstick in her jacket pocket. The fight with Max about it all. She felt like she'd just taken off a huge, heavy coat. 'One of my lipsticks was missing its top. I had no idea why. At least now I know.'

'You should have told me,' Frankie said. 'Maybe I would have realised. Or maybe I wouldn't. I mean, I knew he loved you, and that didn't make me realise, did it?'

'Red didn't love me. He was married to you, Frankie. He chose you.'

Frankie snorted. 'Are you for real? The stupid thing was, I was always so worried about something happening to him at work, or while he was driving. I was so scared of losing him. But it wasn't because I adored him.'

'Oh, Frankie, you did. And that's—'

'I didn't. I have to be honest about at least that. All this sympathy. All these cards. I'm not worthy.'

Verity reached out for the card on top of the pile she'd brought and ripped it open.

Red was such a wonderful man. The world won't be as bright without him.

Verity laid the card down on top of the pile and tore up the envelope into tiny pieces. 'Of course you are,' she said. 'You lost who you thought Red was. I suppose that means you lost a part of yourself. It's all still grief, Frankie. It's all still loss.'

Frankie laughed, even though she was crying. 'Nice. Since when were you a therapist?'

Verity rolled her eyes and threw the fragments of envelope at Frankie so that they rained down on them both like confetti.

Chapter Forty-Three

ALICE

2 January

I wasn't expecting to see them.

'We're moving on, aren't we?' Luna had asked that morning. She'd dyed her hair a dull brown again, making the party night feel like it never happened, even though it was less than a week ago. My heart ached every time I saw her. She'd been so close to having a father. It had been within touching distance. I couldn't tell her, could I? *You almost had something.* It was worse than it never being on the cards. 'Somewhere cheaper, I suppose,' Luna said. 'Somewhere completely different.'

It was natural to her: things go wrong and you run away, move on to somewhere nobody knows you or what you've done or haven't done; whether you were a villain or a hero, or possibly both. Classic learned behaviour.

'We'll have to,' I said. 'We have nothing left here.'

I'd believed it too, at that moment. I was the same as Luna, so used to picking up my bruised little heart and moving somewhere else for a clean start. Only, I'd realised as I watched Luna make us both a cup of tea in our tiny kitchen, the start was never that clean. It was always damp with spores; grimy with other people's muck. You could scrub all you wanted, but some spots would never be clear.

———————————

I'd been scouring letting agents' websites for somewhere new to rent since the day after the party. I looked for places nearby and places further away. Lower Hill was well above my price bracket and there was no way in hell that Max would give me money now. Perhaps he would have done if he'd thought I'd simply saved Harry, but now he might know about the messages. I didn't know who Frankie had told. I'd woken up during the night again and again, sweating, thinking I'd heard a knock at the door and imagining the police there, heads bowed, asking me for my phone and to go to the station. But that wouldn't happen, I reminded myself in the blank January light of day. Red had died of a heart attack, which may have been brought on by the cold water, but then again, may not have been. And Harry was going to wake up, which he probably wouldn't have done if it weren't for me. Frankie obviously knew that, because the police hadn't arrived here, and Frankie had let

Luna go back to the hospital and see her again and sit with Harry and talk to him to try to help him to wake up. Verity had messaged Luna asking if she was okay and Luna had told me, all flushed with relief. *'Verity's speaking to me!'*

So they all obviously knew I hadn't meant for any of it to happen, that what I did was just a tiny piece of a complex jigsaw. Verity had said the lake was shallow. Verity had cut down the trees. They'd *all* left me out and driven me to do something stupid. Max had ignored me. Red had forgotten all about me. Bella had pulled Luna too far in. And maybe Frankie saw all this, and maybe she would call me any day now and I could tell her that we were sticking around.

I left Luna eating a bowl of cereal, engrossed in some YouTube junk. 'Popping out,' I told her, but I didn't tell her where and she didn't ask. I'd swing by the supermarket after going to the letting agent and pick up some nachos and pizza, maybe even let her have a beer to celebrate staying.

I glanced at the agent's papers that lay on the passenger seat as I drove down the pretty tree-lined road through White Fir Lake. The flat was even smaller than the one we had now. It was on a main road. But it was on a bus route to the decent colleges where Verity would still hopefully put in a good word for Luna. The first letter of the postcode was the same as White Fir Lake. It was as close as we could be.

We're not leaving White Fir Lake, I would tell Frankie and

Verity. I would tell Luna. *We're here to stay. We've got a new place only fifteen minutes away. And Luna, those girls you love? They're your half-sisters! And cute little Harry is your baby brother! A ready-made family, just for you. Go on in, help yourself to the fridge!*

It was as I was imagining this that I saw them. I slowed to a crawl along the kerb and gripped the steering wheel as I watched them move down the street adjacent to the one I was driving on. They were with older people I'd never seen before, their grandparents perhaps. Maisie walked solemnly, head down. Bella ran ahead fiercely, her hair streaming behind her in two messy plaits. It was hair that couldn't be tamed. A child who couldn't be tamed. Easy enough to believe.

I'd told myself time and time again that Harry would wake up, and I'd believed it. Just like I'd believed it all before: Max will reply this time, he will offer you money, you can *be* one of them.

I'd been telling myself that if Frankie found out that Luna was Red's child, Luna might be like a gift to her: a relic of Red's. Luna would be delighted to have family. She would slot in, and I could be in the background. Frankie might never really understand me, but she'd grow to love Luna as her own. Maisie and Bella would adore having her in their family.

And Harry, my mind taunted now as I watched Bella, oblivious; Maisie, her life scored with loss; Frankie's parents, doing the best they could to hang on to the wreckage. Where would Harry be in this nice little tale I'd been telling myself? Dead like his father. Beneath the ground and eaten by worms. Gone too soon. Or severely brain damaged. In a terrible accident when he was young.

But I'd saved him.

Hadn't I? I put my foot on the accelerator and changed direction.

Chapter Forty-Four

FRANKIE

3 January

Pyjamas, a grey robe, grey lounge trousers and a loose black top. All soft; cashmere and silk that seemed to melt under Frankie's fingertips. Perfume. A lip balm that shimmered under the hospital lights. A hairbrush.

She looked up from the bag and glanced at her father. 'This isn't from you. Or Mum.'

'No, of course not. Verity asked me to pass it to you.' He stood near the door, not wanting to come too close to Harry or the reality of it all. Her parents were never ones for getting stuck in. Red's parents had handled his death particularly distantly too, and they'd spoken to Frankie only a polite handful of times about the funeral arrangements and his illness. The lack of hugs and howls at

301

the shock of it all made Frankie feel like she had done when she was little, and before she met Verity at school: smaller than she wanted to be, alone and weak with vulnerability. Like a baby bird who had fallen from its nest. *Pathetic*, she told herself. What kind of strong independent woman compared herself to a baby bird in a time of crisis?

Verity had only left a few hours ago. She must have got straight to shopping afterwards. She could shop in any kind of disaster. Frankie put the bag to the side of her and stood up to check on Harry. He was the same; he was always the same.

'Aren't you going to get changed?' asked Robert. 'I can watch Harry for you.'

The nurses kept telling Frankie to get changed too. They had a shower there, just down the corridor, they kept saying. Only two steps away. They'd come and get her the moment there was any change. They made it sound like it could happen at any time, but the longer Frankie sat here, the less likely to her it seemed.

'We're doing okay with Maisie and Bella, your mother and I,' Robert continued. He cleared his throat, signalling a change in direction. 'I know you're beside yourself with worry. I know you don't want to leave him.'

Frankie thought, unexpectedly, of Bella's bed. It was slightly smaller than a single bed with a stocky white frame. Red had twisted fairy lights around the headboard. Bella had a pink duvet with unicorns printed on it and a whole cavalry of stuffed animals and a purple *Frozen* blanket. Now and again (very rarely, if she were completely honest), Frankie would get in the bed with Bella to read a story with her. She'd never really enjoyed it that much. The bed seemed so small, the mattress too soft: it made Frankie feel gigantic and awkward.

When Frankie was little, her mattress had been quite hard and she didn't really have any stuffed animals to speak of. Her mother had never gone near Frankie's bed, apart from to tug at the quilt to make it look aggressively neat. She'd certainly never got in it; the thought of her doing so was almost comical. She'd snapped the light off efficiently each night and told Frankie not to mess about, and that was that.

'If something happens to Harry...' Frankie began, and Robert nodded slowly. 'Do you think Bella will blame herself for wanting to go into the water?'

'No,' said Robert, as though it was just that simple. 'Because it wasn't her fault, was it? It was nobody's fault.'

Frankie was quiet. Really, it was Alice's fault. But once she told anyone that, she wouldn't be able to take it back. The story would be snatched from her, prised from her hands into more efficient ones.

'It was just one of those things,' Robert continued. 'Bella doesn't need to know she was the one who wanted to go in. And we won't remind her of it.'

Frankie nodded and turned to Harry again. Maisie would probably remind Bella every few seconds if she got the chance.

If Frankie told the police what Alice did, would Luna lose her mother? Would she be plucked from her very own blood and bones, and end up somewhere else where she felt like a missing piece to a lost puzzle, a bird without a nest?

Because that would be something that Frankie couldn't bear to happen.

'So, Francesca. Are you going to get changed?'

Frankie sighed and looked down at her tired blue dress. She didn't want to take it off, she didn't want to tell the truth, she didn't want to keep the secret.

Oh, what she wouldn't give to be crushed up, knees bent, spine crooked, in Bella's little white bed.

Chapter Forty-Five

ALICE

3 January

I explained to the nurse at the door of the intensive care unit that I was a relative of Harry's. My daughter was his half-sister, I told her in a hushed tone.

The nurse beckoned me in as though she were taking me into hiding. 'This way,' she whispered.

And then, there I was.

Frankie saw me and shuffled closer to Harry; further from me. Her hand hovered near the call bell. She was wearing some kind of fancy grey loungewear: even in these times, she could ooze casual success.

'Please,' I said. 'You don't need to do that. It's why I'm here. I'll confess. I'll go to the police today, right now, and I'll tell them what I told Luna to do. I wanted to tell you first. It'll be all over the news, and I wanted to warn you because the press will come after you with all sorts of questions.' Luna would be surrounded by art and money, I told myself. She would be better off. Bella would be better off too.

Frankie turned to Harry and brushed his little cheek with her hand. Her enormous engagement ring glinted under the bright hospital lights. A ring and no husband and a forever sleeping child. Was he ever going to wake up? If he didn't, then my promises to go to the police were big ones. Keeping promises, an article I'd read in the early hours had said, was a measure of goodness.

'I don't know,' Frankie said.

I frowned. I hadn't expected this. I'd expected her to take out her phone straight away, and then handcuffs, a police van, maybe some stern Alsatians: all showing me and everyone else that I was good as well as bad. She kept her promise to tell the truth, onlookers would say. 'You must want me to tell the truth.' Isn't this what everyone wanted, all the time? I'd never really done it and sometimes wondered if that had always been my problem. But maybe it hadn't: maybe it had always been something else.

Frankie sighed and looked at me. 'Are you going to tell Luna about Red? She doesn't know he was her dad, does she?'

So Max had told them all. I shook my head. 'No. I didn't tell her. He didn't know either, did he?' He'd gone in the lake to save Luna, apparently, and I'd imagined him knowing somehow that Luna was his; being compelled to dive into the water and save our daughter and be her father. But then Luna had told me that Red had been calling Verity's name. Of course it was about Verity. It always had been, always would be.

'No, I don't think he did know,' Frankie said. 'But I imagine you would have told him in the end. It's why you were here, in White Fir Lake, isn't it?' Frankie looked exhausted. She must do this all the time with her kids. *Tell the truth, I won't be angry if you tell the truth.*

'Yes. Partly. How did you know? Did you recognise me?' In spite of everything, hope burned through my body until Frankie shook her head. Of course she hadn't recognised me.

'I worked it out.'

'Do you want me to tell Luna?' I asked.

Frankie gazed over at Harry but didn't answer.

'We can wait and see what happens if...' My words trailed off. *Wait and see if Harry survives?* Maybe this was why people didn't like me. I always said the wrong thing. I stood up, unable to bear being in this tiny room any longer, where Harry lay frozen in time and secrets were trapped like moths. 'I am so sorry, Frankie,' I said.

And then I left.

Chapter Forty-Six

FRANKIE

4 January

Frankie had gone to the vending machine when it happened. Only for a coffee, she would tell everyone. You couldn't be at the vending machine for a packet of crisps when your child woke up from a coma. In her defence, it was the first time through all of this that she'd felt a flicker of hunger.

When she came back, a nurse greeted her, eyeing her packet of salt and vinegar.

'Mrs Redmond?'

Frankie wanted to throw up. This was it. He'd gone, and the nurse had come to tell her. She felt the wall behind her for something solid. She wanted Red; needed Red, even if he was obsessed with Verity and had kept strange, compulsive secrets from her. Or Verity – could she tell the nurse to hang on until Verity was here? Of course not. 'Yes?'

'Harry's woken up. He's asking for you.'

And now Frankie was sitting with Harry on a different ward where he had his own room. His eyes were open – just slits – but open, and his poor, dry little words were forced from his lips every so often.

Her heart felt as though it might erupt at any moment; molten lava of relief and love and regret spewing from her in red rivulets.

'It'll be a little bit different when you come home,' she told Harry. 'Daddy isn't here now.' She took a breath. 'But you don't need Daddy. You have me, and I'm here and I'm watching. I'm always, always going to be watching.'

Harry croaked something, and Frankie nodded at him, hyperaware. This was how it was going to be now, and she was ready for it. She would call her dad and get him to bring the girls to the hospital, and they would all be together and she would never, ever, ever let them out of her sight.

Chapter Forty-Seven

FRANKIE

5 January

The house, when she returned to it, was like a model of her own; hers, yet not hers. Her mother had obviously been ferociously tidying every spare moment whilst Frankie had been at the hospital with Harry. Every room gleamed and things were organised in new, rather ugly baskets that Ruth had drafted in, obviously in some kind of show of a sense of order. The only room Frankie's mother hadn't touched was Red's office. Verity's bra was still in there, the strange tip of the lipstick where Frankie had thrown it. Maybe Ruth had gone in there, seen the bra and backed away, unsure what on earth it meant. She wouldn't be the only one.

Frankie yanked off the sheets from her bed and tossed

them on the floor. Maisie came in as she was doing it and Frankie pulled her close, so close.

'How are you?' she asked Maisie once she'd released her little body. Had she always been this slight? Frankie would feed her up. Give her lots of butter and cheese.

Maisie thought about the question and then spoke quietly. Perhaps this was how life would be now: never at full volume. 'I miss Daddy. Bella says he'll come back, but that's not possible, is it? You can't come back when you're dead. I let her think it, though. I didn't want to upset her.'

'Well, that's very grown-up and lovely of you.'

Maisie glowed at the praise, and Frankie smiled at her before pulling a pillowcase, Red's, from the goose-down pillow. A lone feather floated onto the floor and Maisie picked it up.

'I'm going to keep this,' she said solemnly. 'I am going to keep whatever I can of Daddy's. Then me and Bella can share it all out and always think about him.' Her voice was brave, cracking like an egg at the end of the sentence so that Frankie pulled Maisie back to her, as though she could pull her back inside and start things all over again.

'That's a lovely idea,' Frankie said, feeling queasy, as an image of Luna – green-eyed, pale, lanky, so obviously belonging to Red – floated uninvited into her mind.

———————————

'What are you looking for?' Frankie's mum asked later that evening. The girls were in bed. She'd thought her parents would go home now that she was back, but they were lingering. Someone from the funeral home was coming round about Red's funeral tomorrow. Perhaps they thought Frankie needed them there for that, to help her tell them things about him for the service. Nice little anecdotes, favourite songs. Perhaps she did.

Frankie yanked out the second drawer in the kitchen. 'I'm looking for an address.' She pulled out a spool of family detritus: a tape measure twisted around a pink beaded necklace; a pack of AAA batteries; a school photograph of Maisie and Bella. She felt her mother's eyes on her and scooped all the rubbish back into the drawer.

'Whose address?'

'Alice's.' On the day when Alice had crashed into the wall, Frankie had shoved the address that Alice had given her into a drawer, she was sure of it. She would transfer it to her address book at some point, she'd thought, but then Christmas had taken over, and then the party and now here they were.

There was a short silence. 'The lady who saved Harry from the water? Are you going to send her a thank-you note?' Frankie's mother thought the world revolved around thank-you notes. She was the kind of person to send a thank-you note for a thank-you note.

Frankie paused for a moment, jamming shut the drawer and opening the next one, which was even more tangled and chaotic. Her mother obviously hadn't been brave enough to tackle these when she was on her tidying binge. *Out of sight, out of mind would have to do*, Ruth would have thought with a tortured sigh.

'Nope,' Frankie answered. 'I'm going to go and see her.'

She took the children with her the next morning. She didn't want to go anywhere without them. It was difficult to extract Bella from Robert. She clung to him like a monkey to a tree. Then she spent ten minutes looking behind doors and under beds for Red. Maisie looked at Frankie with the expression of a particularly patient adult. *See?*

They finally left, about an hour after Frankie had planned to.

'Where are we?' Bella asked when they pulled up. The flat was on a side road, one Frankie had never been down before, on the very edge of Lower Hill. It wasn't far from White Fir Lake, and only five minutes down the road from where she and Red had lived before moving to their big house. Still, it seemed like another world. Affluence had faded away completely at this point. The shops were for sustenance, not pleasure, and the streets were free from trees or anything remotely aesthetic.

'We're at Alice and Luna's. Are you coming in?'

'Yes! Do you think she has paints? She loves painting, doesn't she? And I love painting too!' Bella said, ecstasy in her voice.

'She might not be there. It's her mum I want to see,' Frankie said, watching the girls in the rear-view mirror for any sign of wanting nothing to do with Luna or Alice; of scarred recognition that what they'd been asked to do at the party was horribly, terribly wrong.

But there was nothing.

'Come on, then!' she said brightly, stepping out of the car into the colourless January morning.

———————

Alice looked shaken when she answered the door, as though Frankie had grabbed hold of her and rattled her. She glanced at the children.

'Is Luna at home?' Bella asked, jumping from one foot to the other. 'Does she have paints?'

Alice nodded. 'She's in her room. Are you coming in?' she asked Frankie, pulling her bobbled cardigan tightly around her.

Frankie nodded and forced herself to follow Alice into her cramped hallway. Luna came out of her room when she heard the children and broke into a small smile. Her hair was brown again, Frankie noted with relief. She didn't think she could have looked at Luna for too long if her hair had still been that horrible shade of yellow.

'Luna! Can I paint with you?' Bella asked.

Luna looked at Frankie uncertainly, a carbon copy of Alice's expression a moment before.

Frankie nodded again, unable to say much. The girls and Harry followed Luna into her bedroom and the door shut behind them. Bubbles of laughter floated through the walls, back out into the hallway.

'Should they be laughing?' Frankie asked out loud, surprised by her own voice suddenly bursting into the room.

Alice shrugged. 'Laughter can be quite healing, actually. Do you want a cup of tea?'

'No.'

They stood slightly apart.

'Bella keeps looking for Red.'

'That's normal. She's too young to understand the concept.'

'I know. But it's hard to watch. I sometimes wonder how I'm going to get them through all this.'

Alice stared at Frankie for a minute questioningly, as though Frankie hadn't finished her sentence, but she had, hadn't she?

'I want to know if you're going to tell Luna about Red,' Frankie said quietly.

Alice opened her mouth and then shut it again.

'His funeral is next week,' Frankie pressed on. 'So you'll need to do it sooner rather than later. She might want to be there.' If someone had appeared and told Frankie who her real father was, even if he'd been the worst man in the world, she'd have wanted to know, and she would have gone to his funeral. 'And she might help Bella and Maisie. It's something they can all endure together. I can't. Because Red was their world.' *He wasn't ever mine.*

'You're shaking,' Alice pointed out simply. She gestured to a plain grey couch that looked less comfortable than the floor. 'Sit down if you want.'

'No, I'm okay standing,' Frankie said, gripping her car key tightly, trying to look steady on her feet. Red's *funeral*? Had she really just uttered those words? And was she honestly inviting Luna into their lives, unbalancing their precarious set-up even more than it already had been?

'I'm so glad that Harry is okay,' Alice said.

'I know. But I hate that my children aren't going to have a father,' Frankie said.

Alice hung her head like she'd broken a vase of Frankie's or – ha! – damaged a wall. 'I liked Red, you know, that night when I… when Luna…' She stopped struggling and looked up. Her face was appallingly pale. 'Is that a weird thing to say?'

Frankie sighed. 'It's all weird, Alice.' It was all so, so weird: life stretched out of shape so far that it was unrecognisable, fit for nothing. Red had never frightened Frankie when he'd been alive, until the day she'd found those things in his office. Now his secrets haunted her. In the rare times she fell asleep, she felt his spectre leaning over her, his meaty breath on her face. *I never wanted you*, he told Frankie in his ghostly voice.

Frankie moved quickly to Alice's sofa and sat down with a thud. It was as hard as it looked. Alice looked for a moment as though she might sit next to her, but then thought better of it.

'Is Verity going to his funeral?' Alice asked.

'He was one of her best friends.'

Maybe, Frankie had thought as she lay wide awake in the unbroken black nights, Red hadn't been as obsessed with Verity as it seemed. Maybe there was an explanation. Verity wanted to go to Red's funeral, said she wouldn't dream of missing it, so she obviously wasn't too freaked out by it all. '*It was probably just a little game*,' she told Frankie, '*to stop me taking myself too seriously.*' Yes, Frankie thought in her bed as black turned to brittle grey dawn. Just a little game. *He chose you*, Verity had said, and Verity always told the truth.

'Verity might not want me there,' Alice said, sitting next to Frankie and not meeting her eye.

'I didn't tell her about you telling Luna to take the children into the lake.'

'I thought you told Verity everything,' Alice said, taking a lurid-green cushion from the sofa and fiddling with it.

'I was kind of busy with Harry,' Frankie said. She stood up suddenly, her back aching, and watched as Alice's face flushed rose-red. 'Why did you do it, Alice?'

Alice said nothing for a moment. Frankie waited, listening to the muffled voices of the children, the dripping of what must be a faulty tap in the kitchen, which was only two steps from where they sat in the lounge.

'I honestly didn't mean for anyone to get hurt,' Alice said. 'I just wanted to show you up.'

'But why?' Frankie shouted, then glanced at Luna's bedroom door guiltily.

Alice's face was flaming now, and her jaw was set for a fight. 'I was sick of being on the outside. I didn't think the water was deep, and I didn't think they'd go in that far. I didn't even know Harry was there. You think I would have put Luna at risk? I was doing it because Max wouldn't...' Alice tailed off and pressed the palms of her hands up to her eyes. 'I just didn't know how to make you all let me in. You all thought you were better than me.'

Frankie thought about this. Had she believed that? Yes,

she had, because she lived in White Fir Lake and Alice didn't; because she was best friends with Verity and Alice wasn't. She felt the hot rise of shame on her cheeks. 'That's not true.' She left the claustrophobic sitting area and moved back out to the hall.

'Maisie! Bella! Harry! We're going!'

There was a collective moan from Luna's room, and then the door opened and the siblings all fell out, each face brighter from a few minutes together in a tiny bedroom on a street with no trees and no fairy lights or fancy shops.

'I'll see you at the funeral,' Frankie said to Alice, as they left the flat.

Chapter Forty-Eight

VERITY

1 April

S he never did need to say the words, to ask him that unaskable question.

' It had happened in the spring, when the pale pink blossoms danced down the streets of White Fir Lake in the still cool breeze; around the time when Max was dismantling his studio and Verity was handing over the gallery to Jenny and Luna and they were taking apart their mansion and their life in White Fir Lake piece by piece.

She'd had a choice: ask Max the unthinkable question and let her doubt poison what they had left, or never ask him and run the risk of never knowing. As the days moved them all further from the horror of the party, she watched Frankie live without Red. She'd always known Frankie was some kind of superwoman, but those days made Frankie's strength shine brighter than ever. She'd told Verity, her face flushed, that Red had overspent on the house, on the business, on every single thing he'd done. That she was partly to blame because he'd told her to be more careful and she hadn't been. That, Frankie said, was why his heart problems got worse. And whilst carrying around that terrible knowledge, she'd packed up her house and moved herself and her children back to Lower Hill, and then she'd got herself a job at GLASS as a chef.

So Verity had wondered if she might try to live without Max in the same way, with the same clarity that she was strong enough for anything that might happen.

'Do you want to live without Red?' she'd asked Frankie over a cup of coffee. The question was a strange one, but Frankie understood it, like she always did, and nodded immediately.

'It was my worst fear to lose him, because I didn't think I could cope. And now I can, it's kind of freeing.' She looked at Verity, eyes narrowed. 'Why?'

She'd told Frankie, there and then, about what Max had done that night in America with Alice. She'd put all of her cards, even the bloody, dirty ones she wanted nobody to ever see, on the table. She sat in Frankie's little lounge that was actually quite nice and cosy and safe-feeling and full of dolls and toy trucks and things that made Verity feel scorched with happiness and sadness all at the same time. The walls were painted a soft grey, the colour of drizzle.

'I look at you, and I wonder if I should be moving on in

the same way,' Verity admitted. 'He kept something huge from me. He had a secret with Alice, and not me.'

They'd had to open a bottle of wine in the end to help Frankie process it all, even though they'd done so well at not drinking as much since January. 'Alice never told me about that,' Frankie said, gazing down into her Merlot.

'She never actually told me, although she threatened to. Max told me in the end.'

'It sounds like the guy he killed was better off in the sea, to be honest. Poor Alice.'

Poor Alice. In all of this, Verity had never seen Alice as a victim. But then, as Verity perched on Frankie's couch that was too big for her new, small drizzle-grey room, things shifted into a different shape.

'She's having counselling, you know,' Frankie said, obviously seeing Verity's expression. 'I don't particularly trust her. But she's been through a lot. More than I even thought. It can't have been easy for Max, either, carrying that around for so long.'

'And what about Max? You don't think he should have told me? You don't think it changes everything?'

Frankie put her wine down. 'No, I don't. We all keep secrets, V. He made a mistake. It was one moment. That doesn't change who he is, does it?'

'That's what he keeps saying. It was just one moment.' Just one moment in a web of a million others that had changed everything.

A moment like hearing a faraway splash whilst you painted another coat of Sapphire Sky onto your thumbnail.

About four weeks later, the symptoms started. She'd had some of them before, because she'd had pregnancies before. This time, they weren't subtle symptoms that Verity had to try to notice like a puppy cocking its head and listening to a faraway sound. They were symptoms that blew her off her feet: fierce and all-consuming.

Chapter Forty-Nine

ALICE

One year later

I'd been out in White Fir Lake buying Luna some new watercolour paper in the village when I saw them. The village was full of Christmas shoppers, bright bobble hats and golden fairy lights.

'Frankie,' I said, reaching out and touching her arm lightly before I could change my mind and scurry away. I tugged at my scarf, which suddenly felt too tight around my throat.

Frankie turned and smiled. She was holding Harry's hand. He would be almost three now and was losing the baby fat in his face. He looked like Luna when she'd been that age, except Luna wouldn't have stood calmly and held my hand, not ever. He stared up at me as though he'd never seen me before until I looked away.

'How are you?' Frankie asked. 'I feel like I've not seen you for ages.' She hadn't seen me for ages, and I was glad she'd noticed that I'd worked hard to keep my distance. Luna saw a lot of them all, which I was glad about, but I had stayed back. They had what Luna needed, but nothing for me, really.

'I'm okay,' I said. I supposed it was true, to a point, although the nightmares were yet to subside. Harry, underwater, reaching out for me with wide eyes. Bella crying and crying and pulling sodden reeds from her throat. Teenage Red vomiting black-green lake water filled with tiny eggs. The nightmares would be even worse now, after seeing Harry today. Skulls, glass, rock. The counselling was interesting, but I couldn't be truthful in my sessions about that summer, and so I didn't feel like it would completely cure me. Perhaps nothing ever would.

'I'm glad.' Frankie paused and pushed her fringe from her eyes with her spare hand. 'I'm just out getting some cleaning stuff. I've been renting our old house in White Fir Lake, but it's sold now. It's completion day tomorrow, so I'm going for one last time,' she said. 'You're going to help me clean, aren't you, Harry?'

Harry nodded. 'I'm good at hoovering,' he said to me and I forced myself to mouth 'wow' at him, as though my plan hadn't almost killed him, as though I hadn't arrived in his life a year ago and tried to take it apart, piece by piece.

'And Verity's house is still empty, isn't it?' I asked Frankie. Old habits die hard. I'd driven over to the Bentley mansion a few times over the last year, just to look at it. Now I knew she and Max weren't there, I was free to stare up at the windows, and imagine a life where I had been to every single party there, not just the last one.

'Someone's moved in,' Frankie said. 'Just in time for New Year's. Weirdly,' she added, little blooms of pink appearing on her cheeks as she referred to that night. 'Luna's new friends from college seem nice,' she said next, rubbing her hands together to warm herself.

I hadn't met them, so I wouldn't know, but I smiled. 'Yeah, they're good,' I said. I imagined them hanging out at Frankie's house, eating her homemade pizza and cookies and thinking what a cool step-mum type she was, how much cooler she was than Luna's real mother. Only the scenes of my imaginings were at Frankie's old house, and she didn't live there anymore. I needed to stop it. I took a breath of icy air. 'Actually, I haven't met them,' I admitted.

'No, no, me neither. Luna just told Maisie that they'd been really nice about her artwork. I thought that was a good sign, I suppose,' Frankie said. 'You know, you're welcome to come round with her one time if you want. I think Luna would like having you there.'

I hesitated. 'I always just leave her to it. You're her family, not mine.' After all this time, here was my invitation: a genuine one. And yet I wasn't sure I wanted it.

'I don't think she feels that we're her family yet,' Frankie said, moving closer to me as she was jostled by a rushing shopper and his bags. 'She's pretty quiet, still.'

'She'll just need some more time, I think. But I like her being around you all. It's doing her good.' I'd found Luna's resolution from last year a few months ago. I'd been clearing up and came across a beaded bag that screamed Verity Bentley. I wondered for a minute if Luna had stolen it, then I remembered that she'd had it at the party last year. I looked inside the bag without even thinking. There was a lipstick in it, Evening Rose, the bland colour of plasters, and a little gold card.

I'd ripped it open without thinking about it, remembering as I did that it was one of the cards Verity had got people to write their New Year's resolutions on. I was about to find out what Luna's had been, and I didn't particularly want to know, but I was too far gone to go back.

I looked down at her writing, messy and round.

Tell Max I'm his daughter.

I'd stared at it, horror creeping through me.

'You had all those articles about Max,' Luna told me that night. 'I thought it meant something. And I'm into painting, and he is too...'

'Did you want Max to be your dad?' I asked.

She shrugged. 'Yeah.'

'And what about Red?'

Luna had laughed, the sound unexpected and unfamiliar. 'God, Mum, I didn't go around marking every man we met out of ten as a potential dad. I just got it wrong, and thought you'd come here because of Max. But I'm okay that it wasn't him. At least I know now. And at least I have some sisters and a brother. That's pretty cool.'

So straightforward. She didn't get that from me or from Red.

'Well,' Frankie said now, bringing me back into the present with the crisp morning air and the smell of coffee and chocolate drifting from the café we stood next to. 'We'd best get going.'

I stayed where I was, watching Frankie and Harry disappear through the bustling street until they were nothing but dots on the fancy horizon.

Chapter Fifty

FRANKIE

The same day

'Okay, Harry, I think we're done here,' Frankie said brightly.

She stared out across the lake for one last time. If she squinted, she could just about make out the tiny green heads of the trees Verity had planted a year ago. There was movement in the old Bentley mansion: people had just moved in. Frankie felt an unexpected twinge of regret for Red, who had quite literally killed himself in the process of getting here. Now, already, it all belonged to someone else.

Bumping into Alice in the village this morning had brought it all back. Frankie hadn't seen Alice for months.

'Aren't you still furious with her?' Verity had asked

Frankie more than once. 'She could have killed Harry with her ridiculous plan, and ruined Luna's life in the process.'

'I know you still don't forgive her for the letters,' Frankie said.

'It's not because of those. Max should have told me about those from the start. She was just attention seeking with those. It's more what she did to you.'

'She saved Harry in the end, though,' Frankie pointed out every time.

And every time, Verity's answer was the same. 'If you push someone, then save them falling, you don't get to be the hero. It's fine,' she'd continue, and Frankie would imagine her on the other end of the phone, waving her hand around. She managed, as it turned out, just fine without Verity in White Fir Lake. The things you fear the most often aren't actually so scary. It is the things you don't fear that you need to watch out for, that will reach out and bite you when youare least expecting it. 'I don't have a problem with you being there for her. You're lovely, and that's what you do. But just watch her, that's all I'm saying. And keep an eye on Luna. That poor girl deserves better.'

Frankie didn't need to watch Alice: she barely saw her. Luna came to their house sometimes and seemed to take joy from being with the children. Frankie took joy from it too: the connecting of DNA dots that fascinated her so much. And she couldn't bring herself to still be angry with Alice. She felt sad for her, but she wasn't angry. How could she be, when Alice had only exploited the fact that Frankie hadn't been watching her own children? You were never angry with the burglar who climbed through an open window; only mad with yourself for leaving it open.

'Where are we going next?' Harry asked, bright red from the exertion of pushing around the hoover for the last hour.

'We're going to get the girls from school. And soon, I hope we're going to see Verity and Max.'

'On an aeroplane?'

Frankie grinned and scooped Harry up. Since Red had gone, it was like someone had pulled away a thick curtain that had been between her and the children. It might be a little colder sometimes, a little more exposed, but it meant that she could see them and hear them more than she ever had before. She kissed Harry's hot little cheek. 'Yes, on an aeroplane.'

Her phone flashed and vibrated on the empty worktop, and she picked it up. This would be the call they'd been waiting for, the one that would make everything slot into the shape it should have been years ago.

'Hello?'

Chapter Fifty-One

VERITY

The same day

'She's here,' Verity told Frankie over a crystal-clear line. You wouldn't have thought that there were four hundred miles between them. 'She's here, and she's perfect.' And Red was the worst liar imaginable, although Verity didn't add that part. Where would it get them? It wouldn't get Frankie anywhere, or Luna. There was putting your cards on the table, showing your closest friend that you weren't invincible, and didn't want to pretend that you were, and then there was just telling people too much. It was a hard line to balance on, Verity thought as she looked down at Maria Betsy.

'Oh! Verity! We'll be there tomorrow evening. How is she?'

'She's fabulous,' Verity said. 'She was worth the wait. Max has gone to find coffee and pastries. We're starving. It was a long night.'

'Oh, pastries!' Frankie said in delight. 'I wasn't rushing before, but I am now!'

Verity laughed. 'Are you still not going to just move here? Maria says she wants you to.'

'You tell Maria that I am one of the finest chefs in the Cotswolds, and that they can't do without me.'

'I told her. She says you can be a chef in France.'

'Ah, maybe one day. How was the labour?'

Verity screwed up her nose. 'Vile.' She looked up as Max came into her hospital room, the excitement that had been etched on his face since spring more vibrant than ever. 'My pastries are here. I'll see you tomorrow.'

'Send photos! I want to see her before she goes on Instagram!'

'She's not going on Instagram!' Verity said indignantly and caught Max grinning at her. 'Some things are too good to share.'

———

The following evening Frankie arrived, bringing gifts, a tall Maisie, an excited post-aeroplane Harry, and a Bella who had to be told to not sing too loudly in Maria's little face.

'We're just here for two nights,' Frankie said. 'We'll come again soon.'

'You could stay for a year for all I care,' Verity said, even though nothing could have prepared her for the tiredness that cascaded through her body, dragging her senses off like a fast-moving river. But even with the tiredness, she felt a bright sense of clarity, as though a particularly painful tooth had been removed or a barking dog had gone quiet.

'How's the job, Frankie?' Max asked.

Frankie grinned. 'It's good. I make tiny, rich food for tiny, rich people.'

'Speaking of rich...' Verity glanced at the children, who were dancing around an oblivious Maria in her little Moses basket. She lowered her voice. 'Is there anything left, now the house and business have gone through?'

'Not really. A few thousand with his car and the furniture. I'm thinking of giving Alice some of it.'

Verity gasped. 'What? Is she asking for it?'

Frankie shook her head. 'No, not once. But I just keep thinking of how much our children have had, and how little Luna got. It doesn't seem fair.'

Max came and placed a coffee percolator on the coffee table. 'She wants money. It's all she wants. It's all she came for.'

Frankie sighed. 'I'm not sure, you know. I think she just wanted to belong somewhere. I won't give her enough to be able to do that. I think she'll spend it on Luna, anyway.'

Verity thought about this, remembering dressing Luna up like a mini-me doll for the New Year's Eve party. She'd heard afterwards that Red thought Luna was Verity, and that's why he'd rushed into the cold, black water. 'I hope so,' she said now. She'd spoken to Luna a lot over the last year. She was damaged by what had happened, which made Verity even more angry with Alice. Poor Luna still thought it was her fault, when really all she had done was trust her mother.

Verity hauled herself up and wandered over to where Maria was stirring, leaving Frankie and Max chatting about houses and White Fir Lake and everything they'd left behind. The painting Verity had been doing the night she went into labour was leaning against the elaborate fireplace, its fresh spring greens and blues bringing light into the winter darkness of the room. Discarded Christmas paper lay in crumpled sheets on the soft white carpet. Bella and Maisie were chasing Harry with a length of blue ribbon, and Frankie stopped talking to Max every now and again to tell them to stop, which they ignored. Ava, who Verity and Max had convinced to come with them when they moved, clattered plates in the kitchen down the hallway, and the sweet, heady fragrances of lemon and chicken and tarragon danced into the room. Verity lifted Maria up, pressed her to her tired, scarred body, and looked at the beautiful chaos around her.

Epilogue

'That's the last of it,' Eva said as she put the last box on the floor. She stretched her arms over her head and grinned at her husband. 'I can't believe we're here.'

'I know.' Nathaniel came closer to her, holding a bottle of vintage fizz. 'Our dream house.'

'I wonder what people around here will think of us,' said Eva. She had moved here from New Zealand and hadn't seen the headline: *LAKE HOUSE OF HORRORS*. Eva wasn't the type to do intense research: she'd seen the house when flirting with the idea of moving to the UK, decided she wanted it and that was that. She'd heard vague stories from people a few days ago when she'd first arrived in White Fir Lake: of the legendary parties, of the beautiful hostess and the artist husband. But she'd barely listened. Eva wasn't a big listener. 'I want to outdo the others.'

Nathaniel laughed his big, booming laugh and topped up their champagne. 'Oh, we will.'

Eva turned to him, thrilled. 'Big parties, bigger than the

335

others ever dreamed of. I want everyone to talk about us. I want everyone to be obsessed with us.'

'Oh, they will be,' Nathaniel said. He put his arm around Eva and they were silent for a few moments, staring out at the glittering black lake and all its secrets.

Acknowledgments

I've been so lucky to have this book to focus on throughout such a strange time. Thank you to my editor Charlotte Ledger: inspirational, supportive, wise and an all-round amazing person to know. Working with the whole One More Chapter team is a dream and I am so grateful for everybody's dedication, friendliness and knowledge. Thank you to Emily Ruston for being a part of the story too, and for always supporting me. I'd also like to thank Lucy Bennett for designing the gorgeous cover.

The incredible Creative Writing staff at Manchester Metropolitan University and my fellow MA students helped to shape this book. I am grateful for such a brilliant experience, which shone bright even in the darkest days of lockdown. I'm also grateful to have such wonderful friends who cheer me on in so many ways – thank you to all of you.

Finally, thank you to my family for more than I could ever begin to write down.

Don't miss *The Start of Us*, a moving and page-turning love story perfect for fans of Roxie Cooper, Josie Silver and Isabelle Broom.

Daniel and Erica

From the moment they meet their worlds are changed forever. They know that fate has led them to each other.

Daniel knows Erica is special, but he doesn't quite understand how special she is. Because Erica has a unique gift: an ability to slip between worlds and observe a life she's never lived, made up of all the paths she didn't take.

But just as their lives seem perfect, tragedy strikes. Erica's gift offers them hope – a chance to re-do their lives. But going back comes with risks.

What if Erica can't find Daniel again?
What if their paths were never meant to cross?

YOUR NUMBER ONE STOP

ONE MORE CHAPTER

FOR PAGETURNING BOOKS

One More Chapter is an award-winning global division of HarperCollins.

Sign up to our newsletter to get our latest eBook deals and stay up to date with our weekly Book Club! <u>Subscribe here.</u>

Meet the team at <u>www.onemorechapter.com</u>

Follow us!

 @<u>OneMoreChapter</u>_

@<u>OneMoreChapter</u>

@<u>onemorechapterhc</u>

Do you write unputdownable fiction? We love to hear from new voices. Find out how to submit your novel at <u>www.onemorechapter.com/submissions</u>